Love G‍
Love Broth‍
Book‍
By
Liz Crowe

This is a work of fiction. Similarities to real people, places, or events are entirely coincidental.

LOVE GARAGE

First edition. May 5, 2024.

ISBN: 979-8223007852

Written by Liz Crowe.

Chapter One

J *uly*
"I hope you don't think I'm gonna hire you because you're my baby brother. No, wait. My lazy, bookworm, useless baby brother, who's gone and dropped out of that expensive, fancy writing school he just had to get into, and now shows up here at *my* business, in this ole backwater, hillbilly town...broke and looking like he's been dragged through a knothole."

Aiden flinched in the face of Antony's fury. His hands curled into fists deep inside his trouser pockets, as a too-familiar rush of anger threatened to consume him. He waited and watched, seeking visual cues from their growing up years. Antony merely leaned against the tallest worktable, slowly wiping off some kind of a wrench with a blue cloth, his dark eyes inscrutable.

The sounds of a busy garage swirled around them, filling the real and virtual space between Aiden and the man who'd been his protector and friend his entire life. That gaping hole he'd placed there, with his casual disregard for his family and seeking escape from this very hillbilly backwater. Those were the words he'd used not that long ago. Flung back at him in Antony's overblown, exaggerated redneck accent, they stung like ice pellets.

Not for the first time, Aiden deeply regretted the effort he'd made to keep distance between them—from all his brothers—for the last seven-and-a-half years. It had seemed the right thing then, with him in the full flush of his heady personal expectations as the next Great American Novel Author.

He gulped, and forced his voice to remain steady. Heaven knows he'd had plenty of years to practice not rising to Antony's bait.

"Yes...um, well, kind of. Yeah. That is what I'm thinking." He ran a hand around the back of his neck while Antony observed him without moving or speaking—barely even blinking.

The bastard isn't going to make this easy, is he?

Aiden cleared his throat and tried to find the right words. They failed him.

"Never mind." He turned to shoulder his way through the grease monkeys peopling Antony's successful auto-repair joint. His head buzzed with exhaustion from his trip "riding the dog," as he'd learned to deem travelling by Greyhound bus, and anxiety over the reason he'd made it.

As he reached for the office door, after making it all the way across the garage, a distinct noise like resignation hit his ears.

Ridiculous, of course. He could barely think amidst all the garage noise, let alone hear his oldest brother heaving his patented sigh from all the way across it. But Aiden turned anyway, knowing, somehow, that he had.

Antony remained propped against the workbench, still clutching the blue rag. Still staring holes into Aiden. "You don't even know how to change the oil on a late model pickup. You're about useful as tits on a bull."

Aiden squared his shoulders and tried to look somewhat more useful than that.

"Maybe, but I can clean up after the guys who do know how, or I can keep your books, update your website, get you active on Facebook and Twitter and—" That sounded desperate. But he might as well own that, too.

"I don't use any of that shit." Antony dropped the rag on the bench and scowled as an employee rolled a couple of tires by him. "I don't need it. I have more work than I can handle now."

"Yeah? Well, maybe you should think about it. What happens when the work dries up?"

Antony let out a distinctly unpleasant-sounding laugh. "Little bro, you obviously missed class the day they talked about the recession-proof businesses." He held up three fingers. "Cars always need fixing. People always need to drink beer. Kids always need teaching. By my calculations, the Love family is pretty fuckin' smart. But for one of us, I guess."

Aiden bit the inside of his cheek to keep from lashing back in defense then tried a different tactic.

"Mama is sick. You forget that? Ever think maybe I came home to be here for her?" He had to shut his eyes for a split second to dispel the concept of a world without the formidable Lindsay Halloran Love in it.

Antony grunted and headed toward one of the four lifts. Each had a car hoisted on it and a guy underneath, messing around with whatever they did under there. He reached up and fiddled with something beneath what looked like a big black Mercedes sedan, ignoring Aiden. Given that he had no other viable option, Aiden let him.

His sister had broken the news about their mother to him four days earlier, around 5:00 p.m. He'd never forget the moment—since it happened to be the same day he'd discovered he'd failed a poetry-writing seminar, plus made a serious miscalculation by drinking too much and then coming on to a hot professor at a department social event. He'd seen her next day at the panel "discussion" of his final novel.

Lack of clear plot progression, shallow characters and poor dialogue choices, had been the gist of their "advice."

Jerks. Wouldn't know a decent, modern plot if it bit them all in the collective ass. So what if I want to actually make money with a book, and not just collect a lot of critical admiration?

Shifting from foot to foot, he calculated how long Antony would make him stand there like a supplicant before he caved. Because cave he would. Aiden understood enough about his eldest sibling to realize that. The strains of the latest Luke Bryan song wafted around, chafing his exposed nerve endings.

As Aiden watched, Antony finished under the Merc and hit the button to lower it back to the garage floor. Then he spent a solid ten minutes consulting beneath the hood of a late model F-150, another five wiping down a set of tools, and ten more fiddling with his phone. But Aiden didn't say anything, lest he break into the man's thought pattern. That would only trigger his temper—the last thing Aiden needed at that moment.

Memories of angry explosions past made him sigh, rub the back of his neck, and touch his still-crooked nose. While the Love siblings were fiercely loyal to each other—they maintained zero tolerance for bullshit between them. He took a step backward, regretting his decision to come here first, as opposed to the brewery on the west side of town to beg his father to hire him to pour beer, shift kegs, or hose out brewing equipment, mainly because that would also mean facing Dominic. Between them all, he'd much rather deal with Antony.

He refocused when Antony frowned at him, as if sensing his sudden mental flinch.

Aiden raised an eyebrow in a "well, I'm very busy, and important, and require an answer" sort of way. His stomach churned, reminding him of the disgusting fast food he'd inhaled earlier. He hated being the screw-up little brother. Honest to God, he hated it, almost as much as he despised the country music pounding on his eardrums right then.

Antony crossed his arms over his ample chest, opened his mouth, and something resembling relief coated Aiden's brain. A loud beep of a horn made them both turn to face the one closed overhead door. Thanks to his brother's success with it, Love Garage boasted three new bays in addition to the first, all of which were open onto the soft summer midmorning. Aiden took a step backward to see who couldn't manage to drive up to an open door. He spotted a circa 1990s Ford Explorer, navy blue, filthy, with a crappy spare donut tire on the right front. Antony materialized next to him, a wide smile spreading across his face, replacing the asshole-ish scowl he'd been wearing since Aiden had shown, hoping for a welcome more in keeping with the Prodigal Son's.

Walking past him without a word, Antony opened the passenger's side back door then reappeared holding a little blond boy. As soon as he got released, the kid ran to the patch of pebbles surrounding the giant maple tree shading the front of the garage, plopped down, and started cramming handfuls of them into his mouth.

Aiden frowned then walked over and crouched down in front of him. His eyes were of the clearest, brightest blue, his hair so yellow as to seem Technicolor, or fake. At that moment his cheeks bulged, like a squirrel's hoarding nuts. But at least he'd stopped eating rocks.

"Hey, um...?" Aiden held out a hand in front of the boy's mouth. "Spit. Those are pretty gross."

His face split into a grin and slimy, saliva-covered rocks spilled into Aiden's palm. He grimaced and dropped them before wiping his hand on his travel-wilted khaki's.

"I'm Jeffery. I needs a drink!" he declared, leaping into Aiden's arms as if they were best buddies.

"Me too, Jeffrey," Aiden said, surprised by how comfortable he seemed in his arms.

"Jeffrey needs a drink *now*." He patted Aiden's cheeks. Smelling of dirt, grass, and something a little too much like pee for Aiden's comfort level, Jeffrey pointed toward the SUV. "Tell Mommy to get Jeffrey a drink."

Aiden glanced over toward the truck and saw his brother beaming like a total sap at an attractive, petite, dark-haired woman. Aiden blinked when she looked over at him until the realization she only wanted to keep track of her kid gave him a mental smack. Her green eyes widened and seemed to flash.

"Oh, my Lord." She touched Antony's arm. "That? That is *Aiden*? Little A? Wow...."

Antony scowled at him, then smiled at the woman again, but in a way Aiden didn't quite understand. He forced his eyes to remain on hers, although the temptation to take in all her jeans, boots, and

T-shirt-clad glory nearly bested him. Her flushed face, framed by wild, curly hair barely contained by a headband, deep-green eyes, and full lips, mesmerized him in a bizarre, uncomfortable way. She had to be the most beautiful woman Aiden had ever laid eyes on.

Antony interrupted his internal drooling. "So, what's up today, Rosie?"

Rosie? Rosalee? His memory clicked in then.

"Drink!" Jeffrey flailed around, startling him. "Drink now!"

"All right. Cool your jets." Aiden headed toward the office. Setting the boy down did not seem practical. The number of things he'd find in Antony's garage to stuff in his mouth was myriad, none of them safe.

Jeffrey laughed and patted Aiden's head. "Cool your jets. Cool your jets. Cool your jets!" His volume ramped up with each repeat.

Aiden plunked him on the butt-sprung couch and filled a cup with water from the cooler, his mind spinning as he tried to catch another glimpse of Rosalee. Jeffrey clutched the cup and gulped the water so fast it leaked out the side of his mouth. Antony laughed and leaned into Rosie's ear. Their body language spoke of an intimacy that made Aiden's head pound. Since when did his brother muscle in on another man's wife—a man who'd been his best friend from, like, birth? Antony flirted with the amazingly hot woman who seemed to be giving it back to him while Aiden tried to come to terms with all the years he'd missed out on his family's news.

"Hey, um, how's your dad," he asked Jeffrey.

If he remembered right, Rosalee Kendrick had married Paul Norris, the shooting guard on the Lucasville Broncos state championship-winning basketball team, with Antony as forward their senior year. Paul and Rosie had married while she'd been in college, and he'd had been home on leave from the Marines.

"My daddy is a soldier and he is brave," he muttered, methodically dismantling the Styrofoam cup and flicking the tiny bits around the room. "Jeffrey likes his flag. It's a big triangle. It's my pillow."

Aiden blinked, while Jeffrey stomped on the foam dots, his face furrowed in concentration.

"Uh, hey, Jeff, let's not do that anymore, okay?" He snagged what remained of the eviscerated cup and dropped it into the trash, making a mental note to get something more biodegradable for water cooler use.

Just as he'd concocted a scheme to distract Jeffrey with a no-doubt forbidden high-sugar snack from the vending machine, the door opened and Antony strode in. He glared at Aiden then scooped Jeffrey up, flipping him around so he sat on his broad shoulders. The boy squealed, laughed, and tugged on his hair.

"Jeffrey wants to fix a car!"

"Not today, pal." Antony patted his leg. "You and your mommy have places to go. You're gonna take my car while I work on your—"

"Piece of *shit*!" Jeffrey blurted out. "Piece of shit! Piece-of-shit truck!"

"Cut it out. You know your mommy doesn't like that word." Antony walked out with Jeffrey still on his shoulders then stuck him into his car seat, which now resided in the backseat of Antony's prized blue latest model Dodge Charger. That, in and of itself, shocked Aiden to his core. No one, and that included his own mother, got to touch, much less drive Antony's muscle-car-of-the-moment. But sure enough, he straightened after getting Jeffrey settled and tossed his keys across the hood to Rosie, who caught them, blew him a kiss, climbed in then peeled out onto Hunter Street.

Aiden's head reeled from the memory of Rosie's deep-green gaze, the quick glimpse he'd gotten of the rise of her breasts in the V-neck T-shirt, the way the faded jeans hugged her hips and ass. He gulped then had to repress a yelp when Antony barreled back into the office, his face flushed. At that moment, Aiden embraced a core truth—his brother had it bad for Paul Norris' widow.

Problem at that moment of course—so did Aiden.

Antony grabbed his to-go coffee cup and took a slug, "Lucky for you, Rosie talked me into taking you on as a charity case."

"Oh, uh...great. I guess." He had to look away to hide the flush rising in his cheeks. Antony obviously had something going on with her, in some kind of bizarre, uncharacteristically low-key way. Antony had run through more girls in high school than any of them, even Dominic. He'd been a tough act to follow on many levels. Aiden couldn't quite get his brain around what he'd observed transpiring between his brother and the widow Norris just now.

"It's not what you think." Antony kept his pensive expression turned to the window. "We're just friends. Her SUV is ragged out. The VA moves at glacial speed with her benefits, and she had a day off from her teller job...."

"You don't need to explain anything to me."

"I know that, you little shit."

Ah, now we're back on familiar ground. He banished mental images of Rosie's full red lips, slim legs, and anything else about her from his brain. He had to convince Antony to hire him for a while. Not to mention, he needed a place to sleep until he got up the nerve to approach his father. He stuck his hands in his pockets and tried out the supplicant face once more.

"Be here tomorrow morning at five. You've got the opening clean-up shift and can play gopher for a while, as long as you stay the hell out of my way. Minimum wage. That's the best I can do right now."

"That works. Thanks...seriously, I—"

But Antony held up a hand.

"I don't want to hear it. I, for one, am sick of your excuses. But hey, you'll be the famous author soon, right? After nearly eight years of school?"

The blood rushed to Aiden's face again and his hands curled into fists for the millionth time. He counted to ten then fifteen, then took a deep breath. "Can I crash at your place?"

"Jesus-fucking-Christ. Whatever. Now get the hell out of here before I change my mind."

Aiden stood, heart pounding, fingertips touching the flash drive in his pocket harboring his novel, the one he thought would have passed muster with his stuck-up advisory committee, but had fallen miserably flat. He wondered if Antony still had a computer at home since his own laptop was on its last legs then decided against pushing his luck.

"I'm sorry. But I just need a few...weeks or something. I need to be here for Mama, you know."

Antony's frown deepened. "Yeah, speaking of that. Best get it over with now. She know you're here?"

"Not exactly." Aiden grimaced. Grime coated him from the long bus ride, and he smelled his own sour body odor—hardly presentable to his mother. But he had no choice. "I...um...could use...."

Antony sighed, dug something out of his pocket, and tossed it toward him. Aiden caught the keys, his throat closing with a combination of panic and relief, and the alarming urge to burst into tears.

"Take the truck. Go to my place and shower first. You smell like the losers in the drunk seat. Do *not* smoke in either my truck or my house, got it? Rosie made me give it up and won't tolerate it around me."

Aiden nodded, knowing better than to say a single word at that moment. Antony shot him one more withering glare then turned on his heel and stomped into the garage, yelling and cursing at whatever hapless worker blocked his way.

As Aiden made his way toward the door, he caught sight of the photo hanging over the huge, old-fashioned oak desk harboring all manner of chaos—Antony, his face young and unlined, smiling, with his arm around a lovely blonde woman. A little girl with hair like her grandmother's, and her father's deep-brown eyes sat on the man's shoulders. Aiden shook his head, wondering why Antony let that image torture him every single day.

He'd married his high school sweetheart, like his friend Paul had done, just a little earlier in the game. He and the feisty cheerleader, Crystal Jenkins, had dated from halfway through their senior year then endured a tumultuous couple of years apart while she went to college in Knoxville, and Antony struggled and failed to complete his degree at the University of Kentucky.

Once he'd dropped out for good, declared to their family that he and a now-pregnant Crystal were getting married, and that he wanted to buy a small farm on ten acres across town, he'd also broken the news that he'd be taking over their aging uncle's garage.

Their father had merely shrugged and gone back to eating. Their mother had let out a small, polite gasp then rallied in her usual fashion when confronted by her family's ongoing drama.

"Well, then I guess Crystal's mama and I need to have a chat about a wedding...and a baby shower."

Aiden sighed and observed his bossy, know-it-all sibling for a few seconds, recalling the god-awful moment he'd heard Crystal had been in a wreck on I-75, coming back from a sorority reunion in Knoxville. Antony had gone into a deep hole after that, losing touch with everyone, including his young daughter.

"What the fuck are you staring at, punk?" Antony's harsh voice sliced through Aiden's reminiscing. "Get the hell out of my office. Shower. Go see our mother, and Lord help you if she won't hide you from Daddy."

Aiden nodded, and walked out, gripping the loaned truck keys.

Chapter Two

A iden stood in the office of Love Garage at four-thirty the next morning. He'd not been able to get back to sleep after a nightmare, so arriving early seemed as good a use of his time as any. The memory of his mother's drawn face when he'd shown up yesterday, unannounced, already violating one of her myriad rules of etiquette, had haunted him, making him toss and turn on the small bed in Antony's spare room.

She'd looked so diminished, reduced in a way that made his heart leap into his throat even now, recalling their visit.

"Oh, Aiden," she said with a sigh when he brought her a cup of her favorite spiced tea. *"What am I going to do with you?"*

He stopped and gripped the teacup, those familiar words bumping around like marbles against his near-constant guilt. He'd failed so completely at the one thing he'd wanted, after years and money spent, it made him want to yell, to punch a hole in the wall. The Love family home—a modest, four-bedroom, 1970s split-level on a few acres—had weathered its share of male fists in the Sheetrock.

He took a breath, set the cup down with a telltale rattle then sank into the large leather chair usually occupied by his father, while Mama curled up under a huge flannel blanket emblazoned with basketballs and the Lucasville High mascot—a rearing, slightly demonic-looking horse. Her red hair had streaks of pure gray threaded through it. The freckles on the face that he'd so loved to touch as a little boy, fascinated by them, by her, by the sheer wonderfulness of his mother, had faded, some disappearing altogether in the deep lines around her eyes and on her forehead.

He tried to think of something to say, but words failed him for the second time that day. No big surprise there. Par for the course, really, his inner, self-pitying, wanna-be writer yammered. He glanced around the room, both comforting and familiar, while sickeningly strange and empty.

His mother had a thing for rearranging and redecorating every three to five years, depending on how well the brewery had done the year prior. The most recent iteration involved heavy brown and maroon leather furniture, candles in holders fit for high mass, and a thin, but expensive, Asian-style rug over hardwood flooring the brothers had installed themselves fifteen years earlier.

Framed photos lined the top of a new bookshelf. Each of the Love siblings in their basketball uniforms—but for him in his up-yours soccer kit—were displayed, along with a graduation photo, and each of them at senior prom with some girl on their arm. Antony's wedding photo stood next to baby AliceLynn's newborn picture.

His sister Angelique's photos graced the space as well, taking up as almost as much room as the boys combined. Photos from her dance team, at one of the zillions of competitions she'd won, at her graduation, and one of her in a—to Aiden's mind—too-slinky prom dress for a seventeen-year-old. She and some lame kid in a tuxedo posed in front of their house with his mother's prize half-dozen dogwood trees in full bloom behind them.

He sighed and faced his mother, only to find her staring at him as if trying to figure him out. He grabbed the hand not holding her tea, desperation making him breathless.

"I'm sorry, Mama. I just...I can't deal with the politics of that program. I mean, I have the book written, you know? I need to...I don't know, work on it some more, submit it to some agents?"

"Why don't you publish it yourself? It's what everyone else seems to be doing. Half the books I see on my e-reader are published by the authors themselves."

Aiden grimaced. "I don't want to be a publisher. I want to be an author." He rose from the couch, hoping to end that particular topic. "Anyway, we need to focus on you for a while. It's one of the reasons I came back you know." He kissed the dry, papery skin of her cheek.

She touched his face, her eyes showing a bit of the sparkle he remembered.

"You know, I somehow knew you'd never really leave. I declare I could hardly get you to let go of my legs for the better part of two years before you finally got dragged to kindergarten. It took Antony to convince you of that. You worshipped that boy."

She patted his cheek hard, reminiscent of the smacks she had no qualm bestowing on all of them. Being able to whack her rowdy crowd of children upside the head every now and then had been her way of reestablishing control over her world. And while it would hurt physically, it hurt more emotionally, knowing her temper had been taxed to that point.

At least it had for him.

He took her hand, kissed it then made a few minutes more of fuss over her, aware of the clock ticking its way toward 7:00 p.m., the hour his father always arrived home.

"I should go." He handed her a lap blanket emblazoned with the University of Kentucky Wildcats' emblem.

She smiled, but the exhaustion on her face alarmed him even further. As a little boy, he'd been convinced that his mother never required sleep—that one of the magical mom things included not sleeping. She'd always be up and sipping a beer with her husband when Aiden went to bed then wide awake and having coffee when he'd stumble into the kitchen for breakfast.

It made sneaking out and back in as a teenager tough, if not impossible. The only one who'd ever fully flown in the face of that had been Dominic, the brother just older than him, which had made for some epic battles between Dom and their mother—battles Lindsay always won. Aiden never could figure out why he kept beating his head against the brick wall of their mother's rules. But he always had.

"You're going to have to face him eventually. I'm guessing Antony has already told him you're back and working for him."

Aiden frowned. Antony had always been the worst tattletale.

"I'm glad to have you back, son."

He smiled, unnerved by the tears standing in her eyes, hating to be the cause of it. He preferred it when his mother shed tears over their father, or his baby sister.

"Thanks, Mama. I'll get myself sorted out, I promise." Heading for the kitchen, he turned. "Oh, just curious. Is Antony dating Rosalee Norris?"

Lindsay frowned, her face looking younger for a split second. "Why?"

"No reason." He jingled Antony's truck keys in his pocket. "Just saw her and her little boy today at the garage. She and Antony seemed...close." He cursed his fair skin for the heat creeping up his cheeks.

"Antony claims he will never date again." Her voice sounded stronger now, which encouraged Aiden, as if marshaling her energy to meddle in the lives of her sons gave her a reason to rally. "Rosalee is a lovely girl, although that Jeffrey is wild as a March hare." She shook her head. "A real hellion. And I know one when I see one."

"Have you and Daddy...I mean, with Antony, and...her and Jeffrey?" Aiden hated sounding desperate but he'd sustained a low-level lust and mild obsession with Rosalee since seeing her, and wanted as much information as he could get.

"Why so interested?"

He looked down at his shoes. "Never mind."

"Aiden Leonardo, don't you waste breath lying to me."

"I'm not," he insisted, backing away, needing to escape. "I just want to know, you know, about my brother and...stuff."

She laughed, the tinkling, musical sound he'd adored his entire life. "Oh, you boys are going to be the death of me." Her eyes danced with amusement but her voice got serious. "You let Antony have this one, Aiden. He needs someone like her. He deserves her. You wait your turn."

"Yes, ma'am," he muttered, not terribly surprised she'd sliced through his pretense so efficiently. "AliceLynn still living here?" He had to divert the conversation somewhat. Antony had handed his daughter over to Lindsay to raise after Crystal's accident, while in the darkest depths of *his depression. They'd agreed to do it, "for a while." But that "while" had stretched out over a decade.*

"Yes, she is. But she's at Crystal's mama's house about half the time." *Lindsay picked up her e-reader.* "You know, once that Renee finds out you're back in town I'm guessing you'll have your fool hands full with her again." *She slipped on her reading glasses, pinning him with her unwavering gaze.* "You remember condoms, young man. Do what you must, but know that I do not want that girl spawning my next grandbaby. Lord, have mercy."

Renee Reese. He'd almost forgotten about her.

And now, the sun rose over the tops of the small town where he'd grown up lighting the edges of the Love Garage's bright white interior. The town that had begun life as support to a bunch of horse farms in the picturesque landscape between Kentucky's two largest cities had morphed into an extended, upscale suburb of Lexington. Full of huge, fancy neighborhoods built on those former horse farms' land, complete with a Whole Foods Market, PF Chang's, and a giant outlet mall, with a water park, a driving range, a mini-racetrack, and a sprawling soccer complex, the kind Aiden wished he'd had access to as a kid.

The "charming" downtown remained, but sans a lot of the businesses Aiden remembered. The local hardware store got priced out of town by the Home Depot. The village pharmacy replaced by not one, but two large chain stores. There were a few stalwarts, thanks to the locals who remained. Shug's, the ice cream and soda shop, with red-leatherette benches, and black-and-white-checked floor tile, and Bryant's Burgers, a hole-in-the-wall dump of a place, with seating for about twenty, and a sticky, smelly bar. It had been featured on *Man v. Food* not once, but twice.

And of course, the small corner once occupied by the original Love Bros Brewing Company that had been founded by Aiden's father and uncle nearly thirty years before, prior to the craft beer explosion across America. It still housed The Love Pub—a name that made Aiden flinch every time he saw or heard it. The quaint town square boasted huge, ancient trees, a fountain, and a statue of William Haynes Lucas, owner of the biggest, oldest, and most famously bankrupt horse farm in the nation.

During the summer months, teenagers lolled around on blankets, girls trying to attract boys, boys pretending not to be attracted. Moms and toddlers hung out during the days, playing on the swings and slides in one corner. There were mass picnics for the town, including the annual Labor Day fish fry, festivals galore, and in the winter, a small, manufactured ice rink tucked in next to the Jeffersonian-style courthouse.

To his literary mind, it had always seemed very *Our Town*, both the good and the bad. He'd spent a lot of years yearning to get the hell away from it. But damned if its familiar contours, the scent of distinct maltiness from the new Love Brewing production facility down Hunter Road from the garage, and the ability to order his day by the train whistles every four hours, relieved him in ways he'd never believed possible.

He sipped his coffee and glanced around at the pristine shop floor, the gleaming lifts, the rows of organized, polished tools. His back ached and his legs were sore, but for the first time in nearly three years, he experienced near perfect contentment. On a whim he did a quick phone search, hitting the letters R-E-N- before the name of the girl in question appeared, surprising him a little.

Not a girl anymore. A thirty-one year-old woman, a business woman, he'd heard, who owned some chic salon and spa. Renee's had been written up a lot online when it opened.

His mother had sent him one of the links. "Thought you might want to see what your high school sweetie got up to," she'd said in her email. "All the rich ladies in the big houses go there."

Renee had been in Dominic's class in high school, and her obsession with him had been legend. He'd hooked up with her a few times, before he dumped her like he did pretty much every girl he dated.

She'd shown up at the Love family home the night of their break up, sobbing, begging Aiden to tell Dom she needed to talk. Aiden had eagerly surrendered his virginity to her within an hour on a rickety cot in the corner of the lowest floor of their quad-level house. It had been the most glorious moment, full of whispers, lips, teeth, smells, skin, and sighs of delight.

Moment being the key word of course, since he'd been a raw rookie. After that, she'd taken him on as a project, determined to teach him, the "sweet Love brother," how to really treat a girl.

Aiden sighed and slouched against the open garage door, his skin tingling even now at the memory of her firm, porcelain skin. The way she'd taken his fingers and placed them here, then there, told him to press, rub, stroke, fast...faster...then how to properly use his lips and tongue. He shifted, embarrassed by how his body still, to this day, anticipated the lovely, brash, sexy Renee.

Dominic had spent about an hour threatening him with bodily harm for "stealing his girlfriend," a few weeks later. But their father ended that, nearly shoving Dom through the wall of the upstairs hallway over it.

"I won't have you punks fighting over puss—over girls. Your mama and I have enough on our plates without that shit." He'd poked Dom in the chest then smacked his face when he wouldn't meet his eyes. "You dumped her, Dominic Sean, unless my memory of her crazy caterwauling on my porch deceives me. And I don't think it does. You don't want her. That makes her fair game. I'm not saying I'm thrilled that Little A is letting some woman drive him around but...." He'd shrugged then clapped Aiden on the back. "You must have something going on she likes, eh boy?"

"Don't call me little A, please, sir," he'd muttered, mortified, but glad that his father had intervened. He'd been more than a little afraid of Dominic, most days.

Dominic had walked away in a huff, and left him a gift that night by way of a sticky, still-cum-wet Kleenex under his pillow, where Aiden always stuck his hands when he slept. He'd not mentioned it though—refused to give the jerk the satisfaction. Besides, what other nearly sixteen-year-old had such amazing, upper classman, feminine riches at his fingertips? He'd have been an idiot to jeopardize it.

His parents drew the line at him going to prom with her though, so she'd gone without him, which had driven him mad with jealousy. They'd stuck as an on-again-off-again couple her one remaining year of high school, and nearly a year after that, while she attended night school and worked at her aunt's hair salon. To this day, the smell of hairspray and acetone had the power to give Aiden a painful boner, thanks to all their illicit time in that place.

He snuck one of the two cigarettes he allowed per day out, lit it, and sucked in smoke, reveling in its forbidden satisfaction. Better two than two packs, he claimed. But he'd once been a two-pack a day smoker, working deep into the night on his novel only to emerge, stiff-necked and starving, his mouth tasting like an ashtray when the morning alarm sounded.

Just as he finished the cig, he caught sight of Antony's car in the distance. Wondering when—or better yet, how—he'd made the trade back with Rosalee yesterday, Aiden smashed the butt with his heel, then picked it up and ducked inside, sticking a piece of gum in his mouth.

Antony parked and climbed out of the car, stretching up and then down to touch his feet, before heading to the door. Aiden watched him, the full force of family memory hitting him hard. Antony had always been his favorite. The oldest brother had taken on responsibility for Little A (as opposed to Antony's, Big A) with relish, shielding him from the scary, intense Dominic while they were all more or less ignored by the ginger-haired, family hero, Kieran—the one serious athlete of the group of them, and the acknowledged family peace-keeper, or brown-noser, depending on the situation.

Aiden glanced around the office, reassessing the order he'd spent an hour imposing on the place, where receipts, invoices, and bills had once been lumped into huge, grease-stained piles. He'd brought in some dollar-store plastic bins, labeled them then sorted through the mess of paper on the desk, depositing them in their respective new homes.

He'd wiped down every visible surface, going through mounds of paper towels and de-greaser spray to get the worst of the ubiquitous sheen of dusty grime. All this after he'd mopped down the garage floor twice, used the degreaser and rags on all visible lifts, work tables and tools and even cleaned the garage door windows.

He'd kept rap music cranked, distracting him from his gut-deep exhaustion. Then he'd hunted down the coffee maker underneath six inches of disgusting grime, ran down to Publix for coffee and filters, and now the office smelled less like grease monkey, and more like morning.

"What the fucking hell is that noise?" Antony loomed in the doorway, glaring at him then at the newly neat-and-tidy office desk. "And what the hell have you done in here?"

"Cleaned up. I didn't lose anything or throw away a single piece of paper. I just imposed some order is all."

"Hmph." His brother dropped into the large leather chair with a groan.

"Knee?" Aiden passed him a cup of coffee in a cup he'd spent the better part of ten minutes de-grossifying.

Antony let out another grunt and took the cup, squinting through the rising steam from the coffee. "Stop that cat-in-heat noise. Please," he added.

Aiden reached over and disconnected his phone from the speaker. He had a sort of random, immature thrill of eagerness for approval and resisted the urge to say things like, *did you see the garage floor? How about that bathroom?*

Antony sipped in silence, ignoring him. Aiden had heard him tossing and turning the night before as well, but had been unsure if asking if the guy wanted to get up and join him for a shot of bourbon would have been the right thing to do.

He'd been curious about AliceLynn, Antony and Crystal's now-teenaged daughter, but had been informed of the topic's off-limits nature night before, once Antony had returned home from a date.

"Not really on a date," he'd claimed, as he downed two glasses of water in quick succession. "Rosie's house needs as much work as her car, and she can't afford to hire anybody. So, she feeds me a decent dinner, and I fix leaks, caulk windows, mow grass, that sort of thing."

"Sounds convenient, almost like marriage," Aiden had quipped, as a flare of jealousy hit him square in the chest.

Antony hadn't answered. He'd merely placed the glass in the sink and shuffled past the table still favoring the knee he'd blown out his senior year.

According to their mother, the brothers who remained in the area still gathered every Sunday morning for the weekly round-ball game. Sometimes friends joined them, sometimes not, but they never ever skipped it, no matter the weather. That probably did not help the condition of Antony's knee.

"Don't leave any lights on when you go to bed," he'd said, without looking at him. "I've gotta get some sleep."

He'd lurched down the hallway while cursing under his breath. Before his wife had been killed, Antony had been the most talkative, gregarious, and outgoing of them all, very much a responsible oldest sibling, but in a positive way. Granted, the man had always had a ferocious temper, and suffered no fools. But the morose version of the man who'd championed and protected him from birth now seemed to be the new Antony. Except of course, those few minutes when he'd been around Rosie Norris.

Aiden sighed and dropped his chin into his palm.

"Let Antony have this one," his mother had insisted. And she'd been right.

After making a mental note to call Renee the next day, he'd retired to the third bedroom, feeling tired enough to sleep for weeks, only to lay awake studying the ceiling hour after hour.

Aiden watched Antony as he sat at his desk, his face impassive. "I, um, cleaned everything, so you'll just have to point me where you want me to go for the rest of today."

Antony gave a noncommittal grunt, still not really acknowledging him. Finally, he got up and plugged his own phone into the speakers. Twanging country music exploded into the garage. Aiden rolled his eyes, pondering just how long and crappy this day might be.

By noon, the non-sleep, busy-work adrenaline had fully dissipated. He sat in the office, head dropping back and bouncing forward in the warm room. Weird half-dreams haunted him—memories of Renee's lips, and tits, and skin, mixed in with images of Rosalee's compact sexiness, her thick brown hair, those deep-green eyes. He awoke on the floor after tumbling backward in the chair, then scrambled to his feet, wincing at the tightness behind his zipper.

Wet dreams in the middle of the day, Aiden? Nice.

Gazing into the now sparkling bathroom mirror, he grimaced, studying his own familiar features. He'd been blessed with a square jaw, just like all of the Loves, with a straight nose made crooked by a hard blow from Antony in his senior year, and good teeth. Only two of them had required braces as adolescents, well, three counting his sister, he supposed.

His skin tone fell somewhere between fair and lightly tanned. He had thick brown hair and nondescript hazel eyes. Antony's deep-olive skin mirrored that of their father and uncle. He also had the chocolate-colored Amatore family eyes. Kieran's pale, freckled, red-headed, visage reflected their mother's Irish heritage. Her huge pack of older siblings had declared Kieran the "only decent one of the bunch," based on his old-country looks.

Dom's skin was bronze, a perfect match to his long, golden-blond hair. He'd "cursed" it, according to their mother, with wild, intricate tattoos, and bizarre piercings. Aiden had even heard the guy had pierced his dick, which he simply could not get his mind around despite having seen the ring in his nipple plenty of times.

Of the four brothers, Aiden had always been the least striking. Just a regular guy, but with a face he figured would always seem a little younger than his actual years. Which worked for him because, thanks to the lovely Renee, he'd been totally hooked on older women from the beginning of his sexual history.

He'd even gotten tangled up with a professor out in Iowa.

"Practice makes perfect," she liked to say as she propped on her many pillows and Aiden did whatever she asked of him. Her husband had not been amused. That had ended badly for everyone. He'd been celibate since, which grated on him.

He frowned.

Hi, I'm Aiden, a healthy twenty-seven year-old with two Bachelor's Degrees in Something Useless, and an unfinished Master's in Fine Arts. I've not had sex with anything other than my right hand for going on four years, and I'm back at home, broke, begging my brothers for jobs, and places to sleep, and my mother is dying of cancer. Oh, and I'm too scared to face my own father, so I haven't seen or talked to him yet, although I've been in town for two days already. Plus, the minute Dom sees me, he'll probably deck me.

He made a mental note to call Renee.

Chapter Three

The day ended around six-thirty, when the last of the Love Garage employees called a good-bye and roared away on his motorcycle. Antony glanced over at him as he prepared to shut off the lights.

"I need help with the horses."

"Tonight?" Exhaustion settled deep into Aiden's bones. He'd give a million dollars for a nap.

"Earning your keep and all that, since I'm letting you eat my food, use my water and electricity, plus paying you to be the maid around here." Antony put away his tools and headed for the office.

"Yeah. Right. Okay." Aiden stretched out his lower back and tried hard not to complain. He could knock out the feeding and grooming stuff in a couple of hours.

They shut the place down and rode home in silence, windows cranked open to the suffocating heat. Aiden closed his eyes and let the motion-generated breeze cool the sweat on his face. He jolted awake when Antony braked in the long gravel driveway in front of his house. A strange car, a beater compact of some sort, sat there.

Aiden glanced at his brother, who glared at it, frowning. "AliceLynn's here," he said under his breath. "Wonder what she wants."

Quietly, Aiden opened his door and got out, deciding that heading straight for the barn at the back of the property presented his best plan of action at that moment. As he traversed the expanse of grass, he had another pang of regret for his one-time, upbeat oldest brother. The farm had been a wedding gift from Crystal's parents, allowing him to hang onto his savings. He had started such a great life here with his wife and baby daughter.

The familiar routine of horse care distracted Aiden for another couple of hours. His mother's two dressage beauties—Lucy and Daisy—seemed thrilled to see him, prancing around and nuzzling his armpits with equine familiarity. Once he had fresh hay forked into all five stalls, and had brought them and Antony's three others back inside from the open paddock where they roamed all day, he had to sit on an overturned bucket, lest he fall down in a heap. If he were the type, he'd cry from exhaustion, hunger, and thirst.

Finally, when a bell rang from the vicinity of the house, he got up and stumbled into the waning daylight. Antony had grilled some burgers and set out a salad. But no sign of the beater car, or of Antony's daughter, AliceLynn, remained anywhere. They ate with the television tuned to a Reds game without exchanging more than two words of meal logistics.

Aiden flopped back on the couch and sighed. He hated baseball almost as much as he hated country music. "I'm gonna go out for a bit," he declared at the same moment, remembering he had no transportation. "I mean, do you wanna come—"

"No. I'm beat. Keys are on the counter. Don't drink and drive my truck, punk."

Everything about this day left Aiden deflated. But he rallied, determined to draw Antony out of his funk. "C'mon, Antony, let's go out and get a bourbon somewhere."

"Fuck off." He propped his feet on the ottoman and kept his eyes pinned on the TV screen. "Some of us have to work in the morning."

Aiden gripped his phone, thinking he'd call Renee, hoping maybe she'd have a better attitude about a drink with him. He waited for a couple of minutes, but his brother never glanced away from the screen.

Aiden spent five minutes deciding not to go to his father's brew pub, or to the new wine bar downtown, and ended up at The Cat House, a dive bar on the west side of town that had not changed a lick since he'd last been there. Ostensibly a sports bar, with a ton of televisions, two pool tables, some dart boards, and disgusting food fried in ages-old grease, it provided the perfect venue to get shit-faced in some anonymity.

He greeted a bunch of dudes that he'd swear had been in the exact same position the last Christmas he'd been home. Then he sat, ordered his bourbon, and held onto it, pondering the amazing and rotten new curve fate had tossed him.

After two more bourbons he felt less shitty, and agreed to play pool. He got his ass kicked the first game then picked up a win and a fourth drink. Antony's warning about drinking and driving his truck gave him some pause as he sipped it, eyeing a couple of women who'd just walked in the door. One of them seemed familiar. He wondered if the bourbon had messed with his eyesight.

She and the other girl sat at the bar and ordered beers then put their heads together like they were on some kind of man-hating girl retreat. Aiden attempted to focus on his pool game. After thirty minutes, he'd had another drink and had forgotten about her. When a soft, spicy-smelling perfume hit his nose and he straightened up from a beautiful corner-pocket shot and found Tricia Shelton, Crystal's older sister close to him, he stumbled backward and almost fell on his ass.

"Well, my Lordy, if it isn't the littlest Love," she called out, her blue eyes twinkly. "What in the world are you doing back in this shithole town, Aiden? I thought you were at an Ivy League college somewhere."

Tricia had been one of those girls he'd practically grown up with. Her parents were fellow church members, and owned the insurance company his father used. Tricia and Crystal had been close, bonded in the way children of small-business-owning parents would be—very much like Aiden and his siblings. Like most kids at Lucasville High belonging to the original families of the town, they were all tight, and hung out together in the face of the increasing hoards of invading suburbanites.

When the Love family had gotten an in-ground pool installed, things had taken a turn for the distressing, in his opinion. Both Crystal and her sister would hang around, draped over chairs or floating on rafts all summer long, flaunting their cheerleader bodies—compact, perky, and perfect fodder for young Aiden's vivid fantasy life.

Once Antony and Crystal hooked up and stayed that way as seniors, she and her sister practically lived at the Love pool when they weren't working at Shug's, or in their parents' insurance office.

Aiden watched through a boozy haze as the woman who had fueled his most active, early whack-off sessions loomed closer. She would be in her thirties by now, but looked not a day over twenty, at least thanks to the brown liquor he'd imbibed. Walking right up to him, she gave him a full body hug, hanging on so long the men around the pool table hooted and whistled.

To his surprised dismay, she planted the sort of kiss on him that made him spring a woody like a teenager. She smelled and tasted like heaven at that moment. So he indulged her, even reaching down to grip her firm, jeans-clad ass as the kiss went on beyond anything anyone would consider "friendly."

"Mmm." She ended it by sliding her hand around the back of his neck. "Welcome home."

"I would have shown up sooner if I knew I'd get such a pleasant welcome." He held onto her, reveling in the press of her breasts, and the sensation of her curves under his hands.

Jesus, but I am horny.

He cleared his throat and stepped away, grateful he'd kept his shirttail hanging over his jeans.

When he saw the tears in her eyes, he stepped forward again. He hated when women cried, went out of his way to avoid anything that would cause it. But she wiped her eyes then shook her long, dark-blonde hair back over her shoulders and cocked one hip. Aiden gulped, confused, drunk from one too many drinks, or perhaps mere lust.

What sort of bizarre fantasy-fulfillment moment this was, he had no idea. But he believed he owed it to his recent streak of bad luck to just go with it.

"Sorry. I just keep thinking about the last time I saw you. At the funeral."

He frowned and held out an arm. She tucked in next to him, swaying on her wedge sandal heels, her smallish frame fitting nicely into his side, her hand landing with purpose on his upper thigh.

"I'm a little tipsy," she whispered into his neck. "But I'm so glad to see you!"

He gave her a squeeze, pondering his immediate options. He could hardly take her back to Antony's. That would be way weird on too many levels. She distracted him from his scheming with a hard squeeze to the thigh she'd been stroking.

"Buy me one of those?" She pointed to his half-empty rocks' glass. "I'm celebrating." She pressed close to his side.

"Oh," he said, finding his voice at last, but still frozen in place, unwilling to let go of her. "Sounds like fun. What's the occasion?"

"What else, sweet cheeks." She batted her lashes. "The successful failure of my marriage. Woo-fucking-hoo." A single tear slid down her face.

Her friend appeared then, clutching two beers, and wearing a not-happy-to-see-you expression at the sight of Aiden. Then her eyes softened. "Well, of all people, Aiden Love. I never thought I'd see you again."

Aiden gulped, trying to remember her name. But Tricia's hand kept moving against his leg, and his poor, lonely cock had gone rigid behind his zipper. To keep from cutting off circulation to his entire body, he straightened and let go of Tricia, who was sniffling again.

"Chill out, sister. Good riddance. That husband of yours is a no-good, cheating, dickhead," the girl insisted, sipping her beer, and

giving Aiden a frank top-to-toe checking-out. "Let's flirt with this
handsome young man, play some pool, and celebrate."

Tricia sighed and gripped her beer bottle. Aiden was hypnotized by
the glow of sweat in the scooped-out V of her tank top. He wanted to
lick it so badly he had to clench his jaw not to do it right now in front
of God and everybody.

Tricia had teased him relentlessly for so many years, with those
string bikinis, her sideways looks, and once, memorably, with a quick,
stolen kiss in the lowest level of his house one late summer afternoon.
He'd been shocked, but had opened his mouth, accepted her tongue,
groaned, grabbed her boob, and immediately come in his swim trunks.
She'd retreated, giggling and blowing him kisses. He'd despised her
then, in a strange sort of lust-tinged, hateful way.

He got three bourbons from the bar and turned to find her out on
the small dance floor, swaying to crappy country music oozing from the
juke. Her jeans were dark and formfitting, her waist slim, her arms bare
and tanned. Afraid he might pant like a dog otherwise, he averted his
eyes when the two girls started dancing together.

"Jesus-hopped up-Christ," one of his forgotten pool-playing
buddies whispered, watching them. "Anybody got a video camera?"

"Hit that shit, Love. I'm feeling a three-way in your immediate,
lucky-dog future," said another.

He flushed then downed two of the bourbons fast, not tasting
them. Setting the empties down on a nearby table he scratched his nose,
noting he'd gotten pretty numb around the edges. Best slow down, grab
some water. Because if he didn't get both of them, he definitely planned
to fuck Tricia's brains out tonight.

Yes, indeed.

Where he would be doing that, he'd have to sort out later.

He jolted forward when one of the assholes hit him between the
shoulder blades, forcing him to take a couple of steps closer to the girls.

They parted and held out their arms in encouragement. But he needed very little.

Chapter Four

It took him about an hour to sort out Tricia's friend had no interest in a celebratory three-way. Aiden couldn't remember why by the time he had Tricia in the passenger's seat of the truck. They made their way slowly along back roads, with the windows open, the radio blasting, and it no longer mattered.

They'd had a beer then a bourbon chaser, and danced, kissed, and generally engaged in enough publicly displayed foreplay to make him feverish and overwrought by the time the bartender hollered out last call. Aiden's horniness level at that moment had blinded and deafened him. She'd dropped her hand right on his zipper, giggling into his ear, stroking him through his jeans in a dark, smelly corner near the juke.

"You're not gonna make me blow in my shorts again, Tricia. Stop trying. I'm a big boy now," he'd whispered, letting his lips, tongue, and teeth tease her deliciously sweaty neck. He loved how her nipples poked through her thin bra when he did that, and had to bite the inside of his cheek not to grope her just as enthusiastically. He wanted to savor, to drop into her like the horny teenager he'd once been, but with a skill set honed by years spent with women determined to make a better lover out of him.

"I can tell that." She kissed him again in such a way it nearly did him in. Letting him go, she'd wiggled her way back out onto the deserted dance floor, shaking her hips and ass, closing her eyes, and generally making it a thousand times worse.

Now, she sat with her face up to the warm night breeze, singing between taking long drinks from the neck of the bourbon bottle he'd bought on their way out. When he stopped at the entrance to Antony's driveway, she gasped.

"I can't go in there." She pointed at the house where Crystal and Antony had lived for a few blissful years.

"I'm a country boy, Tricia." He grabbed her hand and kissed it. "I know a place with some nice, dry hay."

She burst out laughing. "I am not going to roll in the damn hay with you, Aiden Love." She unzipped him and he gasped with relief. "Wow." Gripping his aching dick, she kissed him again. "Not-so-little boy, I see," she said into his lips.

"Oh shit," he muttered, and grabbed her hand to make her stop. "No. Wait."

Remaining unzipped, he threaded his fingers in hers and drove past the house. He'd gone for so many hours wanting to touch her, not giving into it other than the kissing and ass-grabbing, he would likely explode if he didn't get his hands and mouth all over her.

But where to go? If she wouldn't do the hay-barn thing, he'd be damned if he knew where. He climbed out of the truck, zipped up, opened the gate, drove through then re-latched it.

"Kiss me some more, Aiden," she demanded when he got back behind the wheel.

He did, allowing a momentary touch to the side of her breast, a flick of his thumb over her nipple while she reached for his zipper again. The exposed skin of their faces and necks were slick. He indulged his earlier compulsion by lapping at the sweat beaded between her full, lush breasts.

She giggled and shoved him off her then jumped out of the truck without another word. He looked in the small backseat and spotted a blanket, grabbed it, and ran after her through the tall grass toward the big pond tucked into the back corner of Antony's property. The expanse of water could hold a couple of rowboats or canoes, and Antony kept it stocked with fish. Tricia's giggling floated back to him, and by the time he'd caught up with her, she stood in the moonlight utterly, gloriously, perfectly naked.

He sent a quick thanks to heaven for her timing that night, and stripped out of his clothes, almost falling over his jeans in his urgency to get at her. She kept backing up, crooking her finger at him. Just as he reached her, she plunged into the water. He saw her surface as the surreal, dream-like moment hit him.

"Come on in, sweet cheeks." She swam up closer, and rose so he got the full effect of the water sluicing off her skin. He followed her, wincing when the cold water hit his dick, but relieved when it knocked some of his edge off.

They swam around, splashing each other, and she let out a scream when she claimed something brushed against her leg. "It's slimy in this end," she said, swimming back to him and wrapping her arms and legs around him. Her warmth pressed against his slightly softened erection, making him grunt. "Let's get out. I want you to make love to me right here, under the stars and moon." She threw her head back, and he buried his face in her neck as he tried to walk out of the lake without falling.

Dizziness struck him between the eyes, but she had her lips on his, and he rallied enough to get them both out of the water. She licked her way down his chest, flicking her tongue over his nipples as she detached herself then dragged him by the dick, literally, about three feet from the pond, before letting go so she could spread the blanket out, which released a definite horsey smell. He blinked, trying to get past the urge to toss her down and plow into her, just to relieve the painful pressure up and down his spine.

"Oh, Aiden." she said, her voice tearful. "I...I'm...."

"Shhh." He kissed her cheeks, nose, forehead, and then her lips. "Shhh." He deepened it, sweeping into her mouth with his tongue, and bending his knees, bringing her down with him. She lay back, taking him with her, keeping their lips locked.

But he broke away, trying to catch his breath. "You are about to fulfill one of my deepest, darkest fantasies, Tricia. And for that I want to thank you." Her nipples tasted like pond water but he didn't care. When she arched her back and moved her hips against him, he kept moving downward, lapping at the water beaded on her skin. Tossing both her legs over his shoulders he focused on his task, one of his favorites.

She yanked at his hair and dug her bare heels into his back. Her orgasm hovered close—he could taste it and smell it and feel it in the way her body tensed. He increased his efforts, wanting it so badly his whole body shook.

"Oh dear Jesus!" she shrieked, making him let go of his suction, having learned that lesson. He adored the female anatomy, and had spent an inordinate amount of time pondering it. And this moment was his second favorite one of all—when he could watch it glisten, pulse, and spasm under his careful attention.

"Holy shit, Aiden, that was...addictive." She tugged at his arm so he crawled up her body, the breeze cooling them both and making his skin break out in goose bumps. He hurt all over, he wanted to come so badly—inside her. But for a little problem.

"I don't have a condom." He exhaled and flopped over onto his back. Tricia dropped between his legs in an instant, her hand cupping his balls, and her lips over his cock by way of response to that dilemma. She did her own teasing, sucking, licking, and had him on the ragged edge, grunting, hips bucking when she stopped and sat up, wiping a hand over her lips.

"I need you inside me," she whispered, still gripping his dick. "So badly, Aiden, baby, please."

He watched her straddle him as if from a million miles away. When her warmth enveloped him, he knew he wouldn't stop her. *God, you are an idiot, Aiden Love,* his upper brain yammered at him, until his lower brain smothered it with a pillow as Tricia rocked against him, tightening and releasing her inner muscles.

"Oh, honey," she sighed and gripped his thigh with one hand, propping against his torso with the other. "That is exactly...it," she ground out, moving faster and faster. He grabbed onto her thighs, dug in his fingertips and angled his hips.

"Come again, Tricia." He'd gotten breathless from holding back. "Give it to me." He yanked her down so he could suck her nipples. Her wet hair shut them off from the world as she shivered and her second climax grabbed him hard.

"Hang onto me." He rolled and pinned her beneath him. "I need....to...." He lowered his face to her neck and called on his grown-up reserves.

She tilted her hips, wrapped her legs around him. "Fuck me hard, Aiden. Just like you always wanted to."

That tore it.

With a groan of satisfaction he let it take him, allowed the orgasm to blind him, deafen him, and he pounded into her. Only at the very last minute, opening his eyes and staring into her face, did he see the tears glistening on her lashes.

"Shit," he muttered, his hips still moving, his body still clenched up with pleasure. "I'm sorry. I didn't mean to hurt you."

"You didn't hurt me, sweetie. That was the best damn divorce celebration a girl could order up." She kissed him, making him wince a little and realize his damn lips were sore it had been so long since he'd done this.

"Hey!" A loud voice cut into his brain's shut-down mode. "Who the hell is out here?"

Aiden scrambled to his feet, trying to avoid the beam of the flashlight slicing through the dark trees. Tricia gasped and grabbed the blanket, wrapping it around her bare body, leaving him with his half-hard dick exposed, and facing his brother.

"Good Christ, punk, you spooked my horses, and my dogs, and woke me up."

Aiden took a long, shuddery breath, trying to figure out what he could say that might make the moment less awkward. He had nothing.

He tried to step in front of the crouching, blanket-wrapped woman about a half second too late.

"Tricia, seriously? Out here in the mud with Little A? Nice."

"Hey, Antony," the girl said, weakly. Aiden shut his eyes. "Sorry we woke you up."

"You're both idiots," Antony muttered as he stomped away.

Aiden released a huge breath before helping Tricia to her feet. She giggled and fell into him.

"Sorry, sweetie. He's really a grump isn't he?"

"Yeah." He tried not to despise his own sorry ass, with yet another example of his extreme lameness, getting caught fucking a woman in the pasture now under his fraternal belt. He groaned and his head pounded, already foreshadowing a nasty, bourbon-fueled hangover.

They got dressed, slapping at the mosquitoes they'd managed to ignore during their screwing session. Thanks to his brothers' various dumb-ass errors, not going bareback had always been a hard-and-fast rule for him—one he'd ignored tonight with relish.

"Don't worry," Tricia muttered at one point as they made their way back to the truck. She slipped her arm around his waist. "I won't get preggers."

"Whatever." Fury made his vision dim—anger at himself, and with her for being such...such....

Oh shut up, Aiden, you idiot. Get her home and pray she didn't give you a disease, but don't even think *about blaming her.*

They didn't speak on their way to her house, which happened to be in one of the new, expensive subdivisions named after the horse farm that had sold the land to a developer. He peered up at her gigantic brick mansion and sighed, wondering why in the hell the woman had not suggested they come there, instead of rutting around in the pond and pasture.

She touched his leg, making him flinch.

"Sorry."

"No, I'm sorry," he said, meaning it. He hardly ever got that out of control. Mortification, plus nausea from the booze, and the smell of pond water filled his consciousness.

"Will you call me? I'll make us dinner."

Even as he nodded, he realized he couldn't face her again after tonight. She kissed him before she got out, and that seemed okay, nice even. But he kept a death grip on the steering wheel.

"I'm usually not that—"

"Eager? Amazing? Great at oral? Jesus, Aiden, I'm not kidding. You are addictive." Her hand trailed along the inseam of his jeans. "I'm up for more. I have a big bed." She raised an eyebrow.

"Thanks for telling me that now. We could have avoided the horse blanket, the mud, and my brother's flashlight."

She giggled, bit his earlobe then jumped down from the cab. He waited to make sure she got in the house then drove out into the empty street, wondering if the loose window in the lower level of his parents' house would still be there, rigged up and ready to receive whichever Love sibling snuck in past curfew. Weighing the two crappy choices—dealing with his brother versus facing his parents, he took a long, deep breath.

With the briefest acknowledgement that he did feel less fraught, thanks to Tricia and the sex by the pond, he kept driving past his parents' street, in the direction of the farm and Antony's fury.

Chapter Five

Love Garage opened bright and early the next morning, a Saturday, a day Aiden had hoped to spend recovering.

"I get so many oil changes and random small jobs on Saturdays, it doesn't make sense to be closed and let the jackasses with the Quickilube at Walmart get the business," Antony insisted when Aiden groaned with dismay upon being awakened after two hours of drunken sleep. It didn't help that the awakening occurred at the business end of a thrown pillow. "Get up, Romeo. You owe me rent money."

He did, slowly, queasily hitting a shower, sore all over, his skin mottled from bug bites. But nothing topped the glorious agony of a bourbon hangover like the one that had him firmly in its evil grasp.

He slouched out the door, cursing Antony, cursing Tricia, cursing her ex-husband for throwing her in his path last night. But mostly cursing his own weak-ass uselessness. He rested his head against the cool comfort of the truck window until Antony hit a bump or two, which sent extra pain jolting down his spine.

"Sorry," his brother muttered, glancing over at him.

"No, you're not."

"Got me there. And you'd better warn me if you're about to toss your cookies. I won't have that in my vehicle, got me?"

Aiden rubbed his neck and nodded, swallowing the urge to throw up all over the pristine interior on principal. "Why d'you hate me so much? You used to like me." He stared over at his brother, heart thumping, ears humming, throat closing up with nausea. He despised waking up still drunk.

"I don't hate you." Antony turned onto the main road headed into town.

"Could've fooled me. You're a real asshole anymore. Worse than Dom."

Antony merely shrugged, not rising to that tried-and-true bait. So they spent the rest of the ride to the garage in silence. Once there, Antony sat gripping the wheel. Aiden waited, hoping he'd get something out of him—something that would assure him that the man he thought he remembered as the protective, funny, and loving guy he'd grown up with still existed inside the guy walking around wearing Antony's skin.

Finally, he let go of the wheel, exhaled, and squared his shoulders as if prepping for battle. Aiden made a mental note to talk to Kieran about how badly Antony had descended into his life of non-stop mourning and jerk-hood.

"So, Rosalee, not putting out for you or what? You need to get laid maybe? Knock the edge off?"

The glare Aiden got for saying those particular words did make him worry Antony might punch his aching head through the passenger-side window.

He clenched his jaw in the way Aiden remembered from their childhood. "That is so far outside the realm of your business as to be in another galaxy. Get to work and don't say her name to me again."

And with that, Aiden was left with the fleeting thought that mentioning Rosalee directly was probably not a good idea. He surely didn't need Antony to guess that her name was on his lips, or front and center of his mind.

He shook his head—a Bad Plan because it summoned the pounding agony back with a vengeance. Groaning, he climbed out and shuffled over to the door.

A new day began at Love Garage.

It passed in a haze of nausea and agony then of exhaustion as his body shifted gears from alcohol processing, to the urge for real sleep. He scurried around after Antony awhile, until the man nearly brained him with a socket wrench for being "underfoot." Then he retreated to a corner, willing the hangover to leave him in peace. That worked about as well as it usually did.

Finally, one of the mechanics motioned for him to help with a tire rotation. Sweat streamed down his face, and his shoulders ached, but the exertion pierced through the agony, leaving him thirsty and hungry. He glanced at Antony's profile, while he sat at the giant desk in his newly clean office, then nodded when one of the other guys asked if he wanted in on pizza for lunch.

After a couple of slices of pepperoni, and a few slugs of sugary cola, he acknowledged he might just possibly live through the next twelve hours. His phone had been buzzing like crazy with texts from Tricia, but he ignored them. Tonight he had a hot date with Antony's couch, giant flat-screen TV, and sleep. He grinned, pondering that potential awesomeness.

By 4 p.m. with another two hours to go before closing, the garage teemed with business. Every lift held a vehicle, and there were three more hanging around in the parking lot waiting for service. Aiden slammed more cola and tried to stay focused on the oil-changing lesson Antony insisted on giving him. By the time he thought he had the hang of it, the clock showed six-thirty and the place had finally calmed.

He collected all the greasy rags, wiped down and organized the tools per Antony's instructions. When he heard a loud screech of tires right outside the garage, he tried to focus as his body processed the carbs from lunch and headed into sleep mode.

Antony stuck his head out of the office door at the sound, his dark eyes angry, until he saw Rosalee jump out of her rattletrap SUV, leaving the engine running and the door open. Tears streamed down her cheeks. Aiden dropped the rags and headed toward the open bay door, heart speeding up, making his head hurt again.

"He's gone," the woman yelped.

Antony caught her arms.

"Who's gone? Calm down, Rosie. Tell me what happened."

"Calm down? Are you crazy? It's Jeffrey, he ran away from the day care!" She whipped her head around and caught Aiden's eye, stopping him dead in his tracks. "He kept talking about you and the garage, so I thought...I thought...oh, shit." She seemed to collapse in on herself. Antony grabbed her and held tight, burying his nose in her hair.

"We haven't seen him all day." Aiden moved closer to the two of them, still tingling from the expression on her face.

Get a grip. She's your brother's woman.

Antony flinched at the sound of Aiden's voice. He held onto Rosalee's arms and spoke to Aiden while keeping his gaze fixed on the hysterical woman in front of him.

"Call the cops. Ask for Mark and tell him to get over here."

Aiden nodded, thanking the gods of small-town life for the ability to "call the cops" and request a specific officer. Mark Garnet had graduated with Antony and Paul, and was also a member of that same state champ basketball team. He'd gone to cop school or whatever one does for that, and now served as second in charge of the local police department.

Once Mark showed up, word had spread and a small army of people was combing the streets for Jeffrey. Aiden had been instructed to stay at the garage in case he showed up there.

Antony left, driving Rosalee's SUV, and headed for his place since Jeffrey loved his horses and the pond. Aiden truly hoped the kid had not taken it in his four-year-old head to walk out the country road that far.

He sat, gripping his fourth, or maybe fifth soda of the day, as the waning daylight dimmed the office. Running away from home had been his own specialty, usually to escape torture from Dominic. He never went far though, hoping someone—preferably Antony—would figure out he'd retreated to one of his usual hidey-holes, and come get him. Which is how things went down, but for one time.

A shiver shot down his spine at that memory. He got up and paced the floor, checking his phone and adding more acid to his burbling stomach. When the phone buzzed, he nearly dropped it.

"Aiden, did they find him yet?" his mother asked. She sounded calm, which helped cool his anxiety.

"Not that I know of. I'm sitting at the garage, in case he shows up here."

"Well, keep me posted." She hung up without waiting for a reply. She could be like that, un-chatty to the point of brusque. But she'd absorbed her fair share of offspring-induced trauma, including runaway moments. Aiden took a deep breath and flipped on the small television in the corner of the office. He settled on the couch and tried to find something other than a baseball game.

His dreams were a tumble of water, bourbon, and the sweet thighs of Tricia. Just as he'd re-lived the horror of being discovered naked, covered in bug bites and God knows what else, he jerked awake, slumped over, and drooling on the couch's arm. He sat, wiping his eyes and coming to terms with the level of dark in the room then scrabbled around for his phone. Which he found on the floor, deader than the proverbial doornail.

"Shit. Fuck. Hell," he muttered, rising and groaning at the aches and pains running up and down his body. When he heard something way out of place, he froze, hands on his lower back. He turned off the TV and walked toward the office door, squinting into the gloom.

The sound hit his ear again—a sort of shuffling, a soft clank then a distinct, childish giggle. Not wanting to scare the kid to death, he cleared his throat, hoping that would make his presence known. The sounds stopped. He flooded the garage with obnoxious light from a single bulb.

"Ow, shit!" He draped an arm over his eyes when pain shot through his skull.

"Shit. Shit. Shit," the small voice echoed back to him. Aiden waited for more. "You snore," Jeffrey said, emerging from behind a stack of tires.

Aiden blew out a breath and grabbed his phone, cursing again when he remembered its dead battery status. He frowned down at the filthy boy, who smiled up at him angelically. Aiden experienced a quick jolt of remorse for his parents just then, acknowledging what he'd subjected them to all the times he'd run away.

"Uncool, Jeff." He crouched down so they were on eye level. "Really not a good idea to scare your mom like that. Do you know how many people are out trying to find you right now?"

Jeffrey avoided his gaze while Aiden studied him from head to toe, seeking blood or obvious injury. A sturdy little carbon copy of Jeffery's dad, Paul, dressed in jeans and a Cincinnati Reds T-shirt, covered in grease and a layer of dirt, met his eyes, tears sliding through the muck on his face.

"I'm sorry." He dropped onto his butt.

"Come on, let's clean you up. Looks like you had a pretty wild time on the lam." When Jeff latched onto him and held tight, it surprised him how natural it seemed. Aiden had always been the one seeking comfort, never the giver of it. He patted the little boy's back as he made his way to the office. "I gotta call your mom."

"Antony's gonna be mad at me," he mumbled into Aiden's neck.

"Yeah, but he'll get over it. Once he knows you're okay. He used to find me when I'd run away, too."

Jeffrey raised his tear and snot-streaked face from Aiden's shoulder. "You runned away, too? Today?" His blue eyes brightened at the concept that someone else might be in trouble besides him.

"No, not today, dude. A long time ago, back when I was your size. Go in there." He pointed to the bathroom. "Use the soap in the bottle and scrub your hands and face so your mom doesn't think you're hurt or anything. I'll call her."

Aiden grabbed the office land line and dialed Antony's number from memory. He waved Jeff toward the bathroom and dropped into the desk chair, relief filling his chest.

When the SUV screeched back into the garage's empty lot, he had Jeffrey mostly tidied up and munching on chips from the vending machine. He sat perched on Aiden's lap, watching the Reds game, but he tensed up and dropped the chips at the sound of his mother yelling his name. Aiden poked his shoulder.

"Go on, little man. You gotta face the mom-music on this one."

Jeffrey sighed and jumped to the floor. Rosalee scooped him up, covered his face with kisses then set him down, keeping his arms in a tight grip. Antony remained beside her. But his gaze rested on Aiden's.

"Takes one to know one, eh, punk?" He moved past the mother-son reunion and flopped onto the couch. "Jesus, but that sucked." He glanced over at Rosalee, who alternated between kissing and shaking her son. Aiden sensed the general anxiety level in the room lessen ever so slightly.

"Yeah, but it's okay now. You knew it would be."

Antony sighed. Guilt flooded Aiden's chest at the worry in his brother's eyes.

"All I could picture was that one time...that van where we found you." Antony leaned forward, elbows on his knees, eyes trained at the floor. Aiden gulped. He remembered that time, too—the last time he'd run away and been scooped up by some drifter on his way through Lucasville. Aiden matched Antony's stance and bumped his shoulder.

"And that worked out fine."

"Only because of sheer, dumb luck. God help me if you hadn't known how to scream so loud the crossing guard heard you...."

"Yeah, well...yeah." Aiden got to his feet, unwilling to revisit that particular nightmare. Antony glared at him a moment, then flopped back on the couch. Jeffrey came over to stand in front of him, his huge blue eyes solemn and watery.

"Jeffrey is sorry."

Antony ruffled his hair. "I'm glad you're okay. Were you in the garage the whole time?"

Jeffrey shot a glance over Antony's shoulder at Aiden, who shook his head and mouthed the word "no" at him. That would really piss Antony off if he suspected that Jeffrey had been hanging around in here the whole time.

"No," he parroted to Antony. "Jeffrey wants Mommy."

"First Jeffrey needs to help clean up a mess he made with Antony's tools." Aiden took his hand and led him out to the brightly lit garage again. He glanced back just as Rosalee ran to Antony, letting him enfold her in his arms. Sighing, Aiden crouched to be on eye level with Jeffrey again.

"Show me where you hid. You know, in case I need to use it someday."

Chapter Six

Rosalee gazed out the kitchen window into the deep darkness of the night. The sounds she understood, the familiar, comforting ones from her childhood and her teen years growing up in the country on the edge of city surrounded her. Frogs singing, crickets chirping, the gentle snort of horses, all wafted in on the breeze lifting the curtain and soothing the chafed skin on her face.

A moth fluttered against the screen, catching her gaze. Mesmerized, she kept watching it. Her addled brain told her to flip off the light over the sink so the thing would give up and fly away, but her body stayed frozen, waiting.

But for what?

After the day's trauma, she'd taken Jeffrey to his grandmother's—Paul's mother's house, and had every plan to stay there with them, until the woman had shoved her out the door right into Antony's chest. He'd been standing behind her, waiting, his dark gaze somber as Jeffrey collapsed into his grandmother's arms.

Rosalee closed her eyes tight, making pinpricks of light and color dance behind her lids. Whenever she did that, she saw him—Paul, her boyfriend, her lover, her husband. The man she still mourned and who appeared to her daily, wrapped up in the skin of their son who looked at her with his father's eyes, smiling his father's smile.

She lowered her face to the cool surface of the table. The bourbon and rocks Antony had poured for her sat untouched, the ice slowly melting and diluting the rich amber color.

Never, ever in a million years would she forget the moment when the day-care lady had rushed out of her house and screamed that Jeffrey must have crawled out of the window during nap time and bolted into the Saturday afternoon sunlight. It would remain etched onto her memory banks forever, like the one when two uniformed officers had appeared at her door to tell her that Paul had been incinerated by a bomb six weeks before she'd given birth. A tear ran down Rosalee's face, stinging her skin chafed raw from sun, wind, and hours of tears.

She and Paul had waited to have a family, figuring he would be done after three tours in the Middle East. And he would have been, if the commander of his squadron had not stepped on an IED in Afghanistan. The man had been Paul's mentor for years, grooming him to take over after he retired, which he'd been within twelve weeks of reaching when he'd been reduced to vapor on the side of some godforsaken road in that fucked-up country—the same country where Paul rushed off to, eager to fill the commander's shoes, promoted, proud, and about to be a father.

She straightened, wiping her eyes, cursing under her breath. The bourbon went fast, smooth and straight to her head, making her blink back more tears. Sensing movement in the kitchen doorway, she rose and met Antony's dark gaze.

She took him in, letting her gaze start at his bare feet then move up his long, jeans-clad legs, taking in his UK basketball-logoed T-shirt, across the wide expanse of his shoulders. Smiling when she reached his Love-family signature square jaw, full lips, and dark eyes. A lick of relief crossed her consciousness. Antony had been Paul's best friend their whole lives. She'd known the Love family since forever. Before losing her fight with cancer, Rosie's mother had been Lindsay Love's canasta-playing, horse-riding friend. It seemed natural for Antony to be so integral to her life after Paul's sudden and tragic absence. And now, he represented something more, yet not, at the same time.

She shut her eyes tight until her head hurt. Anything to drive out the vision that had imprinted in her mind since the second she'd realized Aiden had come back to the fold. God help her, she'd probably babysat him at some point or another. But the sight of him had hit her in the gut, between the eyes, and a few other unmentionable places all at once that afternoon she'd convinced Antony to take pity on him and help him out.

She jumped when Antony's arms encircled her. Trembling in her knees, pounding in her head, the tight grip anxiety had had on her for so long today, all combined to make her shiver, want to scream, and run away from him. He'd been such a stalwart companion, had taken good care of her house, her car, her kid. But yet he'd never, in four years, gone further than a kiss, or once, when they'd drunk too much beer a party, a little mutual masturbation, which had lead to *the* most awkward morning after she'd ever experienced.

Wrapping her arms around his waist, she let him hold her, taking in long breaths of him—the deeply ingrained odors of gasoline and oil, leather and sweat, now tinged with the sweet essence of bourbon. He shifted, his usual maneuver when he got aroused by a hug or a kiss from her. Instead of stepping away out of deference to the physical distance he maintained, she pressed closer to him. As she sighed and turned her face up to his, she forced images of Aiden's dancing hazel eyes and mischievous grin out of her head.

"I need you," she whispered before rising up on her toes and covering his lips with hers. She would admit that she was sick of just kissing him. They were like immature teenagers sometimes, groping but never going "all the way." Anger flushed just beneath the horny roiling through her brain to heat her skin. Antony tensed at first, but opened his mouth, meeting her halfway. His hands roamed, clutched her hair then let go, and drifted back down to grab her ass.

She gasped when his lips trailed down her neck. The night noises encased them as the breeze lifted the edges of her hair. Rosalee sensed the raw, animal need just under Antony's skin, about to engulf them both. He yanked her shirt up, ripped her bra into two pieces, and dropped them into the chair she'd vacated. His breathing rasped in her ears and his hands shook as they cupped her breasts. She buried her fingers in his hair, relishing the almost forgotten, but perfect sensation of a man's lips, tongue, and teeth on her flesh.

He moaned into her skin as she held him close, her desire ramping to a near-unbearable level. Eager to taste him, feel his bare skin next to hers, she shoved his shirt up as tears ran down her face. Tears of what, she had no idea, but the second she had the shirt off and could admire the incredible terrain of his firm torso, he grabbed her shoulders then her hands.

"Stop. Just...don't." His voice sounded hoarse, strange, and unhappy.

Rosalee blinked in confusion. She tried to pull her hands free, but he tightened his grip.

"I can't do this." The words came out pinched through his clenched jaws. A drumbeat pounded at her temples. "I can't do this," he repeated in a whisper, putting her knuckles to his lips then letting her go. They faced each other, naked from the waist up, separated by a few actual inches, and miles of rough emotional terrain.

She touched his dark jaw, willing him to be calm. When she passed her thumb over his lips, he shut his eyes. She sensed him shaking. With a concerted effort not to yell in frustration, she stepped closer, letting their skin touch then went up on her tiptoes again, placing her lips next to his.

"It's okay, Antony. I want it. You do, too." She wrapped her arms around his neck, letting him feel her, loving the warmth and comfort of his body against hers. "Relax."

"You don't understand." He stepped away, his gaze full of a strange combination of lust and fury.

"I understand one thing right now." Taking his hand, she tried to pull him toward the kitchen door. He resisted, which lit a match to her smoldering anger. "You have to let her go, Antony. We are—" She stopped, honestly unsure what came after that.

They were meant to be together. The whole town assumed it. Jeffrey liked him. Antony had become an crucial part of their daily lives and had been nearly from the moment her son had been born. Antony had given her space for a while, provided a shoulder to cry on, a pair of hands to fix things, mow grass, repair her car. His mother treated her like a daughter-in-law. His brothers....

Rosalee sucked in a breath as the harsh and vivid image of Aiden Love swam in front of her vision, choking her. Just as she opened her mouth to tell Antony to do something to dispel the alarming fantasy about his brother, he laid a kiss on her that took her breath away.

He scooped her up and carried her to his bedroom, never taking his lips off hers, or giving her the option to tell him to leave her to her tumbled thoughts and illicit urges. Dropping her on the bed, he yanked her jeans and panties down and off then stepped back, looking like he would just as soon devour her as anything. His dark eyes flashed, reflecting something she'd never seen before, ever. Her skin tingled and she licked her lips, never more ready for this moment—even as she berated herself for being such a craven cougar over Aiden.

"I need this, too, Rosie." He unbuckled his belt slowly, not taking his eyes off hers. She moved back onto the pillows watching as he tugged the leather from the denim loops of his jeans and let it dangle from his large hand. Then, in an instant, his shoulders slumped, and he couched down to his ankles.

She scooted to the edge of the bed and touched his bare shoulder. The odd combination of terror and desire filling his huge brown eyes confused and infuriated her.

"I can't let myself feel it again. I won't go there. It killed me, Rosie. Made me weak and turned me into...I...."

"I don't need you to feel it here." She placed her trembling hand over his heart, which pounded under her fingers. Then she trailed them down the perfection of his lightly furred torso. "That's not necessary tonight." When she got to her feet, he pressed his face into her belly, hanging onto her as if she were a lifeboat. "Stand up, Antony."

He did, sliding against her skin and bringing all her nerve endings to immediate, rapt attention. His lips were on hers, his hands fisted in her hair. She broke the kiss, breathing heavy, desperate for something.

"I need you to feel something else tonight. I need it bad." She unzipped his jeans and wrapped her palm around his dick. This bit of him in perfect proportion to the rest of his physique had made an impression on her that one drunk moment. "Please...Antony...make love to me...."

He frowned and thumbed her chin while she moved her hand. But his hips thrust forward and the skin on his arm pebbled under her other hand. She molded against him, not letting go of his erection, tracing the dark disk of his nipple with her tongue. They'd been here before, that one time. He'd drawn a lovely orgasm from her with his fingers, she'd jacked him off, and they'd passed out, no big deal.

But this seemed like a very big deal.

Antony kissed her hair, took her hand off his cock then pressed her back onto the bed, kissing his way down her neck, fondling and sucking both breasts, licking and nibbling towards her stomach before settling in between her thighs. She closed her eyes and let it happen, loving it, loving him right then as she draped her legs over his shoulders and dug her heels into the muscles of his back.

"Oh, Jesus!" she yelped, as he teased and sucked her flesh, pressing his fingers deep into her. "Oh...my...." Her body pulsed. She threaded her fingers in his hair and held on tight while she rode out a mind-bending climax.

She flopped back on the bed, breathing heaving and contemplating Antony's bedroom ceiling. He got up on his knees between her legs, wiping his lips, and fisting his huge dick. She propped up on her elbows, the erotic energy in the room crackled in her ears as she reached up for him. He hesitated.

"I don't have any protection," he rasped, breathing into her neck. "It's not safe."

"I'm safe, Antony," she whispered. "Are you?"

"I can't do this with you, Rosie. I can't...love you."

"I'm not asking you to love me," she insisted, relieved, but aching to have him inside her. She angled her hips so she could sense his flesh near hers. "Fuck me, Antony, please...we both need this." She wrapped her legs around his waist. "Is that what you want to hear?" Tears prickled her eyes, making her feel empty and desperate.

A slow sound, like a growl seemed to come from his chest.

"Yeah, Rosie, that's what I need to hear." His eyes were twinkling in the moonlight from the open window. The fear tickled her again, but this time it ramped up her lust, dialing it to extra-high, and forcing more words from her lips.

"Okay then." She brushed her lips against his. "Take me. Fuck me with that giant cock. Just...do it now, Antony. What are you waiting for, goddamn you." Gasping, knowing he was holding back, she tilted her hips and covered his lips with hers.

He shoved his tongue into her mouth, but denied her the connection she demanded. "Maybe...." His grin against her lips sent relief shooting through her. "First, this." He rolled over onto his back, bringing her with him. As soon as she straddled him, he thrust into her, drawing exhalations from both of them.

"Hmmm, so that's how Rosie likes it," he whispered, before tugging her nipple into his mouth and sucking so hard she cried out. "Ride me. Take it however you want it."

She did just that, being a good taking-orders girl. When she lay draped over his chest, sweat slicking the nonexistent space between them, he brushed her hair back from her face and trailed his hand down her back.

"My turn on top."

She giggled and got them back to their original position with a few awkward manipulations, gripping the headboard behind her so she could tilt her hips up and take all of him.

"Oh...dear...Jesus," he moaned, still hanging on, in control like always—Antony, the ever-in-control oldest, fixer of things, man of the house, broken-and-crushed widower. She sucked in a breath and let go of the headboard, needing him closer.

"Kiss me. Kiss me now." Rosalee wanted to cry or scream. She had to get out of there. She had to.... "Oh God yes!"

When he lifted his head, his eyes were bright, his hips still moving against her.

"Wow." He shifted back into some kind of neutral gear. Rosalee took a breath as he flopped down next to her. She lay staring at the ceiling, trying to catch her breath and still her mind.

"Thanks," Antony said.

Rosie bit back the urge to scream. More physically sated than she had been in years, an empty, bereft sensation suffused her psyche. Antony's eyes were filled with sadness in the moonlit room.

"Was it that bad?" She flipped up on her side, needing that expression gone from his face.

He took her hand, kissed it, and a smile flickered across his lips.

"It was amazing. You're amazing. And now I'm gonna pass out. No offense?"

"None taken."

"Turn over so I can hold you while I sleep."

She did, loving the warmth of his body against hers, of his breath against her neck. But she couldn't sleep. Once his breathing evened out, she slipped out from under his heavy arm, found a pair of his boxers and a T-shirt, and headed for the kitchen.

Rosalee drank a huge glass of water and lingered at the window, letting the night breeze cool her face, recalling the knowing arched eyebrow Paul's mother had shot her when she'd dropped Jeffrey off. The concept that her own mother-in-law wanted her to be with Antony boggled her mind—well, okay, her former mother-in-law, she supposed.

What a mess.

"Well, that sounded like fun."

She yelped in surprise, knocking the glass into the sink with a crash. Aiden walked in wearing nothing but a pair of sweat pants, sleepy eyed, hair tousled, as tempting and edible as she'd imagined. Anger mingled with mortification when the realization that he'd heard them just now slammed into her psyche.

"Jesus, Aiden. I'm sorry. I didn't know you were...I mean...shit."

He grinned, making her knees wobbly. "Obviously." He pointed into the sink. "We'd better take care of this."

As he did that, he moved with a sort of quick efficiency in keeping with his trim body.

His trim...young body.

Rosalee bit her lip, wrestling her new-found, inner cougar slut back into its cage.

"Thanks," she said under her breath, not trusting her voice.

He winked, drank his own water and walked past her. Before he made it to the hallway, he turned, then to her alarm and horror, put his lips so close to her ear she smelled his toothpaste. "Glad you convinced him. He needed that."

He took her hand and pressed something into it. It had to be her heated imagination because he would never brush her cheek with a kiss. He headed down the hallway, went into a room and shut the door, leaving her clutching the torn halves of her bra.

Chapter Seven

Sunlight forced Rosalee to tug up the sheet to escape its intense glare. When her arm found the empty pillow next to hers, relief hit her sleepy brain. Facing Antony after the intensity of last night's encounter didn't figure too high on the list of things she wanted to deal with right then.

It—he—had been incredible, and the connection had definitely been long overdue. But she needed space to figure out what it meant. A phone buzzed somewhere, so she sat up and rubbed her eyes, relishing the soreness between her legs.

She crawled out of the warm nest of sheets and quilts. The house sounded empty as she made her way down the hall to the living room and into the kitchen. After locating and quelling the offensive alarm, Rosalee took a minute to study the room that still bore the hallmarks of Antony's dead wife.

The lacy curtains, copper-bottomed pots hanging from a dusty rack over the cooktop island, even the patterned hand towels hanging from the oven handle all screamed, "Crystal Love." No wonder the man couldn't—or wouldn't—let go of her. He was surrounded by her every day.

She wandered into one of the two bathrooms, touching the matching towels and shower curtain lightly while sipping the coffee he'd thoughtfully left for her. Something caught her eye, and she paused until she realized her own image in the mirror faced her, looking about as out of place as anyone could in a dead woman's bathroom.

Her unruly hair haloed her pale face, reducing her by its overabundance. She'd never believed her personality lived up to her hair, no matter how much Paul insisted it matched her perfectly. Squinting at the sight of her swollen lips, her faced flushed pink as she put a hand to her cheek.

Oh, good Lord—Antony.

He had been incredible, generous, sexy and all man, just like she figured he would be.

But yet...it had been so strange even after all the time they'd spent together, and no matter the whole town considered them a couple. She trailed her fingertips down her damp neck, reliving the brief moment of connection with Aiden.

"You need to get a grip." She glared at her reflection. "Rosalee Norris. Get a dang grip." She propped her hands on the vanity top and glared in the mirror.

Resolved, she turned away from her image and stomped down to Antony's room. Ignoring the open door to the room his daughter AliceLynn hadn't occupied since Crystal had been killed, she kept going, determined to get dressed and get out. But the door to the room Aiden had entered early that morning posed an insurmountable temptation. She stopped, unable to resist peeking in on the chaos of clothes, the open laptop, and a tall, neatly arranged stack of papers on the makeshift desk near a window.

"Move along." She shut the door and walked into the room where she'd finally fucked and slept with the man who'd been, for all intents and purposes, her chaste and helpful boyfriend for years.

By the time she was back in her truck and headed toward the center of town, Rosalee's chest ached. The windows were cranked down to welcome the overly warm air, radio blaring as loud as she dared on a Sunday morning, when the bulk of the population would be on their way home from church. The perfect blue sky framed by green leafy trees mocked her. The soft air caressing her bare arm dangling out the window reminded her just what a horrific error she may have made, letting Antony Love do...that amazing set of things he'd done to her the night before.

"Goddamn it," she muttered under her breath, shifting around in the faux leather seat at the thought of his skill set. Driving up Paul's mother's drive, she noted the grass needed mowing and figured she'd ask Antony to help with it at the same moment a wave of sorrow slammed her right between the eyes. She gripped the steering wheel, forcing back the memories of her many hours spent in this very driveway, giggling, kissing, and groping her way into adulthood with Paul. The memories still stung. They'd never truly faded, just ran in a near constant loop like background elevator music.

The sight of her son in his grandmother's arms calmed her as she climbed the steps up to the front door with a smile.

"Mommy!" Jeffrey's face lit with joy. He struggled until Paul's mother let go of him. "I was so worried about you." His familiar warmth and body's curvature made her happy and miserable at the same time.

"No worries about me," she insisted. "Remember, we talked about that. When you're with your Grammie, all is well. I'm just doing something I don't need your help with." She sighed, unwilling to address that particular irony even in her head, while her son proceeded to choke her in his relief that she'd remembered to come get him.

She sank to the porch with Jeffrey clinging to her. It would take a while for him to calm enough to let go. Janice Norris sat next to her and bumped her shoulder.

"So...good night?"

Rosalee's face burned hot. This had to be the strangest set of circumstances ever. Janice had adored her own son to the point of despising Rosalee for the better part of her high school and some college years. But once they'd both gotten past the first couple of agony and newborn-baby-filled years after Paul's death, the woman had taken on the role of matchmaker like someone paid her to do it. It was a little creepy, especially since she'd become such an advocate for Antony Love's case.

Rosalee shifted and the old wooden planks creaked. She suppressed a smile at the soreness in all the right places. But a giant boulder occupied her chest, heavy and cold, and just as annoying as her mother-in-law's eager grin over Jeffrey's head. Taking a breath, she tried not to snap at the woman. She meant well, bless her heart. But the way she kept waggling her eyebrows like Groucho Marx made Rosalee want to snatch her baldheaded right around Jeffrey's needy body.

"Yeah." She kept her gaze on the front garden with its fussy rows of foliage. "Thanks."

"Anytime, hon, anytime." Janice stood and stretched. "He's such a little Paul, isn't he? I don't know how you stand it."

Confused by the shift of subject, and struck dumb by the comment, Rosalee stayed silent. Janice walked down the steps and sought out geraniums to dead head.

"So, are y'all gonna watch the game?" she asked, scrutinizing the perfect flowers.

"Uh...what game?" Rosalee tried to loosen Jeffrey's arms from around her neck, but he'd be stuck fast for a while. So she patted his back, waiting him out while sweat gathered and dripped down her back under her shirt.

"You know, the weekly basketball game, down at Vets Park. I swan, I told that new neighbor man to keep his foul dog out of my...."

Rosalee stopped listening. She'd almost forgotten the Love family Sunday tradition. After church and their mother's lunch, the Love brothers would gather at the park for a game of two-on-two basketball. They'd spent a few years corralling various friends to stand in for the missing Aiden. Sometimes their father joined them, but that hardly ever worked out well, according to Antony.

So that's why the house had been empty when she'd left. The Love siblings missed church at their peril, she recalled. Lindsay and Anton Love had struck an Episcopalian compromise, once it became clear the Catholic-Italian stable hand had knocked up the horse farmer's proverbial daughter, and they'd been married in the Methodist church at her father's demand.

And each of the boys followed it, or at least made a show of it every single week, no matter what, or risked the combined wrath of the fiery-haired mother, and the dark and moody father. They still did. Antony never missed church. This morning had just been the first one she'd ever woken up in the man's bed to find him missing, Sunday or any day.

Of course, when Lindsay's longed-for daughter had arrived late on the scene, the energy had gone out of them on that point. The brothers were trained to attend and never question why. But once Angelique Love had been old enough to make a choice about it, she never darkened the church door again.

Rosalee made a tsk-tsk sound with her teeth then forced her thoughts away from the gorgeous, wayward Love daughter. She had enough to worry about. Besides how could she judge? She'd stopped attending church the second she'd gotten her mother's cancer diagnosis on the heels of Paul's accident. That had been the beginning of her life as single, grieving, widow mother, with a crap job and a too-big mortgage. She had no room for mythical fantasy requiring her to get dressed up every Sunday morning and force her mule-headed son to do the same.

"No," she called down to Janice who'd gotten on her hands and knees to yank at invisible weeds. "I should get him home."

"You should go to the game," the woman called out from below her. "Let Jeffrey play with them. Anton started the whole thing when Antony and Kieran were only learning to walk. He'd add a son to the nursery and then to the basketball court as soon as it could walk. It's a nice tradition. Jeffrey could use something like that. You know, men he can...."

Unwilling to tolerate any more blather about how Jeffrey needed more male influences in his life, Rosie resumed ignoring her mother-in-law. She didn't know if Jeffrey could get any more "boy-like," being a handful and three-quarters already.

Her conscience prickled. Janice only wanted the best for her dead son's child. Rosalee knew that. She also knew her son could stand a heavier hand—something that Paul would have definitely had, but Antony seemed reluctant to provide.

"Thanks again, Janice." After peeling Jeffery off her, she stuffed him into his car seat. By then they were both drenched in sweat. Her head pounded. Paul's mother waved at her as she backed out into the quiet street.

Rosalee chewed on her lip as she drove home, trying not to make the turn down River Road leading to the park. But when she found herself there, gripping the steering wheel, and staring at the four men going at it on the basketball court, two of them shirtless, it didn't really surprise her...much.

"Mommy." Jeffrey mumbled, half-asleep. Once she unhooked him and set him on the asphalt, he ran off toward the court like he'd been shot out of a cannon. She remained by the truck, leaning on the hood, content to observe from afar.

Apparently today, Antony and Aiden were shirtless, taking on the other two, Dominic and Kieran. A shiver shot down her spine at the sight of Antony. The man's tall, broad-shouldered, slim-hipped, long-legged physique drew her eyes like a magnet. All four had that going for them, but each had his own twist on the theme.

Jeffrey had reached the fence and was waving at the men, who ignored him, intent as they were on what might look like a friendly pickup game of round ball, but what really passed as an excuse to beat on each other and work out their "issues." She recalled broken noses, black eyes, one dislocated shoulder, and several smashed fingers in high school, or on holidays back from college when all four of them would be around.

Easily the biggest of the four men, Antony dominated the court, but Kieran had always been the true athlete, and his slick moves had the sort of practiced professionalism the rest of them lacked. All of them had played high school sports, but Kieran and Aiden were the only two to play in college—Kieran as guard for the Kentucky Wildcats basketball team that had gone as far as the NCAA tournament final his senior year. Aiden bucked the family trend, playing soccer in both high school and college.

"Hey," a female voice interrupted her musings about the relative physical merits of each of the brothers.

"Hey, Renee." Rosalee glanced back and spotted Reese, who'd graduated from Lucasville High a few years after her. The owner-operator of the sort of salon and spa Rosalee only wished she could afford to go to, stood, smiling at her. Rosie noted the other woman's dolled-up hair and makeup, the pretty sundress and sandals over carefully tanned skin. "Come from church?"

"You know it." Renee pulled her sunglasses down over her eyes and joined her.

Kieran, ever the peacemaker, tried to force the brawl into an actual game. He stopped the action at one point, holding Dominic and Aiden at arm's length. She was too far away to hear him, but could read the fury in his eyes as he spoke.

Antony had the ball under one arm, a smile playing around his full lips. Finally, they all took a water break. Kieran spoke to Antony then ran his fingers through his Halloran-family red hair. He had his mother's family's build, tall, but lanky, not stocky like Antony and Dom. His sort of spin on the Love family handsome endeared, didn't startle like Dom's, mesmerize like Antony's, or charm like Aiden's.

"How're things?" Rosalee said, for lack of anything better.

Renee's smile shone so bright, Rosalee figured it might very well glow in the dark. "Oh honey, if things got any better I might have to hire somebody to help me enjoy it."

"Ah. Okay, good."

The women waited in silence as the game progressed, or devolved, depending on your perspective.

"I hear that fiancée of his, some lady lawyer over in Louisville, is a real bitch on wheels," Rosalee said by way of striking up conversation with Renee. "Antony says she has him pussy-whipped to within an inch of his life."

Renee snorted, but kept her eyes on the action. Kieran threw up his hands then and took the ball from Antony, and started shooting free throws. "That one is a real sweetie. Don't know what came over Cara Cooper, dumping him like she did. Always figured those two for one of those perfect couples, you know?"

Rosalee kept her eyes on the men, three of whom sat draining water bottles, the other dropping shot after shot into the net. "Yeah," she agreed, unable to tear her eyes from the vision of Aiden as he poured water over his hair and shook it. The water dripped down his bare torso and she experienced the distinct and alarming urge to run over there and lick it off him. "He sure is the politest of the bunch."

Renee laughed again. "Out of a passel of sons who got politeness beat into them. Where'd he meet her anyway? I heard it was some online dating thing."

"Yes, that's what Antony told me. I so wish he'd marry someone nice, who deserved him. But I've never met her, and Antony tends to exaggerate about his brothers and women, so..." She glanced over and found Renee studying her, like a bug under the microscope. "Who knows? After what he went through, breaking his leg and all, and having to move back home."

"So you and Love bro *numero uno*?" Renee pointed at the court where Antony had just poured water over his dark, sweaty hair and shook like a dog, splattering everyone for the sake of doing it. She got a girlie tingle, watching him, her...what? Boyfriend? Lover? Fix-it man? She blew out a breath and decided to just enjoy the view. All of them were the dictionary definition of "very easy on the eyes."

"Yes, well...yes," she said, confirming it for herself as well as Renee.

She let her eyes flicker over Aiden a half second, noting how his shorts rode low, below his belly button, giving her a view of the dark line of hair below it, and the way his hips flexed when he grabbed the ball from Kieran and ran to the other end for a dunk. She swallowed hard and actually whispered "watch out" at the sight of Dominic barreling straight at Aiden, just outside of the younger man's line of vision.

While not shirtless, Dom wore a thin undershirt, revealing the copious body art he sported on his sculpted arms. He had his dark-blond hair pulled back in a ponytail, which gave her a view of the many ear piercings.

Renee made an alarmed sound and gripped Rosalee's arm. They both winced when Dom slammed into Aiden's shoulder, ostensibly for a rebound, but knocking him into the fence hard enough for the women to hear it and the man's curse. Jeffrey jumped up and down on the other side of the fence, clapping his hands.

"Rat bastard," Renee muttered under her breath and loosened her death grip on Rosalee.

"He was your boyfriend awhile, right?" Rosalee had always been intimidated by Dominic. Paul had hated him, called him a show-off asshole, a thrill-seeking man-whore. Antony had never directly disagreed with him during their high school years.

Renee sighed and fussed with her still-perfect updo. "Yeah, but one of many. Made the mistake of falling pretty hard for him for a few weeks or so, I'll admit it." She smiled at Rosalee then focused back on the court again, where Kieran tried to break Dom and Aiden apart again. "Luckily that sweet hunk of man there helped me over my heartbreak." She cocked her head and kept her gaze on Aiden. Rosalee suppressed an irrational rush of jealousy. "I heard he'd made it back to town. Tricia hooked up with him already, the slut."

Rosalee's face heated up. Antony had told her about finding Aiden and Tricia screwing by the pond a few nights ago. Tricia and Renee had been as thick as thieves in high school. She assumed they still were.

"Is it true that Dom has a pierced...you know...." Rosalee gestured in the general vicinity of her crotch.

Renee giggled and bumped her shoulder. "That came after we were together. But of course, I only know because my girls wax his junk every other week." She winked. "That man has poked holes in more places on his own body than I care to contemplate. I caught him fucking my best waxer just last week. He had that girl bent over the table, ruttin' like the pig he is. What does he say to me when I open the door and see it all there, spread out like some porno? 'What's wrong, honey? Don't be jealous. I had to see how things felt down there. I can let you try next.'"

Rosalee blushed harder. Renee shook her head. "I tell you I nearly grabbed both those nipple rings and yanked 'em clean off him." She straightened and wiped her hands together, reminding Rosalee of the truck's constant dirty state. "He may look like a cover model, but he acts like a stone-cold slut."

Rosalee observed the man in question, who had calmed down and moved to the other end of the court. Rumors and gossip flew nearly constantly about Dominic. Hands down the best-looking of a set of perfect brothers, he had bronze-colored skin, not olive, like Antony's, or pale and freckled, like Kieran's. Prone to borderline violent outbursts of temper, he could have stepped straight out of a high-fashion men's magazine with his sculpted cheekbones, signature Love family square jaw, with the added bonus of a chin dimple deeper than any of the others'.

"He sure is mysterious," she said, for lack of anything better.

Renee nodded. "You know, as tight knit as that family is, and as small as our little community was before it became a rich-bitch bedroom suburb for Lexington, he is still the one no one really understands. I swan but I don't get how he's the only one of the four who works with his daddy in the family business."

"He dropped out of college, but nearly had his chemistry degree at UK," Rosalee told her, recalling once when Antony got talkative about Dominic. "Took a night flight out to Germany, Antony says, studied to be a brewer. Remember that scraggly hippy he brought back with him?" She blew out a breath, recalling the rumors of loud family arguments while she'd been away at college, pining for Paul. "But whatever happened to Diana? The Brantley girl he kept going back to over and over?"

"Diana has been a Dominic Love doormat for a lot of years, bless her heart." Renee studied her perfect manicure. "She got married, I heard, but divorced almost as quick. Remember the restaurant she tried to open with that New York guy? What a shyster. But now she helps her sister Jen and their business is gangbusters—you know, Brantley's, with all the farm produce and goat's milk cheese, and whatever. I'm right proud of her, breaking loose of Dom's hold after all those years."

"What about the skinny hippy girl...I mean, wasn't she pregnant?" Rosalee thought she recalled that being part of the problem.

"Out to here." Renee held her arms out miming a large belly, keeping her eyes on the men. "I hate that for Miss Lindsay. I know the thought of a grandbaby wandering around New York City, not knowing his people back home makes her crazy."

"I'm sure of that."

"Dominic Love is as crazy as a bedbug, I shit you not," Renee declared. "I know he and his daddy fight like cats and dogs every day. I hear people come in and say they can hear 'em all the way down Hunter Street."

"Antony says the brewery is doing great though. Better, since Dom is in full charge of production."

A woman ran by them, dressed in a sports bra, shorts, and running shoes, with earphones stuck in her ears. Tall, athletic, with a long, dark-blonde ponytail bouncing, she gave a shy smile to the two women. Rosalee figured her for another city transplant.

Renee raised a hand and called out to the woman who waved and kept going around the track.

"Who's that?" Rosalee couldn't help but admire the fitness level of the woman's long legs. "Newlywed suburbanite?"

"Oh, no, honey, that there is Margot Hamilton. She's a psychiatrist, or some such thing. Or maybe she's a preacher. I don't know for sure. She's the new chaplain at County. And freshly divorced, too."

Rosalee frowned. "How d'you know all that?"

Renee laughed, showing her perfectly straight, bright white teeth again. "Don't you know that owning the most popular salon in town is a perfect job for a silly old gossip like me? We do her highlights—have done for a year or so, since she moved here with her husband. We also talked her into a Brazilian, you know." Renee nodded, as if Rosalee should understand this reference. "He up and left her a month after dragging them down from Michigan for his job in the athletic department at UK. Men are such assholes." Renee's eyes softened, and she grabbed Rosalee's hands.

"I can't tell you how happy I am for you though, Rosie. You deserve a fine man like Antony. Maybe now he can finally let go of Crystal. Those two were so strange together—happy, but fighting all the damn time. I never understood it. And that daughter...." She surprised Rosalee by folding her into a huge, perfume-scented hug. "Y'all will be so good together. I hope you make more pretty babies, too." She stepped back. "I'm gonna go. I don't want Aiden to see me yet. I have such nice homecoming plans for that one, mmm hmmm."

Rosalee had to consciously unclench her fists while Renee sauntered back to her sexy convertible Mustang. While she was mentally formulating a plan to get Jeffrey away from there and home for a nap, something caught her eye, some movement on a picnic table nearby. She sucked in a breath when she spotted AliceLynn, Antony's estranged teenaged daughter. The girl sat on the table, dressed in the exact sort of way that made her father red-faced furious. Too short shorts, slutty halter exposing so much of her fleshy real estate, she might as well have on a sports bra and not bother with calling it a shirt.

"Oh, my Lord," Rosalee said under her breath. She'd had quite enough of the smart-assed girl lately. She would show out and Antony would say nothing as usual, letting her slink back to her grandmother's, defeated in her latest effort to get the man's attention.

AliceLynn had a room in Antony's house she never visited, and bounced between Lindsay and Anton's, and Crystal's mother's house even farther out in the country. She and her father barely acknowledged each other, and according to Antony's mother, who'd taken her aside just last week about it, things were escalating, thanks to AliceLynn's recent spate of skipped days at school. The girl had a destructive streak a mile wide, and the will to express it to go with her scary book smarts.

As Rosalee approached, she heard the ball game escalate again. But she ignored the grown men acting like little boys, and focused instead on the pretty girl who'd chosen that moment to flip around so she sat straddling some straggly looking kid, kissing him in a way that embarrassed Rosalee.

"AliceLynn," she called from a few feet away, hoping her voice had the same effect as a water hose pointed at a pair of dogs in the yard. "I know you've been skipping school."

Still perched on the boy's lap, so close Rosalee couldn't see light between their bodies, AliceLynn took her tongue out of his mouth and turned to her.

"Not your business, Rosie. You aren't my mama."

A shout came from the court and the kid jumped up, dumping AliceLynn on her ass in the dirt.

"Hey," she yelped, smacking his calf. "What's wrong with—"

"Gotta go. See ya 'round." He flew past Rosalee so fast she almost missed the whiff of pot smoke.

"Asshole," AliceLynn muttered, rising to her feet. Dominic had taken off after him, chasing him into the parking lot. The other three men stood facing AliceLynn and Rosalee.

"Aiden!" Jeffrey took advantage of the break in the action to storm the court and clamber up Aiden's sweaty body until he clung to his neck and had his face between his hands. "You were playing very rough."

"Get on home." Antony glared at his daughter. "And don't come here acting like a slut, trying to piss me off."

"Worked, didn't it?" The girl lifted her chin, matching her father's profile to perfection. But Rosalee caught the glint of tears in her eyes.

Antony blinked and took a step back, then wiped his forehead, his expression confused for a split second by the sight of Rosalee together with his daughter. A spike of sadness hit her then, making her hesitate. These two were worse than ships passing in the night. They were more like Jeffrey's mini-magnet set, faced the wrong way around, their repelling power stronger than the attracting one.

"You know, calling her that in front of people isn't helping," she said to Antony.

"Don't take my side, Rosie. God. I don't need your stupid, busy-body, goody-two-shoes help." AliceLynn grabbed her purse and took the first steps away from the tableau. Antony had the girl's arm before she could blink.

"Do not speak to her like that."

"Just because you're fucking her does not make her the boss of me, Daddy. I don't want a *stepmama*." The last word dripped with angry sarcasm. "Excuse me. But I have to go find my date before Uncle Dom kills him. Call him off next time, will ya? Jesus."

Rosalee had to hand it to the girl. She could press all the right buttons. Antony let go of her and stepped away.

"Oh, hey, Uncle Aiden. Welcome home." The girl gave a jaunty wave, winked at Rosalee, and held her middle finger high in the air on her way to the parking lot.

Rosalee stood, frozen by the girl's nerve. Glancing at Antony' stricken face, she honestly believed the man might explode with rage.

"Mommy! That girl flew her bird at Antony. That wasn't very nice."

Aiden chuckled. Rosalee tried not to laugh. Antony blinked at her.

"Sorry," he muttered.

She shook her head. They'd shared minimal information about AliceLynn and his distance from her. Rosalee had told him more than once he bore half the responsibility for the girl's bitchiness, and if he'd just pay some positive attention to her, maybe they could repair their shattered relationship. That comment had gotten her exactly nowhere.

"She's better off without me altogether," he said, watching her drive off before glaring at both Aiden and Rosalee. "I don't want to talk about it. God damn Dom. We weren't done with the game."

"Jeffrey will play! Jeffrey will play!" her son screamed.

"No, mister, we have to go home."

Aiden walked right up to her. She could smell him, and had to bite her tongue not to reach out and touch his shoulder, or to lick her way up his neck. She took a step back. But he just handed Jeffrey over.

"Next time, Jeff. I gotta go back and school these guys, you know."

They bumped fists, then without a word to her, Aiden ran back to the court where Antony and Kieran were already playing one-on-one.

Chapter Eight

The week after Aiden had lain in bed and listened to Antony make love to Rosalee, things only got stranger. The reunion on Sunday had gone down about the way he'd expected. The days he'd spent avoiding Dom and Kieran did not help their attitudes about his silent return to their midst, at least the way Dominic measured things.

Good to know at least some things never changed, Aiden mused as he fired up the coffee maker his second Friday morning at Love Garage. His book, the one his professors at the snooty MFA program in the middle of a cornfield had dissed for being "too much like popular fiction" centered around family dynamics. He figured he'd be a fair expert on that topic, especially as it related to ones as large and complex as his. Every family had its own dysfunction, but the Loves really cornered the market on it.

When Aiden had made his surprise appearance in the birth order, followed quickly by the only Love daughter, Dominic had not taken it well. He'd always been a hotheaded super-competitive asshole. Nothing about his "new baby brother" had pleased him. Local urban legend had it that Dom had tried to give Aiden away as a newborn, standing out on the street, holding him and asking passersby if they wanted a "stupid baby" to take home with them.

Luckily, thanks to their small town, that effort got nipped in the bud the second somebody called Lindsay, who'd been taking a well-needed break at a spa in Lexington, leaving a sitter in charge for a few hours.

Aiden studied his image in the bathroom mirror. He'd developed his own coping strategies for Dom's blatant hostility. Running away had worked a few times, until the one time that had scared him so badly, he'd never considered it an option again. Confronting him came next, with Antony in his corner.

That had netted Aiden his first black eye and three broken fingers.

The patriarch had come down hard on his third son after that, administering a patented "go get a switch off that tree, pull down your pants, and grab your ankles" sort of treatment. Then he'd whirled brandishing the switch, to face his other sons and their mother who had been made to watch.

"Get yourselves straight on one thing; I will not stand for y'all treating each other like this. You—" He'd faced the stoic, red-faced Dominic, who had his jeans back up and waited to be told he could leave. "You will not treat your own brother that way." He'd pointed to Aiden who was trembling in fear, fingers stiff and taped together, his eye socket aching. "Look at him, Dominic. You did that. You beat up a kid who had no means of defending himself yet. And I won't put up with that."

He'd tossed the stick down and stomped away from the crowd, muttering about "ungrateful spawn." Dominic had glared at Aiden. But their mother had shooed the other three away, telling them to get her purse so she could give them money to go down to Shugs on their bikes for ice cream.

Aiden had gone into his parents' bedroom and grabbed it then had run past the others who were hanging around in the kitchen, silent and cowed by their father's aggression. Ice cream had never sounded better at that moment. He'd run down the steps to the back yard, stopping a half second when he didn't spot her right away.

He'd skirted the recently installed pool, and the small pool house where they were required to put away every ball and float every night.

"Mama?" He'd made his way toward the large detached garage that housed the horse trailer and the riding lawn mower he'd been dying to learn how to use. "Hey, Mama, I've got—"

Rounding the corner of the garage, he'd caught sight of her, sitting in one of the old lawn chairs. Dominic's face had been pressed against her shoulder as he shook and sobbed. She'd been running her hands down his back. Aiden couldn't hear her words, but he saw her eyes swimming with tears.

Dominic had stepped back and hiccupped, rubbing his eyes. It had struck Aiden how very young Dom seemed just then. To him, Dom had always acted so many years older, stronger, bigger, more experienced, and better at everything. But at that moment, he'd resembled nothing more than a hapless kid, tear-streaked, dirty, and miserable.

Their mother had taken Dominic's face between her hands. "Why are you so angry all the time, my love?"

"I don't know," the boy had wailed, flinging himself into his mother's arms again, sobbing as if his heart had broken.

• • • •

"YO, PUNK."

Aiden jumped at the sound of Antony's voice. He must have been standing here mooning around for nearly twenty minutes.

"Yeah?"

"I need you to play secretary today. File all that shit I paid there." Antony gestured toward a pile of invoices and tax forms stacked on the corner of the desk. "Then line up the crap I still owe over here." He pointed to the ancient, cracked leather desk blotter that he'd inherited when he'd taken over their uncle's business.

"Sure, no problem." Aiden poured them both a cup of coffee. He'd weaned Antony off the cheap grocery store brand in the last week, ignoring complaints about the five-dollar-a-pound difference. "So, what's Rosalee up to? Haven't seen her in a few days." He tried to appear innocent, as if he were just inquiring on Antony's behalf. His weird obsession with her had only ramped up by a thousand, however.

"Why? You her fucking social secretary now?"

"No, just wondering. Seemed as though you guys sort of hit a, ah, milestone the other night and all. I figured she'd be over some this week. I don't know...." Antony always did have the foulest mouth of them all, even growing up, which had netted him his share of parental whacks to the back of his head and, later, more money in the family swear jar than anyone.

"She is not coming over to make you dinner, if that's what you're hoping for. And my milestone with her is not for your consideration, perv."

"Dude, you knew I was home. That didn't stop you."

"Whatever." Antony's eyes darkened in a way that forced Aiden to drop the subject.

They sipped in silence, listening as the mechanics arrived, opened up the bay doors, and cranked the horrible country music. Aiden wanted a cigarette so badly right then he nearly took his battered pack out of his jeans pocket and offered one to his brother.

"I'm not good for her. I'm just an old grumpy asshole anymore. She deserves someone better."

Aiden raised an eyebrow at the impressive contiguous string of sentences that had just emerged from the other man's mouth. "Well, let's start with 'yes, you are a grumpy asshole.' But you aren't old. And while she is pretty awesome, I'd say that you're not a bad catch yourself." He winced at that; he'd just talked Antony into something he wanted. But he went on, mostly as a distraction from the nicotine craving hammering at his nerve endings.

"I mean you're a successful business owner. You have your own home, with land, and horses. I'm not sure what the hell is going on with your daughter but—"

Antony held up a hand. "*That* topic is off limits. You've been gone too long to have a say in it anyway, out getting college degrees so you can mooch off me and learn how to change a fucking tire, finally, at twenty-eight."

"I'm twenty-seven." Petulance crept into his voice.

Antony shot him a grin and Aiden's heart lightened. "I stand corrected," he said, and got up.

Aiden remained seated. "Listen, Antony, you've been letting Crystal's ghost browbeat you for too long. You owe it to yourself to move on. Maybe you owe it to your daughter not to be such a dick. You still have time to save that girl from herself you know."

"Funny, I didn't realize you had a degree in deep psychoanalysis, Dr. Freud."

"You're a miserable shell of yourself, Antony, seriously. I'm...Mama is worried about you. She told me. She thinks that Rosalee...." He stopped and gulped, recalling why his mother had voiced this fact to him before going on. "Rosalee is great for you, if you'd just let her be. She's hurt too, but she...she loves you, right?"

Aiden tried to keep the questioning tone to a minimum. He had no idea how Rosalee felt, but she and Antony had been "together" for all intents and purposes, a more or less recognized couple, according even to the increasingly drunken Tricia and her gal pal the other night at the bar.

There'd been plenty of girlfriends right up until Antony got the proverbial smack between the eyes by the lovely Crystal. Guy had been a regular cocksman, if rumors were true. Before Crystal, his urban legendary prowess conquering girls had even been more impressive than Dom's. The concept that Antony had gone without pussy for the better part of twelve years boggled his mind.

"You don't understand. You'll never understand."

"Maybe not, but I do know this—you are going to 'grumpy asshole' yourself into a heart attack or a stroke, and then our mother will kick my butt for not taking better care of you. Go out with the woman again, Antony, for God's sake. Be romantic. I figure you know how to do that. Then get laid again. A lot. It makes you slightly easier to be around. Rosalee is smart, gorgeous, funny, she tolerates Dominic, her son is kind of a pain, but she's pretty...and hot...and...."

"Watch it there, punk. If I didn't know better, I'd think you wanted to be in my shoes right now, with the pretty and hot woman, who is *my* girlfriend last I checked."

"There, see, you said it. Was that so hard?"

"Fuck off."

At that moment, Aiden acknowledged he absolutely had to let go of his Rosalee fantasies. His mother had been right, as usual. Rosie belonged to Antony. They needed each other. Besides, Aiden had a date tonight with Renee.

The sound of a familiar throat clearing made them look up to see their father standing in the office doorway. He tossed a set of keys, and Antony caught them.

"Differential's fucked up on the van again."

"What's wrong with it this time?"

"How the hell do I know? It's why I have a mechanic in the family." He glared at Aiden. "Two of them, it would appear."

Aiden swallowed the urge to rise to that bait, his ingrained anti-swear training making him wince. "Coffee?" he asked, holding up an empty cup.

"Sure." Their father took his cup and sat on the couch, staring down into it as if it held the universe's secrets. Antony met Aiden's eyes over the top of his head. "Boys, we need to call a family meeting."

"Oh?" Aiden sat in the chair across from his father, the man he'd hardly known at all growing up, since by the time Aiden had joined the Love throng, the brewery had expanded, the pub had opened, and things were going full throttle, requiring Anton's full attention seven days a week. "Why?"

"Your mother is...well, she's sicker than we thought." Anton ran a shaking hand down his face. "I need you to call Kieran for me. I already told Dom. Let's make it tomorrow night. I'll grill. Bring Rosie."

"Dad, Rosie is...." Antony's face flushed.

"As much a part of the family as anyone. You're the only numb nuts who can't see it." He rose and left his half-finished coffee on the desk. "AliceLynn will be there, too. This affects her."

"Dad...."

"No. No arguments. We have to make some changes. And you," he pointed at his oldest son, "You are going to have to man-up regarding your daughter." He left without giving either of them a chance to speak.

"Fuck," Antony muttered. "I've got work to do. And a date tonight." His eyes held nothing but anxiety for a second, before the mantle of eldest brotherhood slipped over him. He squared his shoulders. "Call Kieran. Tell him to bring that bitch of a fiancée if he wants to, although she's steered pretty clear of Love family business so far. We aren't sophisticated enough for her, I don't think."

"Will do." Aiden picked up the stack of paid invoices, his mind spinning in a million different directions, but all around a single concept.

His mother was dying.

Chapter Nine

"**A**iden."

He sat straight up, blinking in the bright sunlight, confused by his surroundings. Whiteness from pale walls assaulted his optic nerves. Combined with the sunlight, it seared his brain with the force of a lightning bolt. Turning his aching head slightly to the left, he saw her, Renee, she of the expensive red wine and blow job skills he'd almost forgotten.

She held a cup of coffee, and wore a short, silky robe, and a smile. He groaned and flopped back on the pillow. While he didn't exactly regret a night spent between the thighs of a woman, at that precise moment Aiden wished he hadn't done it—had just driven her home, kissed her good night, and gone back to Antony's house. He needed to edit his book. The thing sat there flashing on the junky laptop screen, and piled in yet another printout, mocking him.

"I won't sell myself to an agent," it taunted him. A lot.

"Aiden, your phone is blowin' up with texts. I think you'd better—"

"Come over here." He let his mind shut down. Way too much adult world lurked outside the four walls of this strange, pale, virginal-white bedroom. "I have something for you."

"You are so bad. You always were." She slid between the sheets and curled against him.

"Hmm, well I'm pretty sure you're one of the ladies who made me this way." He sighed with satisfaction when she ran her hand across his chest and tweaked his nipples. "Lower," he whispered into her hair, closing his eyes and sucking in a breath of her just-showered soapiness.

Music wafted in from some other room—The Eagles, one of his oldie favorites, and one of the bands they used to listen to while screwing around in the lowest level of his house across town. She lifted the sheet, climbed on top of him and kissed her way down his body. When her lips covered his erection, teasing, sucking, and messing with him in that lovely way only she could do, Aiden thought he might just move in and stay here forever. He'd yet to find a woman as adept at this, or as willing to bestow it.

Threading his fingers in her hair, he tilted his hips and gave into it, moaning when her finger teased his balls and then went lower, circling his ass while she continued that delectable suction.

As he observed her head bobbing up and down, the sensation of acting like a selfish pig stole over him.

But she liked it or at least she sure used to. I didn't tell her to do it.

"Holy shit!" He dropped his head on the pillow and arched when her finger hit his prostate and stroked it. He held her head, hips pumping, thinking he might never stop coming, until finally, he did.

Renee released him with a loud, wet pop, before heading to the bathroom, leaving Aiden spent, gasping for breath, and with that creeping feeling of uselessness slipping over him again. He closed his eyes, giving in to the rush of hormones to his brain, wishing he could sleep the rest of the day.

"Honey, you gotta get this phone. It's buzzed itself clean off the dresser." The device hit his chest. He sighed and grabbed it, observing Renee as she stuck dangly earrings in her ears, loving the sight of her fully dressed, sexy self.

"You're amazing. Let's stay in bed all day. I need more Renee time."

Her expression bordered on annoyance, the way she might ponder a toddler unwilling to pick up his toys at bedtime. He frowned and swung his feet around to floor, biting back a rush of queasiness from to much wine the night before.

"Never mind. I know you have a business to run."

"And you have to go mow your daddy's lawn, I think." She nodded to the phone that he kept ignoring then click-clacked over to him in a pair of fuck-me pumps that mesmerized him for a split second. Feeling drugged and goofy, he grabbed her ass and pressed his face into the thin fabric of her shirt. She ran her hands through his hair, but stopped him before he could lift the silk and get at her tits. Such amazing tits on a woman he'd never had since Renee—huge, firm, with nipples so sensitive, he could lick one and make her come.

"You spoiled me for all other women."

"Really. Might want to tell Tricia that." She tucked another strand of her hair into a glittery clip then crossed her arms over her chest.

"Um, huh?" He flopped back once more, the phone clutched to his chest. "How did you—"

"It's so cute how quick you forgot the way things get around in this town, lover boy." Renee sat next to him and ran her smooth, warm hand along the inside of his thigh. When she hit his balls she cupped them then squeezed a little too hard for comfort.

"Hey," he yelped, lunging up. "Watch out. You don't wanna hurt the Love family jewels."

She grinned and planted a wet kiss on him, her small tongue exploring until he tingled all over. But she kept her hand on his nuts, distracting, and a little alarming. He moved it away.

"What? You're jealous?" He got up and stretched, sensing her gaze crawl all over his back view. His head buzzed at the thought of Renee threatened by anyone.

"Not exactly. Tricia's my friend, you know. We don't keep secrets from each other. We tend to compare notes, too, sweet cheeks." She smacked his ass so hard he winced. She got to her feet slowly, inch by curvy, perfect inch, and stood close, up in his grill, her hand on his flaccid cock, her bright red, fruity-smelling mouth hovering over his.

His brain had already concocted ways to get back there, tonight, with her in nothing but those killer high heels. She ran her finger across his cheek then kissed him, sucking his lower lip into her mouth and biting it once.

"You're feisty this morning, Miss Renee," he whispered into her neck. "I like it."

"Well, just so you know, I heard all about your little fuck session in the grass. Bourbon sure does strange things to my boy."

He let go of her, embarrassed. But she held on to his dick, which rose to the occasion albeit slowly.

"I'm not your boy, Renee." His temples pounded.

"Oh, relax, lover. I'm just jerking your chain." She gave his cock another somewhat too-tight squeeze then let him go. Aiden blinked, willing it not to get any harder at the sight of the woman in front of him, and the memory of her many talents. It didn't work, so he was left there, like a dork with a boner, glaring at her.

The buzzing phone broke the moment. She grinned and blew him a kiss. "Let me know next time you and Tricia want to party. I know a place a lot less buggy, and with no one around to catch us."

He stared at her swaying hips, processing her words. Finally, without letting his mind wander into the realm of a possible three-way, he picked up the phone.

"Yeah," he said, rubbing his eyes and wandering into Renee's fussy, hot pink-accented bathroom.

"Son, you had better be talking to me from the grave," his father growled in his ear. "I've been sending you texts for an hour now."

"Uh, oh, sorry. I was...."

"I don't care whose thighs you're using as earmuffs. Get your sorry ass over here and mow my lawn. Antony doesn't need you, but since you aren't answering I guess you knew that."

Aiden opened his mouth to respond but the device lay silent in his palm.

Chapter Ten

A iden managed to skirt the edges of a hangover with a lot of water and a decent meal at his mother's kitchen table. When his father made an appearance after spending the morning at the brewery, he smacked the back of Aiden's head and told him to stop mooching and get to work, kissed his wife on the lips then dropped into his leather recliner with a tall glass of iced tea.

"Don't be mean, Anton," his mother stated mildly as she cleared the table and shoved Aiden out the door.

"I can be however I like in my own house." His usual reply.

Aiden trudged out to the garage for the riding mower. By three o'clock that afternoon, the five acres were mowed and trimmed to his father's specifications, and Aiden had parked the mower in its designated spot between the horse trailer and the four-wheeler. His back ached and his shoulders stung from the sun.

Now, his parents were setting up the two patio tables for the "family conference cookout." He admired for the millionth time how seriously his parents took each family meal, never skimping on the courses, the drinks, the tablecloths, and fabric napkins. He'd missed it more than he'd been willing to admit, in his hurry to fulfill his long-stated goal to get the hell out of Kentucky and never come back.

"Need help?" he hollered across the lawn.

"No, take a dip in the pool. I'll get you to fill the outdoor fridge in a few," his mother replied. Aiden noted her face seemed more flushed than usual, her eyes sunken and worried. She caught his gaze, smiled, and gestured to the glimmering surface. "Go on. I know you want to get in."

He saluted her and jumped in the deep end, coming up at the opposite side with a gasp of relief. A few light laps later, he stretched out on a lounge chair before drifting off into la-la land to the sounds of birds and the baseball game on the outdoor radio.

A loud screech and a splash of ice-cold water woke him, sending him off the chair to his hands and knees on the concrete. Jeffrey Norris jumped up and down, laughing and clutching one of the buckets from the toy box.

"Jeffrey made Aiden fall over! Mommy! Did you see?"

"Yes, honey. Don't lose your floaties. I need to help inside. Ask Aiden if he'll play with you."

Aiden raised his head and saw Rosalee, dressed in a batik-print sundress over her swimsuit. He grinned through the wet strands of his hair and got to his feet, yanking Jeffrey up, and holding him over the pool.

"Make me fall over will ya, Jeff? You look hot. How about a dip?" After a glance at Rosalee to make sure he could handle it if he got dumped in, he had to gather his wits. Her nod and smile, the way she tucked a strand of curly brown hair behind her ear made his skin tingly.

"Go for it. He loves it. I'll be inside." She waved at him, leaving him blinking, before a squeal brought him back to earth.

"One, two, two-and-a-half, two-and-three-quarters...." He kept holding Jeffrey over the water, delighting in his excitement, while still admiring the kid's mother sashaying across the lawn to the back patio.

An hour later, both of them were waterlogged and exhausted. Aiden collapsed into a chair and tossed his water cannon to the ground. "I give. You win. Go get me a Coke. Will ya?"

"Coke!" Jeffrey yelped as he ran, bowlegged, toward the patio. "Mommy! Aiden wants a Coke!"

Aiden closed his eyes once Jeffrey disappeared into the house. The sudden rush of memories overwhelmed him. He could picture his brothers, their various girlfriends and friends, little sister and her passel of friends, and his parents gathered there around the pool so many years, so many nights of play and fun. And of course, later, various misbehaviors and illicit parties that had gotten them all in trouble but were part and parcel of his life here. It all filled his head, until his eyes burned.

He must have drifted off again. Bloody-murder-style screaming woke him up facing the blue sky, confused and disoriented, until he jumped to his feet. Pool water sloshed around in his ears and nasal cavities. But the screaming would not stop. Panicked, he ran across the lawn toward the house, fearing the worst—that his mother had collapsed and died on the kitchen floor.

Something dashed past his legs, nearly tripping him. The noise seemed to be coming from it. He stopped, regarding Jeffrey's naked butt as he headed straight for the edge of the pool. Without another thought, Aiden ran after him, snagging him by the arm just as he poised to jump in, sans floaties or a swimsuit.

"Let go of me!" he screeched. Tears streamed down his beet-red face. "Jeffery wants a Coooooooke!" He thrashed so hard Aiden had a hard time corralling him, but he set his jaw to the task, putting his twenty-some years, and a hundred-and-fifty pound advantage to good use.

"Noooooooooo!" The kid kept it up at dog-deafening decibels, but Aiden held tight, grabbed a towel and wrapped him up in it, swaddling him so his legs and arms were immobile. "Jeffery doesn't like this! Let go of meeeeeee. Jeffery wants Mommy!"

Aiden held on tight to him, making shushing noises, and rocking him back and forth until he stopped screaming and was reduced to chest-heaving sobs. The sun went behind a cloud at that moment, casting everything in late afternoon shadow. Rosalee appeared at the open sliding glass door, eyes wild.

By then, Jeffrey had fallen asleep as fast as he'd run naked out of the house. Aiden rose, heart still pounding, but enjoying the child's warmth against his chest.

"Caught the escapee," he said, trying not to leer down the front of her dress.

Rosalee touched her son's head and sighed then slipped her arm around Aiden's waist. Aiden just stood, loving her pressed against him, while having an utterly inappropriate reaction to her proximity.

She is Antony's woman. Stop fantasizing. Now.

"I'll just, uh, set him down somewhere?"

Rosalee sniffled and nodded, stepping back. "Thanks. Let's stick him in the back bedroom, farthest from any noise. He hardly slept last night, as usual. He's like an owl—up all night, but raring to go every morning."

Aiden walked up from the lowest level of the house that opened onto the backyard, past the kitchen where his mother puttered around—not lying dead, thank God—and past his father in the hall, who touched Jeffrey's head.

"Reminds me a lot of somebody else around here." He smiled at Aiden. "Thanks for your help today, son."

Aiden gaped at the bizarre, out-of-character gratitude, but kept going, following Rosalee. He entered the far back bedroom, one that had housed his little sister most recently, but that now served as the guest room since she'd left for college. After sitting and attempting to settle Jeffrey onto the pillow, Aiden was surprised when the kid wrapped damp arms around his neck.

"Hey, buddy, relax. It's okay." Aiden patted his back, feeling awkward, but not exactly unhappy at the close contact.

"He may hang onto you a while, fair warning." Rosalee was as far from them as possible, while still remaining in the room. "Sorry. He's a little clingy when he gets upset."

"What the hell happened?" Aiden asked, keeping his eyes away from her on purpose. "He's not gonna pee on me, is he?"

Rosalee giggled. Aiden glanced at her. Big mistake. She looked devastating, hair wild and framing her small face, her eyes huge and bright, her petite form barely concealed by the light fabric of her swimsuit cover-up. He took a breath and words he probably shouldn't speak formed themselves in his brain and were about to emerge from his mouth. But at that moment Jeffrey relaxed enough to let Aiden know he'd fallen back asleep, so he laid him down on the pillow, loosening the towel. His lips pursed and he mumbled something then flipped over on his back and flung both arms over his face.

"He even sleeps like Paul did, Rosalee whispered, right next to him.

Aiden shivered as a chill ran down his spine. A hand touched his bare shoulder. Aiden kept his eyes focused down, his brain rushing three or four steps ahead, playing this out to its only conclusion—a bad one for all concerned.

"I'm sorry," he said, also in a whisper. She made as if to move away from him so, in desperation, he grabbed her hand. She bit her lower lip, which made him want to do that very thing to her, and tugged at her hand. But he held on, like he'd done with Jeffrey. His brain clanged with warning bells, reminding him of his vow to stop fantasizing about Rosalee, of how much fun he'd had with Renee, of the implied ménage with her and Tricia.

But his eyes were fixed on Rosalee's, on her lips, the tempting line of her jaw, that wild hair he wanted so very much to bury his hands in while he kissed her. She shook her head, but let him hold her close, so close she had her feet on either side of his, straddling his legs, her breasts at eye level.

Without thinking about it, he threaded his fingers in one of her hands then took the other and did the same thing. The sunscreen and shampoo smells filled his brain. Staying silent, he tugged until she bent her knees, sat on his lap, and was kissing him so fast it shocked him. But he closed his eyes and let it happen, unable to keep from making a noise when her tongue breached his lips. Their hands stayed clasped—odd, yet somehow perfect.

She tasted exactly as he imagined she would—ghostly flavors of beer and the minty gum she must have in her mouth registered in his addled brain—mostly like perfection. After about three seconds of "Oh no, you did not do this" guilt, he relaxed and gave in to the moment. And when his body hardened, she sighed and pressed even closer.

With reluctance, he broke the kiss, let go of her hands and touched her lips. "Wow. Glad to know I wasn't the only one thinking about doing that."

Her face flushed beet-red as she leapt up off him. "Oh, God, Aiden. I'm...I didn't...I can't...I'm sorry." She ran out, leaving him sitting next to the slumbering Jeffrey, her taste on his lips, her words in his ears, and his heart pounding so hard it hurt.

"Aiden?" He almost leapt out of his skin at the sound of Jeffrey's voice.

"Yeah, buddy? Thought you were sleeping." Aiden had a moment of worry, wondering what he'd seen.

"Are you gonna be my daddy?"

He blew out a breath and thought carefully about his answer. "No, Jeff. I'm just your friend. Now get a little more rest. We have a party later, remember?"

The boy frowned as if he wanted to say something else then rolled over onto his belly.

Chapter Eleven

Rosalee took one step outside the bedroom, heart in her throat, and ran straight into Antony. She yelped and pressed her back against the wall, hand to her sweaty chest.

"Lord-a-mercy, Antony, you scared me." Her voice wobbled.

"Sorry." He kissed her lightly. "Mama told me you were back here putting Jeffrey down for a nap." He bent down to meet her eyes, but she couldn't do it, not now, not on the heels of that bizarre encounter with Aiden. "You all right? You're shaking." He held her tight and she buried her face in his chest, sucking in familiar scents, some of them hers, from the night before. She clutched the back of his T-shirt, gripping so hard her fingers ached when she finally let go of him.

"I'm sorry." She wiped her eyes and smiled, banishing all thought and memory of Aiden from her mind.

She wanted and needed *this* man. And he needed her, too.

End of story.

No discussion necessary.

She took a breath. "Thanks. Needed that."

His smile didn't quite reach his eyes. It was something she'd gotten used to, but she figured she'd take what she could get from him, considering he offered a hell of a lot more than many women ever got. When his gaze sharpened as he glanced over her shoulder, she froze, sensing Aiden near as if he'd triggered her internal radar.

"What's up?" Aiden brushed past the two of them in the close hallway. Rosalee closed her eyes, furious that he'd had the nerve to touch her arm, on purpose, right under his own brother's nose.

"Would ask you the same thing." Antony tucked Rosalee under his arm and guided her toward the short flight of steps down to the main living area.

By the time they got to the kitchen, Rosalee had her breathing under control and her mind fixed on one thing—forgetting Aiden, and focusing the full force of her attention on getting Antony to marry her, quick, before she did something utterly stupid and irretrievable.

Going up on her tiptoes, she whispered in his ear. "I had a great time last night." She let her hand trail down his back to his swim-trunks-clad ass.

The man had gone full-romance on her for the first time, leaving behind the tried-and-true pizza, beer, and movie days, or her boring meatloaf and mashed potatoes, post-house repair. Dinner at a fancy restaurant in Lexington, meant to be followed by some kind of concert, but she'd been so worked up by the time dessert arrived she'd practically jumped him in the parking lot.

They'd driven home with the windows down, music blaring, and holding hands. Rosalee marveled at how much of a mystery Antony remained, even after a long night of slow, luxurious, incredible lovemaking. Even when he'd been inside her, wearing a condom that time, after nearly an hour-and-a-half of mind-bending orgasmic activity for her, he seemed distant and detached. She'd cried at the realization, and he'd held her until she calmed down, but when he asked her why, she'd deflected.

"Only really crazy women cry after sex," she'd sniffled, burying her face in his neck. "You should get far, far away from me."

He'd chuckled and thumbed her chin so her eyes met his. "Nah. I think I'll keep you close by."

She'd lain awake again while he slept, pondering how heavy her heart weighed in her chest even as she reveled in how sated she felt everywhere else in her body. That very morning they'd shared eggs and bacon cooked by him, and coffee made by her then she'd kissed him goodbye. But now she'd just gone and tongue wrestled his younger brother in a way that left her weak in the knees. Her own capacity to shock and dismay continued to blindside her.

She heaved a sigh. Antony blinked as if he'd been daydreaming.

"Me too, Rosie. You're amazing."

"You say that a lot. I'm gonna get a big head."

His smile almost reached his eyes then retreated, leaving her frustrated.

"Hey, you two." Antony's mother interrupted them. "Come on and see who's here!" She motioned them forward into the kitchen. Antony dropped his arm from her shoulders, took her hand and kissed it. She had a sinking sensation when her intuition told her he was about to say something important when he got interrupted by a squeal of delight, and a body launching into his arms.

"Wow, whoa, hey there, little sister. Didn't expect you." He set her down and grabbed her cheeks in one hand, making her lips pucker like a fish.

"Leggo me," Angelique squawked, her eyes dancing with delight, then greeted Rosalee with a grin and a quick hug.

"So glad you guys are finally getting together," she said under her breath. "Maybe he'll go back to being the fun guy he used to be."

Rosalee opened her mouth to answer, when Aiden swooped in and picked his sister up, tossed her over his shoulder then ran out the back door. The sounds of her shrieks and laughs echoed around the family room. A breeze blew in and cooled Rosalee's overheated face. She bit her lip and administered a not-so-gentle inner lecture before facing Antony, only to find him staring out the kitchen window. His mother stood between them, pondering her with a serious expression.

Rosalee gave her a weak smile then averted her gaze, unwilling to contemplate what kind of mess she may have set in motion with her ill-conceived notion that kissing Aiden resembled anything like a good idea. But Lindsay Love's eyes held no malice, just a sort of gentle study. Rosie acknowledged her scary maternal ability to sort out who'd misbehaved or needed her support with very little provocation with a nod.

The sound of new arrivals diverted her attention. Kieran appeared, wearing his swim trunks and a polo shirt, sunglasses pushed up on top of his thick, red hair. He held the hand of a tall, whip-thin woman with ebony hair swept back in a casual, but classy chignon. Her turquoise linen sundress looked both out of place and impossibly chic. Her nails were trimmed and polished to match her toes, which peeked out of a pair of wedge-heel shoes that Rosalee had seen on sale for no less than seventy-five dollars—way outside her price realm for a pair of summer sandals. She took a moment to touch her own messy updo and wrinkly, cheap swimsuit cover-up.

As she tucked her expensive-looking sunglasses on top of her head and glanced around with a fake wide-eyed-innocent expression, Rosalee swore the corner of her lipsticked mouth curled in a sneer, revealing her identity immediately as "that Melinda," who had the sweet, amenable Kieran Love pussy-whipped.

"Hey y'all." Rosalee stepped into their line of vision in the sliding glass doorway. Trying not to tug at her unruly curls, she gave Kieran a quick hug. Melinda took a noticeable step away from them, smoothing down her perfectly smooth linen skirt, as if Rosalee might have sprayed cooties over it on her way past.

Kieran tugged her closer. Rosalee held out a hand and pasted a friendly smile on her face.

"Hey, Rosie, I'd like you to meet Melinda, my fiancée." Kieran gazed at his brittle future wife with a rapt and moony expression. Rosalee tried not to snicker.

"Hello there." Melinda held out a manicured hand, sort of sideways as if she expected Rosalee to bow and kiss it. She gave it a quick squeeze then released it, and swore to high heaven Melinda wiped it on her skirt.

Kieran had not peeled his eyes off her the entire time, while Melinda stood there appearing both out of place and above-it-all for a solid thirty seconds. Rosalee let her, going against everything she'd been raised to do, by not making random conversation just for the sake of putting the snooty bitch at ease.

"Well, so, I understand Melinda is here." Lindsay Love joined Rosalee, wiping her hands on a kitchen towel. "Hello, honey, nice to see you again."

Rosalee heard the tightness in Lindsay's voice. She hadn't been wrong in assuming Melinda had not made a good impression before this. Melinda remained still, peering down her long nose at the mother of her fiancé. Rosalee's ears burned.

"Kieran, be a good host and get Melinda a cold drink," Lindsay said, and headed back into the kitchen. Rosalee followed her without comment.

"Wow, what a bitch," Rosalee said, taking the beer Dominic held out to her in the kitchen.

He chuckled around the mouth of his bottle. "'Bitch' is too nice a word for that one."

Antony hadn't moved from his position at the kitchen window. When she touched his arm, he jumped as if he'd forgotten she'd been in the general vicinity. "Sorry." He frowned at something in the yard. "Somebody's coming up the walk. Mama must have made another rescue."

Dominic muscled them aside. "Hmmm, nice one, Mama. I might just take her on myself." Both men gawked so hard, Rosalee thought their eyes would pop clean out of their heads. She shoved between them, bumping them both aside with her hips, giggling when Dom smacked her on the ass. Antony didn't react, keeping his hands balled into fists on the counter. Ignoring both men, she joined the sets of eyeballs to see what was so mesmerizing.

The object of their concentration was making her way up the long front walk from the road. Without the contacts Rosalee had managed to leave at Antony's the night before, she could only tell that she had long blonde hair and carried a big plastic box.

"I thought this was just for family. She squinted, trying to make out more details.

"Yeah, well, knowing our mother, she's probably adopted the poor soul, and is gonna toss her into this mess today. You know how she likes to collect people," Dom said.

"Only those who need her. Your mother is great that way." Rosalee elbowed Dom, who snorted.

"Whatever."

When she drew closer, Rosalee could see her five-foot-nine framed dressed in bright white Capri pants, a sleeveless blue shirt, and flat sandals, with her hair piled half up on her head, long tendrils trailing around her face and shoulders. Athletic, tanned, pretty, and nervous were all things Rosalee would use to describe her right then.

"Come on 'round back, Margot," Lindsay called out. The woman looked up, waved, and changed her trajectory.

Dom blew out a breath. "Now that is what I call a real Amazon beauty. I think I may be in true love." He reached around Rosalee and punched Antony's arm.

But Antony kept frowning. "How in the hell can we have a family conference with some stranger hanging around?"

"Who cares? Maybe she's matchmakin' for me. C'mon, let's go meet the future Ex-Missus Dominic Love." He smacked Rosalee's butt one more time on his way out of the kitchen. The stress line between Antony's dark eyes deepened.

Rosalee put her arms around his waist. He stayed stiff and apart from her a few minutes, until she placed herself in front of him and took his face between her hands.

"Chill, mister. You don't have to manage this thing. It's your parents' deal and they will handle it the way they want." She went up on her tiptoes and pecked his lips, surprised when he gripped her hips and dove into her mouth with the kind of kiss he didn't normally bestow in public. She closed her eyes then opened them, recalling Aiden's lips earlier, and how different that moment had been.

"Mmm." She broke away, needing some space, and maybe another beer or three to get through the rest of the day. "Nice. Thanks. Now, let's go be sociable and meet the new lady. I saw her once before. Renee told me she's a preacher, or chaplain, or something. At least she would be, before becoming Missus Dominic."

"Oh, Lord, anything but that," Antony groaned but held her tight, eyes narrowed as he seemed to study her. "I...I don't know what to think about you right now, Rosie, but...I...."

She touched his lips. "Shhh...no reason to get all mushy. I'm great in bed, I know it."

He grinned and bit her fingertip. "Yeah? Well, that makes two of us, I guess." He released her and took a deep breath. Rosalee knew at that moment how hard it must be for a caretaker like Antony, facing the facts about his mother. This might be more than his still-fractured heart could take.

"Yep, that it does. Now, come on, let's find some beer. I hear there's some decent stuff on tap outside."

Chapter Twelve

As they came out onto the patio to join the family, another person emerged from the front of the house. Antony tensed beside her. When she placed her hand on his arm, he slowly exhaled. But his jaw stayed clenched, and his eyebrows furrowed as AliceLynn picked her way across the grass in a pair of wedge sandals not that much different from the ones worn by the snotty Melinda.

She had on a nice sundress, thank the good Lord—no slutty shorts and halter top. Her red hair framed her face, which appeared devoid of its usual layer of makeup.

"She looks real nice," she whispered to Antony.

"Hmph," he grunted, stiffening as his daughter got closer.

Rosalee elbowed him. "Go on and say hi. Jesus, man, it's your own daughter."

Lindsay grabbed the girl and gave her a huge hug. AliceLynn shut her eyes, and held on tight to her grandmother, one of the two women who'd essentially raised her after her father went off the deep end when she'd been just shy of three years old.

Happy noises wafted around the tension-filled tableau. Screams and laughter from the pool, soft music from the outdoor speakers, quiet conversation between Dom and the tall woman, all hit Rosalee's ears, making her think that maybe, just maybe, they could make a normal life out all this. She grabbed Antony's hand. He glared down at her, his eyes dark and wary.

Lindsay tugged AliceLynn into the group and shoved her in front of him. "Go on, give your daddy a hug."

After a second of hesitation, she stepped forward. Rosalee nudged Antony closer. They mimed the polite embrace of a couple of strangers then backed away from each other.

"Who wants some snacks?" Lindsay said.

"I'll help," Rosalee said, eager to escape.

They brought out hummus and pita bread, a tray of veggies and homemade yogurt dip, sliced tomatoes and mozzarella cheese, and a huge bowl of plain, ridged potato chips—the boys' favorites.

AliceLynn perched on the edge of a chair, fiddling with her phone, and ignoring everyone. Melinda sat, stiff-necked next to Kieran, who was chatting with Margot and Dom. Antony remained where she'd left him. Aiden ran into the middle of everyone and shook like a dog, getting cold pool water on the entire group. The shriek that issued from Melinda's lips seemed entirely out of proportion to the situation, in Rosalee's opinion.

She leapt up. "I'm *allergic* to chlorine!"

Rosalee tried not to giggle at the fact she had borne the brunt of the prank, likely on purpose. Dominic laughed, and Kieran's lips twitched as he watched his moderately waterlogged fiancée stomp into the house.

"Oh, honey, I'm so sorry. Aiden, you are very bad." Lindsay winked at him then followed the furious woman.

Rosalee shoved Antony into a chair at the table where Dominic kept flirting aggressively with the tall blonde woman. She seemed more at ease now, holding a beer and picking chips out of the bowl in front of her. With her dark-blue eyes, high and sculpted cheekbones, she could be a model, Rosalee thought, glancing at Antony.

Aiden flopped into the chair vacated by Melinda, rubbing his wet hair with a towel. It took all Rosalee had not to gawk at his bare torso. She exhaled and kept her eyes fixed on the new lady.

"Hey there, I'm Rosalee." She stuck out her hand. "Since that guy doesn't seem to remember his manners." She nodded at Dom, who shrugged and sipped a beer.

"Hi. I'm Margot." She shook Rosalee's hand and gave her a wide, genuine smile.

"So, where did Lindsay find you?" She took the beer Dom handed her and sipped.

"At a book club, actually. I joined a few weeks ago." Rosalee noted the lack of wedding rings, and that her hands were rough, like she gardened, or shared Lindsay's love for horses.

"New to town?"

"Kind of. I...we moved here about ten months ago. From Ann Arbor."

"I thought you sounded like a Midwesterner." Dom gave her his best smoky-eyed gaze.

Margot blinked in surprise then focused on Rosalee, who suppressed another giggle at Dominic's aggravation in the face of Margot's apparent immunity to his charms.

"We?" Rosalee asked, a little unnerved by the way Antony kept his eyes locked on the woman as if she were an oasis in the desert. Jealousy's foreign, pointy daggers hurt. She didn't like them, and had zero reason to feel that way, considering what she'd done with Aiden not an hour ago.

"Yes. I'm...was married." She took a sip of her beer, her hands shaking. Margot's eyes begged Rosalee to change the subject.

"Wait, I thought you were a family counselor," Dom interjected, eyeballing Margot again, second wind obtained. "Isn't that kinda counterintuitive? I mean, 'physician heal thyself,' and all?"

Margot pondered him as if studying a bug under a microscope. "Well, I guess so. Unless you'd say the same thing to a cardiac surgeon who dared to need a bypass. Or, perhaps to use terms you can relate to, a gynecologist who requires a hysterectomy."

Antony burst out laughing—an odd sound to Rosalee's ears, as she hadn't heard a sound like it from him in years.

"Touché, my lovely Amazon." Dominic raised his bottle to her. She clinked hers to it then faced Rosalee and Antony with a more relaxed smile.

"So, we moved here for my ex-husband's job. He's a sports psychologist. Still handles all the UK teams. I came along and started up my practice again. I have an office near campus, and I just got hired as chaplain for the small satellite hospital here in town."

"Huh, maybe he can psychoanalyze the basketball team into a national championship next year. That'd be a nice change," Dom said, gazing out over the yard. "Or maybe you can just pray over 'em. Are you are preacher, too? Sounds fun. I like women who invoke the Lord's name a lot." He waggled his eyebrows at her. Rosalee reached over the table and smacked his arm.

Margot ignored him. "Well, anyway, turns out we moved here not necessarily for the job, but for the coach. The women's soccer coach that is. She got hired just before we moved. I guess they'd been...together a while. Whatever."

"Sorry." Rosalee patted the woman's rough hands. "Men are animals." Something made her place a possessive hand on Antony's thigh. Startled out of his frank perusal of Margot, he flinched and swallowed while Rosalee watched, her heart sinking.

"Only around women we love," he declared, giving her a brief peck on the cheek.

Lindsay plunked a tray of glasses and a pitcher of gin and tonics on the table and took a seat.

"I met Margot at book club. She and I got to talkin'. We've had coffee a few times afterward. And so I invited her here today." She looked right at her oldest son. Antony stiffened again, anxiety coming off him in waves. Rosalee supposed they were that in tune, they'd been together as friends for so long now, and had finally connected, physically speaking. It made sense. But it saddened her, all the same.

She caught Aiden staring right at her. Kieran had gone inside to hunt down the pouting Melinda. Angelique dropped into his chair and punched Aiden's shoulder before meeting Rosalee's eyes. She frowned then turned back to Aiden.

Her face flushed and she focused back on Antony and his mother, and Margot who'd been invited, apparently for a specific reason. Kieran reemerged, holding hands with Melinda, who was definitely a bit less linen dress crisp. He poured her a gin and tonic then brought a couple of chairs close to the table. Anton appeared, looking haggard and stressed. Lindsay held out a hand to him. He took it, reserving his gaze for her.

Rosalee was struck dumb by the force of the connection between them. The fact that her own parents had once been madly and passionately in lust and love still gave her pause. But they had been high school sweethearts, right there in Lucasville.

The story of Lindsay Halloran and Anton Love had been something out of a romance novel—one of the steamier ones, complete with young, handsome, unsuitable stable hands, angry fathers, and shotguns at weddings.

Lindsay kept her eyes on her husband for a moment then faced her children and one grandchild, who remained separate, as if only observing. She tugged on Anton's arm until he took the seat next to her, his arm around her shoulders. The patio silenced as if someone had flipped a "quiet" switch. Terrified, Rosalee clutched Antony's hand under the table.

"So, it appears that my cancer is worse than we thought. It's at stage four, and has spread to the lymph nodes in my armpit. The doctors up at University Hospital are adamant that I have the double mastectomy as soon as I can get myself in there, and have the chemo and radiation right after."

No one spoke, but every face wore identical expressions of panicked horror. Angelique Love stood and walked over to stand next to her father. Anton kept his eyes on his wife.

"Have you obtained a second opinion?" Melinda seemed somewhat more relaxed after one of the famous Love cocktails. "I don't trust the doctors here. You should come to—"

"Shut her up, please," Dom muttered out of the side of his mouth. His eyes were the wildest.

"You're doing the therapies, right, Mama?" Aiden asked. "I mean, you're young still."

"Yes, I'm doing 'em for the first round, even though your daddy had to talk me into it. Go find a shirt please, Aiden." She patted his knee. "You'll catch a chill. You've already heard what affects you the most."

"Yes, ma'am." He brushed past Rosalee's arm in the process of heading for the door. She set her jaw, determined to ignore him.

"AliceLynn'll be moving back into her own house. Next week. It's the best for everyone," Anton said.

Antony glared at his parents. "You can't make that call," he said, jaw clenched so tight she could hardly hear his words.

"Oh, yes we can." Anton pointed to his son. "You dropped out of her life, and we all know why, and we're sorry for you. But I didn't raise you to shirk this duty another minute. That girl is out of control. She's wild, willful, borderline rude to her elders, and we can't have her here anymore. We need to concentrate on gettin' your mama well again."

"Hey, you do know the wild, willful, rude girl is right here, participatin' in this conversation," AliceLynn piped up.

Antony jerked his head around to glare at her. "Don't sass."

She rolled her eyes and flopped back in her seat. "Nobody wants me, Daddy. I get it. I've already told y'all I could go live with Janey."

Anton's dark eyes flashed. "That is absolutely not happening. You have a home, and a father, and it is high time he broke you to a more civilized manner of behavior."

"I'm not one of your stupid horses, Granddaddy." The girl's eyes were filling with tears. Rosalee resisted the urge to jump up and go to her, hold her close like the little girl she resembled at that moment.

"If I may," a voice interjected. Everyone's attention shifted to the opposite end of the table from Lindsay and Anton. Margot sat, competent and in control. Rosalee choked back another nasty surge of jealousy.

"Ah, I get it now," Dom said lightly, his face also red, but his eyes neutral now. "The family shrink gets invited to the family conference. Nicely done, Mama." He raised his beer bottle.

"Show some respect, Dominic. Or I'll beat it into ya," his father growled.

"No need. I'm sorry. But seriously, this is ingenious." He squinted at Margot, who had her eyes pinned on Antony in a way that made Rosalee blind with furious possessiveness.

"No." Antony rose so fast, his chair fell backward. "You do not get to decide how I handle my daughter. You do not sign me up for head-shrinking sessions with some divorced stranger you picked up off the street, Mama." His eyes were full of pain. "AliceLynn and I will work ourselves out. Sorry." He turned his gaze to Margot. His expression was instantly recognizable, at least to Rosalee. "We don't need your help but thanks anyway."

He stalked into the house, leaving the group blinking around at each other in silence.

"I warned you," Lindsay said as she sipped her drink.

The tall, pretty, blonde head shrinker, who had somehow imprinted on Antony in a way Rosalee thought she understood, but rejected out of sheer irrational female jealousy, got to her feet. Rosalee wanted to smack her right in her perfect aquiline nose. Instead, she sat on her hands, waiting.

"It's fine, Lindsay. That went about as well as I thought it might, based on what you told me about Antony." She looked over at AliceLynn, who still sat, arms crossed, pouting like a two-year-old. "I'll see you guys at my office on Monday, AliceLynn. It's already been arranged."

The girl ran toward the pool, nearly breaking her ankle on the high-heeled sandals in the process. Angelique kissed her father on the cheek and squeezed her mother's hand.

"I'll go talk to her."

Anton snorted into his beer. "In the land of the blind, the one-eyed man is king."

"Stuff a sock in it, Anton," Lindsay said, dropping back in her chair, more exhausted than Rosalee had ever seen her. She got up and poured the woman a tall gin and tonic. "Thanks, hon." Lindsay patted her hand. "Go on and find him." She gestured toward the house with her glass. "I think I'll just sit here and get drunk. That sure was a lot harder than I figured it to be."

"Me, too," Melinda slurred, pointing at the pitcher. "Pour me another will you, sweet cheeks?" She smiled at Kieran. Dominic made a gagging sound. Anton glared at both of them.

Rosalee went inside, shivering when the air conditioning hit her bare skin. She figured Antony would either be down in the basement or in his old bedroom, the one he'd shared with Kieran growing up. But her quick check of both places revealed empty rooms.

After peeking in on Jeffrey to make sure he remained asleep and hadn't peed the bed, she wandered back down to the lowest level of the house, the "bottom basement" as the Love siblings had grown up calling it. It had served as their rec room, illicit party, and screwing-around space, according to Antony. It still bore the hallmarks of years spent hosting rowdy athletic boys, and their various buddies, and, later, girlfriends.

The couch and chair cushions were squashed flat. An ancient, boxy model television complete with multiple video games, old-school videotapes, and a ton of DVDs sat, dusty and unused on an army trunk. An indoor-basketball hoop, ratty floor rug, and piles of back issues of *Sports Illustrated*, *Road and Track*, *Horse and Owner* and, likely *Penthouse* magazines completed the decor. A couple of cots were stacked in a corner. Neatly folded blankets and sheets, plus five sleeping bags were stacked on a large shelf.

Rosalee had been down there a few times, with Paul of course, making out, drinking the beer they filched from the brewery, smoking the occasional joint. The Love family enjoyed nothing more than throwing pool parties. As the brothers got older, the parties tended to go on way beyond what the parents expected. She sank down onto the smoky-smelling couch and dropped her head to her knees.

A hand settled on her shoulder, making her jump, with the words, "Where were you, your Mama's worried," on the tip of her tongue.

Aiden touched his lips and tugged her into the darkened alcove beneath the short set of steps. Before she could say a word, he had her pressed against a stack of plastic boxes labeled "XMAS," and kissed her without a word of warning, clutching her hair as if he let go, he would drown. Rosalee wanted not to respond. She truly did think she would act shocked, indignant, and demand that he stop acting like an infatuated teenager and leave her be so she could go find Antony, her future husband.

But she didn't.

He tasted too good. His lips were too perfect. His firm torso under her hands, and his touch, made her want to scream and cry at the same time.

Rosalee Norris, you must have the menopause already because you are going right around the bend, never to return.

She sighed when he untied the string of her bikini top and cupped her breast beneath the thin batik fabric. "Yes," somebody kept saying over and over again, sounding suspiciously like her own voice.

Their tongues tangled, teeth clicked together in over-eager, unpracticed urgency. His other hand had gone up her skirt, dipping into her bikini bottoms and she, Rosalee Slut Norris, let him. She even spread her legs so he could have easier access.

"Rosalee," he whispered into her neck as he touched her, stroked and teased her.

"Please, Aiden." The words flew out of her mouth, making her sound like some kind of sappy soap-opera heroine. When she came with a squeak into his sweaty chest, the first thing she thought was that she wanted more. She reached into his swim trunks and gripped him.

He moved his hips, encouraging her. "Kiss me, Rosalee. I want to...oh...shit...." He moaned into her lips then forced them open with his tongue. And she jacked him off, under the steps, right under the feet of his parents, and Antony, the one she'd meant to find and comfort.

Wow. Some lady of comfort you are, Rosie.

"Holy mother of...Aiden, stop." She pulled her hand out of his shorts. "I think I'm going to pass out. Or puke." She banged her head against the boxes.

He kept grinning and tweaking her nipples, which betrayed her with their eager poking through the dress's thin fabric. She smacked his hands away, but he kept at her, his eyes shining with playfulness and lust. It made her want to do things to him she couldn't even imagine doing with Antony. She shivered.

Eyes darkening, Aiden held her close, stroking her hair, and saying soothing words she couldn't hear for the roaring in her ears.

"We can't do this," she whispered into his chlorine-scented skin. "We *cannot* do this."

"We just did," he whispered back, thumbing her chin so she had to meet his eyes. He stood a good six inches shorter than Antony, which made him easy to reach without having to stand on her toes for a kiss. Which she did, for a good, long, dizzying while.

Finally, she broke away, tears running down her face.

"Yes, we did. And won't ever again. Do you understand me? I need to be with Antony. It's what...people expect."

"Screw that." He nuzzled her neck, making her sigh.

"Aiden?"

They jumped apart as if someone had cattle prodded them both at the sound of a voice on the stairs.

"Yeah, Mama?"

"Have you seen Rosalee? Her boy is awake."

"Okay, I'll come see to him. I think she's...uh...."

Rosalee smacked him when he snaked a hand back up her skirt.

"Well, anyway. I found Antony. He's gone for a swim. Daddy is gonna fire up the grill in a minute."

"Coming," he called up the steps, before yanking Rosalee close again. "I'll find you later." He laid a kiss on her that left her breathless and furious.

She shoved him away. "No, you won't. Mission accomplished. You finger-fucked and got jacked by your brother's girlfriend. Now leave me alone." She could barely control her shaking.

"That's what you think this is about?"

She nodded and pointed to the steps. He snuck around the corner and fished under the couch a minute, emerging with a half roll of paper towels.

"Some things never change," he said, handing her one before bounding up the stairs without a word.

Chapter Thirteen

"**I**s Margot still here?" Aiden walked quickly past his mother, who sat holding Jeffrey. "Give me a second. Need to use the restroom."

Phrases like "take a leak" flew about as well as F-bombs around their mother. But he had to get into the bathroom, throw some cold water on his face, and wash his hands. He stood, braced against the vanity top of the main level half bath, glaring at his flushed face in the mirror.

"You are the biggest idiot on the planet," he said. He'd had no intention of doing that, of kissing Rosalee, and touching her, and...he groaned at the memory of her lips and hands, of how incredibly responsive she'd been, hair-trigger, glorious, and perfect.

His phone buzzed in his pocket. He lifted it out, noting yet another dirty text from Tricia. If she and Renee were as tight as she claimed, he sure didn't get how the woman believed it appropriate to send him messages outlining what she wanted to do to him.

He ran a hand down his face, noting the drying white mess he'd made on his shirt. Knowing from direct experience plain water did not hide that particular stain, he yanked the shirt off, snuck out into the back hall, and up the steps to his old bedroom. After locating a shirt of Dominic's and tugging it over his head, he stuffed the dirty one into the hamper, intending to grab it before he left.

When he came back down, Jeffrey still sat on Lindsay's lap, thumb lodged in his mouth, staring at a book. His mother had kept nearly all of their old toys and books. "For the grandbabies," she always claimed. Aiden listened for a moment, hearing Jeffrey's soft questions mumbled around his thumb, and Lindsay's gentle reading cadence that Aiden could sometimes still hear as he drifted off to sleep. She used to read to them every night as a group, until they were too old for that, leaving her with Aiden and the antsy, restless Angelique, who could barely get to sleep at night anyway, and who didn't like being read to.

When Jeffrey caught sight of him, his eyes brightened and he raised his arms. "Pick me up." Lindsay gave the child one of her patented politeness lessons under her breath to Aiden's amusement.

The little boy nodded. "Pick me up, please."

He did, loving the way Jeffrey clung to him, sitting down across from his mother who remained in her rocker, frowning at him.

"I told you not to do that."

"Do what?" His face flushed, as he anticipated the coming lecture.

"To covet things that aren't yours." She leaned back and closed her eyes. The sudden vision of her sick, or in any way reduced, made him dizzy with terror.

He shook his head. "I don't."

No, I don't covet her. I just groped her like a stupid teenager at a house party.

"I can read you like a book, Aiden Leonardo Love."

"Yeah, Leonardo," a familiar voice called from the shadows in the upper-level family room. "Hey, Mama, I think Margot is fixing to leave," Kieran threw over his shoulder as he passed by them on his way to the bathroom.

"But we haven't eaten yet." Lindsay got slowly to her feet, her slight frame engulfed by her sundress. How Aiden had only just noticed she must have lost twenty pounds since he'd last seen her at Christmas boggled his addled mind.

"Hang on a sec, I'll help." He got up with Jeffrey still clinging to him like a barnacle then froze at the sight of Rosalee in the kitchen. The breeze lifted the hair framing her face, and stirred her thin dress, molding it around her frame. Noting the tears running down her cheeks, he cursed under his breath for the millionth time, swearing off it, off her, and his bizarre, sudden obsession with the woman who'd been nothing to him once but the girlfriend of Antony's best friend—a nice girl, pretty and all, but older and unattainable.

She bent over the sink, shoulders shaking. Aiden hated himself then—utterly despised his weak-willed inability to keep his stupid, lust-addled mind and hands off the woman.

Jeffrey stirred. "Mommy!" he yelped.

She wiped her eyes and fixed a smile on her face, until she saw who was holding her son.

"Jeffrey, thumb." She mimed pulling her thumb from between her lips. Her eyes were full of remorse. Aiden took a breath, and willed something decent to materialize out of his mouth. "Stay away from me." She moved past him.

He touched her shoulder. "I can't."

She stopped, her hands on either side of the patio doorframe. "You have to."

"What's wrong with my mommy?" Jeffrey patted Aiden's face, his brow knitted with worry.

"Nothing, Jeff. Everything is fine. Let's go find Dom. I'll bet he'd play some soccer with us."

"Soccer!" The kid's shriek nearly deafened him.

Aiden set him on the wide expanse of grass between the patio and pool then scanned the yard for Dom. He spotted Kieran and Melinda in a dim corner of the patio, heads together. Rosalee sat with her legs in the water, clutching a gin and tonic. Antony had propped up on his elbows, his body in the pool, his eyes dark and stormy. Margot was talking with Lindsay. His father and Dom were huddled around the grill. AliceLynn and Angelique had disappeared somewhere, probably to smoke a joint.

He wished he had one right now, truth be told—anything to ease the guilty ache in his chest. Not to mention the clear, memory sensation of rightness when Rosalee had been in his arms.

Margot waved in his general direction then turned to leave. He watched her go, pondering how a woman that attractive would get dumped for someone else.

"Show me a beautiful woman, and I'll show you a man tired of fuckin' her."

"Shut up, pig," he said, catching the soccer ball Dominic tossed his way. "You're ruining a new generation." He pointed to Jeffrey, who ran around chasing butterflies.

"All in a good day's work, I'd say, little bro." Dom kicked another ball toward a goal he must have dragged out of the shed. "I'm proud of how you turned out."

"Right," Aiden muttered as his brother dribbled and kicked the ball around like a pro. Bastard always managed to be good at any sport he tried.

After a few minutes of playing keep-away from Jeffrey, and running him ragged from one end of the yard to the other, Aiden saw that Margot had returned. She worried her bottom lip and held her hand up to shield her eyes from the sun.

"Hey, um, I think I need a jump or something. My car won't start."

Antony reemerged from the house, dressed and holding a beer. "I'll check it out," he said.

"Antony, he's our car-fixin' hero," Dom crooned in falsetto. He slung Jeffrey around to his shoulders and raced around the yard to the boy's delight. "Let me know when you need a beer brewed, gorgeous!"

She waved him off. Aiden was struck by her beauty again, but more so by the expression on her face at that moment. Antony seemed uneasy and unsure. Not something Aiden had ever known the man to be around anyone, especially anyone female.

"Sorry," she muttered.

"It's fine. But I'm still not coming to therapy."

"That remains to be seen."

"You don't know me very well do you?"

As they headed down the driveway chatting, Aiden was shocked to his core when Antony roared with laughter and bumped Margot's shoulder.

Now that is a funny turn of events. Funny. And perhaps to my advantage.

But when he caught Rosalee observing the same thing, his heart clenched at the sight of her dismay.

A few hours later, post burgers, brats, and his mother's secret-recipe baked beans and rice, Kieran and Melinda left, her claiming she had a deposition in Miami she had to catch a flight for Monday, and Kieran mooning after her like a stone-cold fool. AliceLynn and Angelique reappeared to eat, both of them giggly and red-eyed.

The awkward silence between a grim Rosalee and a somewhat dazed-looking Antony made Aiden's teeth hurt. He kept shifting his gaze from one to the other of them during the candle-and-tiki-torch-lit meal, at one point intercepting an angry, thin-lipped frown from his mother.

After the sun, pool, food, and extreme emotional swings he'd endured, he was utterly drained. He lay in a lounge chair by the pool, under the glow of a large mosquito-repelling torch, drifting back and forth between sleepy and horny, between tired and exhilarated. His phone had buzzed nonstop, but he ignored it in favor of studying the drama unfolding in front of him.

AliceLynn had been given a week to get her stuff packed from both houses with Angelique's assistance. In the meantime, the two of them were staying in AliceLynn's soon-to-be old room upstairs. Aiden had hoped to snag that room tonight. The thought of driving back out to Antony's, only to be confronted with sex sounds he dreaded held little appeal.

By the time he'd lost count of how many beers he'd consumed he figured that maybe he'd just sleep by the pool, if the mosquitoes didn't carry him away. The floaty, dreamlike sensation got more intense. Sounds around the patio quieted, but the music kept playing, coming from the outdoor speakers attached to somebody's portable player.

Finally, on a desperate whim to get away from there, he sent a text to Renee.

Come pick me up from the Love Estate? I've had about enough.

In what seemed like seconds, she stood by the pool, wearing a bikini and a smile. He sat up and rubbed his eyes, wondering if he was dreaming. Without a word she sat on the edge, giving him a great view of her perfect, hourglass shape, before slipping into the water and disappearing.

After checking around to ascertain that no one remained nearby, he dove in. He caught her up against the edge and kissed her, grabbing her tit with one hand, and her ass with the other. He ached for something, and figured he could purge it with the agreeable Renee.

She slipped her hand into his trunks then shifted so her legs were around his waist, and he was inside her, still drunk enough to be a bit fuzzy on the details. All he knew at that moment was how great it was to be there, so he held onto the side of the pool and got off, thrusting and grunting like some kind of loser while she clung to him, whispering encouragement into his ear.

He shuddered and kissed her, wishing very much that he were not that guy, the one who would lust after his own brother's girlfriend while taking advantage of a perfectly nice woman in his family's pool. Not that he hadn't had sex in this pool, probably in this very spot with this very woman, plenty of times.

Renee drew back as he gathered his wits, post second orgasm of the day.

Talk about going from drought to monsoon.

He sighed and pulled out of her accommodating body, keeping his hands on either side of her. "Sorry," he muttered, cupping her breast. "I owe you for that one."

"I know a fun way to pay me back," she whispered, before biting hard on his earlobe and tucking his softening dick back into his shorts.

"Go hop in my car, sweetie. I have a surprise waiting for you at my house."

A slow smile spread across his face. If a nice three-way won't snap a guy out of a funk, then he should probably turn in his man card. But something about it made him wish he had the nerve to declare something along the lines of, "No thanks. All done for tonight."

He heaved up and out, grabbed a towel then assisted Renee out. She giggled and slapped his hands off her nipples that stuck out so nicely behind her wet bikini top. When he heard a dramatic throat-clearing noise, he realized who made it before he saw her.

"That was disgusting." Rosalee's eyes blazed with fury. "I had to turn the television up and convince your parents not to look out the window at your noise."

He rubbed his eyes, anger settling deep in his chest. Renee tugged her cover over her suit and grabbed her bag then Aiden's elbow.

"Come on Aiden, honey. We don't need lectures. We're grown-ups."

"Really," Rosalee said as they passed by her at a quick step. "Might want to think about acting like one, Renee. You know Miss Lindsay is right inside and awake."

Renee crossed her arms over her chest. Aiden could almost taste the fury oozing from her pores.

"Rosie," he croaked, sick at his stomach and more tired than he'd ever been in his life.

"Don't call me that, you pig," she insisted, her voice tight as she sat with her arms full of pool paraphernalia. "Antony and I are getting married. He asked me tonight. Right before we saw you out here screwing in the pool like a couple of teenagers."

Aiden opened his mouth, but no words would emerge.

She held up her hand. "No, save your congratulations for another time." Her eyes were bright with tears and her voice wobbled.

Finally finding his own voice, he said, "Rosalee, don't. He's not ready." And he meant it. Not because by marrying her Antony would remove Rosalee from him, but recalling the strange interaction between Antony and the newcomer Margot all afternoon.

"Don't give me advice. Now go on, let your *girlfriend* take you home." Her emphasis on the word made him flinch.

"Renee, go to the car."

She sucked in a breath, but he pointed to the darkened driveway, needing just a second alone with Rosalee. Once Renee stomped off, he faced her again. "Interesting way to end a day like this, eh, Rosie?" he said, unable to stop the words from tumbling out. "I mean, you know, considering."

She stood, sending all the toys crashing back onto the concrete. "Do not call me that. Don't touch me...don't ever speak to me again." Her jaw clenched, not unlike Antony's when he got his temper up. "And at least I ended the day in a way that your parents could appreciate. Unlike some people." With that, she flounced off in a huff, leaving him breathless with anxiety and the words, "Antony and I are getting married," whirling through his brain.

He barely registered the ride home in the dark, with the Mustang's top down and radio blaring. Renee prodded him through the front door, and he headed for the kitchen seeking water. He gulped down three full glasses then set the empty on the counter, eyes closed, processing all he'd seen, done, and experienced in the last few hours. Exhaustion crept up and pounced, until he wanted to sink to the floor and curl up in a ball.

"Aiden, sugar bear," Renee called from the bedroom.

He groaned, remembering he "owed her" for the quick-and-dirty in the pool that had so distressed Rosalee. "Coming."

"Come on in here and just settle down, let me take care of the rest," she crooned, soothing him, and making him horny all at once. Three times in one day had to be some kind of personal record, but he flopped back and let her tug his shorts down and off. The room faded on him then, and he sighed, stretching his arms over his head.

"Aiden," a female voice whispered. "Open your eyes."

A womanly shape appeared in front of him—full hips, lush breasts, thin waist, thick hair tumbling around her shoulders. She walked closer, a breeze from the open windows lifting her hair. She stood at his knees then straddled him, fisting his miraculously hard dick. Her lips found his, no...they were on his cock. Wait...there were two sets of lips.

He groaned and reached for the woman who had him down her throat, wanting to see her face, but finally surrendered and arched into her efforts.

When the second woman straddled his face, he gripped her hips, licking and sucking, teasing, fingering, and moaning when she came all over him. At that moment, luscious suction girl stopped, leaving him on the knife-edge of orgasm. As he lay there gasping like a beached fish, one of the girls crawled up his body and settled onto him, gripping him so tight he grunted as she rocked her hips.

Where in the hell am I? Still poolside? At my parents' house? Lord, I hope not. I'll never live this down.

Shit.

Goddamn that feels good.

The woman on him ground down, using her inner muscles to clench and release him, tugging him back to the edge. But then, she disappeared, too.

Confused, heart hurting, chest aching, and ready to explode down below, he blinked, trying to sort out what, exactly, was going on right now.

"Aiden," a voice whispered in his ear.

"Aiden," another said, nearer his crotch.

"Huh," he croaked.

"We want to watch you come."

A set of lips found his balls, the other his nipple. He fisted his own dick and let it happen as warmth flooded his brain just before it coated his hand. A blanket covered him. Soft female lips kissed him one by one, teeth nipping his lip, fingers teasing him over the fabric. Then, they were gone.

He woke in the morning with a pounding headache, stickily sandwiched between Renee and Tricia.

Chapter Fourteen

September

Rosalee shifted in the uncomfortable faux-leather recliner next to Lindsay's hospital bed. She glanced at her phone to confirm the time—well past midnight, but not enough to justify giving up on sleep just yet. Her over-caffeinated brain spun, making her eyes burn.

The room door creaked open and a nurse peeked in. "She sleeping still?"

Rosalee nodded, getting up to stretch her lower back, thinking she might as well walk around, as sit and be miserable.

"Bless her heart." The nurse held the door open so Rosalee could exit. "She's such a fighter."

Rosalee nodded. The last couple of months had been such a blur she got tired thinking about it. Waving at the nurses on night shift, she headed for the lounge, needing a change of scenery. Lindsay would likely wake in another couple of hours and she'd want someone nearby.

Dropping into a chair, Rosalee let gravity tug her down as she stretched her legs out in front of her. She'd been living on crappy food for nearly two weeks since Lindsay had been sent back to the hospital. A post-operation infection after Aiden had found her shivering, burning up from fever, crouched in her bathroom and babbling like a crazy person, put everyone in the Love household back on edge.

They kept pumping that god-awful poison into her, in an aggressive attempt to kill every healthy cell she possessed, on the off chance they'd kill the cancer ones, too. Lindsay alternated between practically comatose from painkillers, and puking her ever-loving guts out—brutal and awful to observe. But her family had worked out a schedule so that not one of them stayed with her longer than a couple of days in a row for sanity's sake.

Rosalee flat out refused to leave her alone at night, something everyone else seemed willing to do, which infuriated her. She'd actually screamed at Antony when he'd dared suggest they come home the first night and let the nurses deal with her.

"Goddamn you to hell, Antony Ian Love. If that were any of you ungrateful shits lying there, do you honestly think she'd 'let the nurses deal with you at night?' Really?"

"Well, she'd charge you two bucks for all those bad words if she could hear you."

He'd collapsed into a chair then, fueling her guilt. He'd been dealing with so much with AliceLynn back at home, trying to be a dad, while not throttling her at the same time. A challenge, Rosalee knew. The girl did her level best to make life miserable for the man, despite their regular therapy sessions with that Margot person.

Rosalee tried not to let her low-lying jealousy about the time Antony spent with his therapist overwhelm her. She held her hands up over her face, reassured by the sight of the diamond ring he'd given her the weekend after that bizarre "family-conference cookout" when he'd rushed back from fixing the therapist's car, grabbed her, kissed her, gone down on one knee, and asked her to marry him.

The expression on his face that night had been one of desperation and despair. She preferred to think about it as concern that she might say "no." But more than once, something made her think otherwise, especially lately.

Rosalee closed her aching eyes, willing images and memories of Aiden out of her brain. She had to be done with him. He's an immature punk, like Antony frequently stated. Spoiled rotten and ruined by it, but hopefully willing to work back into some kind of usefulness now that he'd landed a teaching job at the community college to round out his hours at Love Garage.

"Hey," a soft voice teased her half-waking dream state. She stretched, relishing the memory of Aiden's lips on hers.

"Rosalee," the voice spoke again, making her smile at the sound of Aiden's voice in her dream. Something tickled her cheek. She brushed at it, still reliving that first kiss, when he'd threaded his fingers through hers.

When her chair tipped back, making her gasp and grab the armrests, she cursed and opened her eyes, coming face-to-face with the man in her dreams.

He grinned, which did not ease her pounding heart. "Truce. Seriously. I just thought you might be hungry." He held out two chocolate-dipped ice-cream cones.

She frowned but her mouth watered at the sight. "Fine. Give it to me."

He raised an eyebrow and held the cone closer to his body.

"I'm not in the mood, Aiden," she warned, her face growing alarmingly hot.

"I can see that. When did you last shower? I mean, really."

"Fuck you. Give me the ice cream now."

"Such a delicate desert blossom." His grin widened and he handed hers over then settled back to eat his.

Rosalee inhaled it, relishing every creamy, fattening bite.

"How is she tonight?" he asked, after he passed her a napkin.

"Better I think. A lot better than last night. Which is good, they say."

"Infection is gone, right?"

"Yeah, but she's fighting the chemo, too, so she's just so worn out. She can hardly hold her head up when she's awake, which is about five hours a day."

"How's Jeff?"

"Freakin' out, most days. Paul's mama deals with him mostly. I don't know."

"You don't have to be this person, you know—the one who watches over our mother twenty-four-seven, making sure the nurses and doctors don't screw up."

She glared at him. "Don't make me give you the same speech I gave your brother."

"Want me to grab Jeff tomorrow? Take him to the pool and keep him at the house, maybe spell Mrs. Norris for a couple of days? I don't start teaching until next week."

A bolt of relief shot through her. Without thinking she reached out and grabbed his hand. "Yes. Thanks. That would be great."

After following his gaze down to their joined hands, she tried to pull away, horrified at how natural it seemed to touch him. But he held onto her, using just enough pressure to let her know that he wouldn't let go.

"I miss you." His words sent a jolt down her spine.

She sucked in a breath. "I look a fright. I don't think I've showered in two days, if you must know."

Aiden made a show of pinching his nostrils shut. She smacked his shoulder but couldn't bring herself to let go of his other hand. An awkward silence descended between them.

"Does he know?" Aiden's voice stayed low and intense.

Rosalee blinked, processing that. She frowned and tugged at her hand, but Aiden held on tight, boring into her with his intense hazel eyes.

"Does who know what?"

"Does Antony realize how lucky he is?"

She tried not to giggle, or burst into tears.

You don't get to have them both, Rosalee. Get a hold of yourself.

"Spare me your sweet talkin'."

He let go of her hand and moved back, stretching his legs out so they were on either side of her feet. "I suppose he does," Aiden said, softly. "When do you think they'll let her come home?"

Grateful he'd changed the subject, Rosalee blew out a breath. While she'd never admit it to him, his presence soothed her. It must be his place in the Love family pecking order that made him so relaxed and calm and seemingly drama free. As she opened her mouth to reply, a nurse stuck her head into the lounge.

"Hey y'all, she's awake and askin' for you." Her eyes flickered over the somewhat intimate way the two of them sat, Rosalee with her elbows on her knees, Aiden with his legs framing hers. "Hey, Aiden."

"Hey, Sherry." He flashed his wide smile at the attractive girl, who blushed.

Rosalee had an irrational jealous spike, the same one she'd endured during that terrible display in the pool the night of the family conference. She'd had to drag Antony away from the window, saying he had to help her distract Lindsay and Anton from the noise.

Her face flushed hot at the memory so she fiddled with her hair, hoping to smooth it and wishing she'd slapped on some makeup that morning, however long ago that was, of course. She'd lost track of time.

You're engaged to this man's brother. You do not have to primp for him.

Stop staring at his ass.

She shook her head and she followed Aiden and Sherry the adorable nurse back down the hall to Lindsay's room.

Chapter Fifteen

"**A**iden! Aiden! Aiden!" Jeffrey jumped up and down and clutched at his jeans.

"Yeah, pal, now tone it down to a dull roar a second, please. I need to talk with your Grandma." He took the boy's hand. "I'll keep him overnight and tomorrow Mrs. Norris. Get some rest."

She nodded, but gave her grandson a fierce hug, seemingly unwilling to let him go despite the fact she looked like ten miles of bad road after ten days of one-on-one with him. Jeffrey struggled away from her in a typical, selfish, four-year-old way. Aiden picked him up and fastened him into the car seat Antony now kept in all of his vehicles.

A sign, Aiden. They are getting married, hitched, 'til-death-do-they-part. Lord forbid that would happen to either of them again. Stop obsessing. Stop. Stop. Stop.

They sang *Old MacDonald* all the way across town to his parents' house. He wrestled the squirmy, over-excited kid into swim trunks, lathered sunscreen on him as best he could, stuck his floaties on his spindly arms, and tossed him in the pool. Aiden stood, trying to catch his breath, wondering how in the hell his mother had done this thing, not once, not twice, but five different times.

Jeffrey spluttered and spat then grinned so wide something in Aiden's chest did a strange sort of twanging. A kind of pang of missing something he wanted, that had nothing to do with getting laid, filled it—a wholly new sensation and one he didn't know how to take. He shook his head, took off his T-shirt, and jumped in, bringing squeals of frightened delight. After endless rounds of Marco Polo, some quick, but ear-splitting efforts to go without the floaties, a cannonball-splashing contest, and a water-gun war, they sat together on a lounge chair, covered in a dry towel.

"Hungry," Jeffrey insisted, half-asleep. "I wants a hot dog."

"Gross." Aiden hauled them both up and out of the chair. "How about a peanut butter and jelly sandwich? It's my specialty."

"I am allergic to peanuts." Jeffrey had a grip on his neck with one hand, his other thumb lodged in his mouth, eyes at half-mast.

"Oh, right, good to know. Okay. Let's see what's floatin' around in the kitchen. Go pee and then sit on the couch." He wandered into the kitchen, hoping something resembling food could be found. He hadn't been to the store in over a week, ever since they'd readmitted his mom. His father went from brewery, to hospital, to home, in a weird, uncharacteristic daze, so Aiden figured he hadn't thought through the food thing yet. He paused as a shiver shot down his spine at the realization if what they all prayed would not happen, did happen, they'd be fending for themselves a lot more pretty soon.

He shook it off and opened the pantry, shocked to find it overflowing with staples. Grabbing spaghetti noodles, he set water on to boil. The fridge practically overflowed, chock full of tinfoil-covered disaster-oles from the neighbors, two gallons of milk, a huge pitcher of lemonade, and a bunch of fruit suspended in jello. A couple of gallons of homemade ice cream sat in the freezer. He wouldn't have put it past Rosalee to have devised all of this, but he figured it for a group effort. In a small town, one where Lindsay had grown up, raised her family, and organized similar efforts for sick folks, word traveled fast, and the good Christians in town moved faster with their help.

He found the butter and Parmesan cheese, poured a giant glass of milk, downed it then poured some more.

"Hey, come on in here. I found something."

Jeffrey wandered in, rubbing his eyes and looking alarmingly red on his shoulders and cheeks, making Aiden wince and wish he'd applied more sunscreen. But the boy had his dad's complexion, slightly darker than Rosalee's, so he figured it would fade, no harm, no foul.

Placing the milk on the table, he told Jeffrey to grab a seat then cut up an apple and a banana, and stuck them in front of him.

After glaring at the fruit, he said, "Jeffrey doesn't like it."

"Okay." Aiden hadn't been a fan of fruit when he was little either. "Well, what do you like?"

"Hot dogs."

"Here's the thing," he said as he drained the noodles then mixed them with plenty of butter and cheese. "I know for a fact that your mama would not let you eat hot dogs. So try that with some other babysitter. It won't work with me." He divided the noodles into two bowls and sat, holding up his fork. "Dig in, little man. This is gourmet stuff."

Jeffery just glowered at him then crossed his arms and stuck out his lower lip. Aiden braced for an outburst, but kept eating.

"I don't like s'ghetti."

"Really? Cool. I'll eat yours then." He grabbed his bowl, wondering if he should just drop him into bed and worry about eating when he got up.

"Jeffrey wants a hot dog!" The last two words were a high-pitched screech, accompanied by the crash of the milk glass hitting the cabinet. "Aiden gets me a hot dog now!" Before he could launch off the chair and into the glass shards, Aiden snagged him and hauled him up onto his shoulders.

He managed to avoid piercing his feet on his way out of the now-destroyed kitchen, and keep his cool. Finding a towel, he tried the wrapping up trick that had worked at the cookout. But this time, Jeffrey used every ounce of his furious energy to thwart it, managing to punch Aiden twice in the eye and stomp on his nuts.

"I hates Aiden!" he screeched. "I wants Mommy, now!"

At that moment, Dominic appeared, arms loaded with grocery bags. He set them down and took two steps across the room, picked Jeffrey up, and held him over his shoulder until he stopped struggling and lay limp, sniffling, and sucking his thumb. Aiden dropped onto the couch, rubbing his sore eye while Dominic carried Jeffrey upstairs.

After coming back down, he sat in the chair opposite Aiden and pinned him with a dark, Love-patented glare. "You gotta stop this."

"Stop what?" Suddenly bone tired, Aiden wanted nothing more than to crawl in bed to take a nap.

"Oh, little A, you're gonna cause trouble no matter what you do, aren't you?" Dom got up and smacked his head hard enough to make him yelp.

"I have to teach Monday. It's my first class," he said, apropos of not much, but feeling a need to justify his existence.

"Okay then, Professor Love, try to keep out of co-ed panties." Dom picked up the grocery bags and headed into the kitchen. "Shit! Motherfucker...you could have warned me about the minefield, Aiden. Get in here and clean this up."

Once they got the kitchen back in order, their father came in, ate something, and took a shower then sat in his recliner, clutching a cup of coffee and staring into it. "Need to spell Rosie. Antony's headed over, too. You all keep things together here."

"Sorry, Pops, I've got a hot date." Dom emerged from the downstairs bathroom rubbing his hair with a towel. "I have Monday and Tuesday with Mama."

Anton pinched his nose. "Good Lord Almighty, son, I don't need your swingin' dick in my face. Get some clothes on." He sighed. "Docs are saying we might have her back home by Tuesday."

Aiden stayed quiet, watching a late season Reds game without really seeing it.

"You gonna ever publish that novel, Aiden?"

"I don't know," he said, sipping lemonade. "It's sort of back burnered now."

"Huh. Sounds like an excuse to me."

He studied his father, shocked by the comment, but not terribly surprised. Anton Love never expected less than one-hundred percent from his children, whether at school, in their athletic endeavors, or in terms of a tidy bedroom and a mowed lawn. "Can't never did do nothin," was a many time stated and much hated phrase of his.

"Maybe." He wondered where this conversational line had come from. "I should tweak it some. Just go ahead and send it out to agents. My advisory board hated it though. Not terribly encouraging." Unwilling to tread too far into that minefield with his father, Aiden left it at that.

"Well, at least now you'll be making money teaching the next generation how to write shitty books, eh?" Anton got up and stretched.

Aiden was struck by how old his father seemed then. A strange sort of terror gripped his chest. "Something like that." He knew better than to say more. His dad did not do well alone. He drew a lot of his strength from his wife. Holding it together by a thin string, worried sick about Lindsay, unable to focus on his brewery, all combined to make him more of a hard-ass than usual. "Still working with Antony though, three days a week."

"Good thing. You'll need a real job to fall back on." He patted Aiden's shoulder. "It's good to have you home where you belong. I'll be in tomorrow."

Aiden couldn't think of anything useful to say before his father left the house. He stretched out on the couch then woke on the floor, with the front door open revealing Rosalee, her face streaked with tears.

"Where's Jeffrey?" she asked, dragging him to his feet.

"Uh, asleep? What time is it?"

"Aiden...." She pulled him closer.

"What?" He gripped her arms. Her eyes were half open. "Come on." He tried to guide her toward the steps.

Rosalee nearly collapsed against him as Aiden fought the urge to pick her up. He had no idea what had happened, but hurt, fury, and exhaustion rolled off her in waves.

"He...he...." She gripped the back of his shirt. "He was...with her."

"What the hell are you talking about?" She clung to him so tightly, he had to grab her arms and peel her off so he could hear her. He had an idea what she was talking about, though.

"That therapist. Margot." Rosalee stepped back, rubbing her arms. "Her. Antony was...." To Aiden's surprise, the one woman on the planet he would never expect to be jealous of anything, or anyone, screamed like a banshee and stomped into the kitchen, leaving him slack-jawed in her wake.

She drank water and he waited, unable to fathom what she must have seen. The tickle of guilt blossomed into a spike of pain in his gut over what he wanted to do—shit, what he'd done—with Rosie. "You must have imagined it. Antony would never—I mean, you're tired and stressed out and...."

"Shut up, Aiden. You weren't there. You didn't see what I saw." She whirled on him. "This is my fault. I brought this on by screwing around with you!"

"No, no, no, it's not that." He took a few steps closer, itching to get his arms around her, to comfort at least. But she dodged past him, and they switched positions in the room. He heated up at the thought Antony would do anything to hurt Rosalee, even as his logical brain rejected that entire concept.

To his horror, she collapsed in on herself like a wilting flower, sliding down the kitchen wall in tears. Brain spinning, he hesitated then walked over and tugged her to her feet.

"My fault," she kept saying, even as he took her chin, tilted it up, and kissed her.

With a sigh, she wrapped her arms around his neck and met him halfway for a few seconds. Despite the weirdness of the moment, he wanted nothing more than to just be here, with her. As he moved his hand down her back, a slamming door made them leap apart. She nodded at his tented shorts so he grabbed the first thing he could find to cover it.

"Nice apron, Julia Child." Dom sauntered into the kitchen wearing a smirk.

"What are you doing here?" Aiden backed away, hoping to escape, and pissed off Dominic had chosen that night to hover around the Love family homestead.

Rosalee smoothed her hair and wiped her lips, her gaze anywhere but on him. Dom took a cola from the fridge, popped it open, and drank half of it before setting it down and appraising the two of them, a knowing gleam in his eye.

"I'm here to get Jeffrey and take him home," Rosalee blurted.

"Stay here," Aiden said to her, then locked eyes with Dom. "I'm going to talk to Antony. He's still at the hospital, right?"

"Yeah." Rosalee wore a defeated expression. "But the good news is your Mama is rallying, big time. She'll probably come home by Tuesday."

"Great," Aiden muttered, resolved as he untied the silly apron, hoping his boner had gone down enough not to show. "I'm still going there. Now. You should just stay here. Crawl in bed with Jeffrey. He's in the back bedroom."

Dom gave him a high eyebrow as he pushed past. After he found a clean shirt in the laundry and pulled it over his head, he tried to ignore the buzzing in his ears. A strange sort of fury he had no decent explanation for gripped him hard. Grabbing his mother's car keys, he headed out, driving the twenty minutes to the suburban hospital with all the windows open, fingers tapping the steering wheel.

Chapter Sixteen

He hadn't known what to expect, but finding his mother wide awake, smiling, and sipping ginger ale at two in the morning, surrounded by Anton, Antony, and Margot, had not been among the options. When they all looked up at him as he pushed open the door, the spit dried up in his mouth. He had no business getting into this.

Then again, he had even less business kissing his brother's fiancée. He gulped, and pasted on a smile. "Just wanted to see the miracle for myself." He walked over to kiss his mother's thinning hair. Trying to get the adrenaline-fueled trembling in his knees to stop, he lost the battle and grabbed a chair to hide it.

Antony moved ever so slightly away from the tall, blonde, exceedingly attractive Margot the Therapist. "Is Rosie out—"

Aiden interrupted him. "No. She came to the house." He kept his voice light and his gaze on his mother and tried not to let his dismay at the sight of her thin, sunken-in face show too obviously. "Do you mind if I talk to Antony a sec, Mama?"

She smiled and patted his hand. "No. He and Margot were just keeping me company. I'm trying to get your daddy to go home and rest."

"Okay, I'll drag him with me in a few minutes. Antony? A word?"

Antony narrowed his eyes before glancing at Margot then back at him. The man's face was one of pure deer in the headlights. Aiden had to repress the urge to tease him, or laugh like an idiot.

Has Antony, the moody, self-declared bachelor, now betrothed to his dead best friend's widow, fallen for the very pretty preacher-lady-therapist? Now? Dear Jesus, what a mess.

Aiden led the way out into the hall. He waited until Antony had joined him in the empty family lounge, kicked the door shut with his foot then grabbed the older, bigger man by the collar and shoved him up against the wall, catching Antony off guard. His stunned expression made irrational giggles rise in Aiden's throat, but he fought them back.

"What the hell are you doing to Rosalee, hmm, big bro?"

His face darkened in a way Aiden would normally run away from. Instead, he tightened his grip and shoved his face way up in Antony's grill. "I mean it. I won't let you hurt her just because you've got the hots for the preacher lady. That's pretty much not allowed anyway, I don't think—fucking your therapist."

Antony shoved him hard, so hard Aiden spun backward and tripped over a chair, landing on his hip, before scrambling back to his feet.

"You're an idiot." His brother loomed over him. "You don't know what you're talking about."

"Oh, really? Well then, maybe you can tell me why your fiancée ran to our parents' house in tears over finding you here with...her...doing...I don't know what, I couldn't get that out of her." Aiden rose slowly, chest heaving.

"What? Rosie saw...I mean...there's not anything to...fuck!" Antony raked his fingers though his hair and stared out the latticed window into the darkened hallway. Aiden grabbed the back of a chair. "She couldn't see anything because there wasn't anything to see, I swear it." Antony turned back to face him.

Aiden nodded, willing to accept that there had not been, at least, not yet.

"Margot just came up to spell me actually. I had a shit day at the garage, had to fire Ben. You were off today. I had...she is...." Antony's dark eyes were wild with anxiety. "I can't lose Rosie, Aiden. I can't let that happen."

Aiden closed his eyes a split second, unwilling to recall the taste of Rosalee's lips, not an hour ago.

This is a disaster in the making, Aiden Love. And you are in the middle of it. Best get the hell out now.

"I'll go get her. I'll explain." Antony dropped into a seat.

"Okay, listen." He attempted to rally his inner, not-obsessed-with-Rosalee, smart guy. "I think I get it. Rosalee's over-tired. She saw something, misinterpreted it, and got her back up. I just wanted to find out for myself from you."

Antony groaned and kept his eyes on the floor. "I do love her," he declared into his palms.

"I'm sure you do." Aiden headed for the door, wondering how in the world this could possibly resolve well for anyone concerned. Antony grabbed his hand, jerking him back. "Hey!"

"I know what *you* want, Aiden." Antony's low, menacing tone gave him a brief chill. "I'm not an idiot. I have eyes. And you need to understand one thing."

He jerked out of Antony's grip and crossed his arms over his chest, hoping the other man couldn't hear his heart pounding. "I understand everything I need to."

Antony rose, using his six-inch-height advantage to tower over Aiden. "I know you're sniffing around my woman. And whatever this bullshit confrontation might be about, you better get it through your head now—Rosalee Norris is mine. There is nothing going on with me and anyone, *but* her. Keep your dirty paws to yourself."

Aiden shrugged out from under the heavy hand on his shoulder. "You're crazy," he muttered, needing to get out of there, and already calculating how he could afford his own apartment sooner rather than later.

Opening the door, he spotted his father, standing with his arms crossed, observing them. Aiden shrugged and tried to arrange his face in calm lines. Anton frowned at him then at his oldest son, who glared at Aiden.

"I don't know what you boys are fussin' over, but I'll tell you now, it had better not be what I think it is. Go home," he told Antony. "Sounds like you need to be there. Your mama's good. She's gone back to sleep."

"Where's—"

Anton clenched his jaw. "Your therapist lady left, and said to tell you she'd see you Tuesday. At your session with AliceLynn."

Antony seemed to deflate a little at that. But then he squared his shoulders. "I need to go see Rosalee." He shoved past them. "I'll talk more with you later," he muttered under his breath to Aiden.

"Go on, son." Anton yawned and stretched. "I've got this tonight."

Aiden arrived back at his parent's house about ten minutes behind Antony, but sat in the car awhile, gripping the wheel.

No more. No more. Stay away from her. It's not good and it's causing more trouble than anyone needs.

He finally climbed out and trudged up the walk. Dom's car sat in the drive, along with Rosalee's and, of course, Antony's truck. Exhaustion blinded him by the time he hit the side door into the mudroom. The kitchen and the family room were dark.

He drank some water then headed for the steps up to the bedroom hall, his heart heavy and his head fuzzy. After brushing his teeth, he stumbled toward an empty bedroom when he heard Antony's voice.

"Marry me, marry me now, Rosalee. I don't want to wait anymore. I can't stand it."

Aiden froze. Unable to make out her words, he tiptoed closer to his parent's bedroom. The door gaped open enough for him to see Rosalee sitting on the edge of the bed, Antony on his knees in front of her, gripping her hands. Her thick curls curtained her face so Aiden couldn't see her eyes. But he saw Antony's, and the intensity in them.

"We need your mama to get better first. She can't be—"

Antony slid his hands around her back and kissed her then, gently at first. When she made that small noise down her throat that Aiden had heard so many times it made him nuts, he had to step back to keep from barging in and telling them this whole thing had to stop—that Antony wanted to deny his feelings for someone else by diving in headfirst with the woman everyone expected him to marry. And that Rosalee wanted him, Aiden, not Antony.

God, man, what are you, a romance novelist? Cut the crap and leave it alone.

He took a long breath then peeked in again. Antony's head lay on Rosalee's lap. She ran her fingers through his hair.

"It will be fine, honey. Just a simple misunderstanding. I know that now."

"I would never hurt you, Rosie. Never, ever." Antony touched a finger to her lips.

She gave him a weak smile and nodded. "I know."

He laid his head in her lap again, and she rested her hand on his hair. Aiden moved so he stood directly in her line of sight on purpose, for reasons he couldn't have articulated, even if pressed. She caught his eye and shook her head. "Let's move the date up." She spoke to Antony while looking right at Aiden. "You're right. We shouldn't wait. No reason to."

He had to bite his tongue to keep from protesting, and had to watch as she turned Antony's face up and cradled it between her hands. "So, let's talk about December, instead of a June wedding."

He nodded, cupped a hand behind her neck, and kissed her. Aiden slumped against the wall outside his old bedroom, chest tight, but head clear for the first time since he'd laid eyes on Rosalee Norris at Love Garage. Serenaded by the sounds of kissing advancing to more, and yet more, he ducked into his old room and shut the door.

"I told you not to go there," Dom whispered in the darkened room they'd once shared, and now would again, until their mother returned home.

"Fuck off," he muttered, flopping down onto the twin bed he'd occupied every night for the majority of his life to that point.

"Buck in the swear jar," Dom said, with a yawn.

"Whatever."

Chapter Seventeen

October

      Aiden made a valiant attempt to focus on the words coming out of the female mouth across from him. Instead of giving away his newfound habit of drifting off and pondering Rosalee while with Renee, he sipped his wine and nodded, hoping that would suffice for a response.

"You didn't hear a word I said, did you?" Renee picked up her fork and speared a cherry tomato in a way that made it clear she wished it were one of his balls.

Desperate to make amends and not sleep alone that night, he reached across the small table, using his best Aiden puppy-dog eyes to get her to soften. She held the tomato to her lips and glared at him then blew out a breath and put the fork down so she could take his hand. Her smile made his chest loosen ever so slightly.

"Sorry, Renee. Just have a lot on my mind is all." He squeezed her palm, allowed his finger to trace the inside of her wrist then let go.

"Did you submit to those agents yet?" She placed the tomato between her teeth and commenced chewing, as if pondering its future nutritional value. Eating slowly, one miniscule bite at a time kept her figure, she claimed. It drove him crazy, but he figured it for a small thing to tolerate, in exchange for her other charms.

"Yeah." He frowned down at the plate of food he didn't remember ordering. "Sent out ten more yesterday. It's hopeless."

"Oh, honey, no, it's not." Her eyes brightened as she sipped her wine. "It's a lovely story, at least the bits I read."

Aiden pushed the sea scallops around on his plate. She'd read about three chapters of it, after begging him one morning, post-second threesome of his life then set it down and declared it "perfect."

"How would you even know?" he'd asked, miffed that she'd stopped.

131

"I just do. It would be even better if you had more sex in it though."
She'd been lolling around on her couch, wearing nothing but that
short, silky robe at the time.

"More sex? Renee, it's a story about a family of brothers. Not
incest." A tiny bit of misplaced superiority had crept in then. This,
coming from a woman whose favorite books bore covers of shirtless
men with impossibly perfect abs, had caused a thrill of irritation to
shoot down his spine.

"No, no, I mean the guys...they're a little...I don't know, not like real
men, you know, in the real world I mean. They're sort of, I don't know,
insufferably perfect. Getting all mad at each other when one of them
does something not perfect. And that father...he's just way too stupid to
live."

Aiden had spluttered and self-justified it, calling it "literary fiction,"
not "pulp for the masses." She'd smacked his ass and told him not to
be a snob. Something about her then, the tousled, well-fucked, older
woman, lounging on her couch after a night of the sort of debauchery
that would have made a central theme of one of her favorite novels,
made him so horny he'd picked her up, tossed her over his shoulder, and
made her squeal with pleasure for another few minutes. That had been
the end of the book talk. But she reminded him daily about his goal to
send it out to agents. Not to let it sit and rot on his computer, forgotten
and unloved by anyone.

"How was school today?" she asked, glancing around to take in
whoever had walked into the restaurant.

The way she called the community college writing classes he taught
"school" set Aiden's teeth on edge. But he reminded himself not to be
a dick. She meant no harm, as usual, only making conversation, being
nice, whatever.

"Fine, thanks." He stuffed a bite of the garlicky seafood into his
mouth.

"Hey, isn't that Antony? With a woman not his fiancée?" Renee whispered, leaning over the table and giving him a class-A cleavage view. He blinked at it, processing her words.

"What?" He started to turn.

"No, don't look, jeez." She picked up her glass.

But he did anyway. And there they were, tucking into a booth toward the back of the cheesy chain restaurant with the addictive breadsticks. Aiden squinted and tried to understand what he saw. Antony's face split into a wide, genuine smile, like Aiden remembered on his formerly easy-going, yet responsible, oldest brother. He'd not seen anything like it in years, even since he'd been back and dropped into the middle of the Rosalee/Antony courtship.

Margot looked like a million bucks, as usual, in a short skirt, silky blouse, her long blonde hair tumbling around her shoulders. She matched Antony's grin. Aiden blinked. He was a fairly decent reader of body language. And the borderline-intimate way they were talking made him suck in a breath. At one point Antony crooked a finger. Margot tilted her head and they seemed to whisper about something then they laughed and accepted drinks from the waiter.

What in the hell would possess the man to bring her there on some kind of a date, in plain sight? He had to know gossips like Renee would be around and see them. It must be some extension of therapy, a friendly dinner.

But the expression on Antony's face right then, the intense manner in which he seemed to be studying the striking woman across from him, told a different, and more complicated story.

"Well, if I were Rosalee Norris, I would not like that one bit," Renee declared, before chewing a single lettuce leaf in a thoughtful way.

"It's nothing," he muttered, fiddling with his fork. "I'm sure of it. He wouldn't bring her here on a date. That's too dumb, even for Dominic."

"Speaking of...." Renee prefaced her next launch into some random, latest illicit bit of gossip about his pussy magnet of a brother.

Aiden sensed them behind him, burning into the back of his head like a branding iron the entire time.

"Aiden," Renee said sharply, as they waited for the check. "You need to wipe that moony look off your face right now. I think maybe you all need to talk, you know, about her." She raised a carefully arched eyebrow.

Alarm bells rang in his head. Handing the credit card he'd just obtained to their waitress, he asked, "About who?"

"About Rosalee." Renee stood and shouldered her purse. "I am not sharing you with her. Get your head straight, Aiden Love. I mean it."

He sat, frozen, watching her go, in all her hip-swaying perfection, trying to sort out how in the world she'd figured that out. When a hand landed on his shoulder, he nearly jumped a mile.

"Problem?" Antony nodded toward the door where Aiden's date had just departed in a proverbial huff.

"Um, no." He signed the check. "You?" He made a show of craning his neck around to see Margot, who seemed uncharacteristically flustered.

"Nope, no problem. Just finished therapy, thought we'd eat before...." Antony stopped and glared at Aiden. "I don't owe you any explanations."

He shrugged. "Nope, I guess not."

Margot stepped out from behind him. "Hi, Aiden." Her classic, cool beauty struck him once again. The way she kept blinking as if she'd been caught in the dark, confirmed his worst suspicions.

"Hey there." He accepted the folder from the waitress, signed, and tossed the receipt on the table. "If ya'll will excuse me, I need to try and go salvage my date." Part of him was furious, part of him hopeful, and a very small part of him sad for the situation, and for Antony. The brief thought of going to Rosalee straightaway and telling her what he believed might be evolving between Antony and the beautiful therapist flashed in and then straight out of his brain.

None of your business. Go. Find Renee. Get laid. The end.

But when he walked out onto the sidewalk of the cookie-cutter suburban strip mall, he didn't want anything but his laptop and a beer, preferably one brewed by Dom. He had some new ideas, ways to freshen the manuscript and the urgency to get back to it hit him hard.

The rejections were bombarding his inbox fairly regularly by then. After the first dozen or so, he'd become immune—and stubborn—determined to find a place for what he honestly believed to be a classic novel of southern family life based, not to loosely, on his parent's relationship.

He tucked his hands in his pockets and whistled while he walked out to the car his father had sold him—one of the old family junkers, a hideously ugly Oldsmobuick of some age. But thanks to Antony's deft hand, it ran like a charm, and had an FM radio. Not bad, even if Aiden did have to hand crank the windows open.

Once home, he let his mind enter a place he'd inhabited twenty-four-seven while at the Masters of Fine Arts writing program at Iowa. After popping open a Love Brewing Heartshaped IPA he fired up the laptop, sipped, and opened up the one-hundred-thousand-plus word document he'd slaved over for the last two years. Then, with a satisfying knuckle crack, he highlighted three chapters, hit "copy" then "delete." After sticking them unceremoniously in a side document, he dropped into the cool comfort of his writing cave, where there were no disapproving, or possibly cheating siblings, no girlfriends of siblings to tempt him, no girlfriends at all. Just Aiden, and his words, and his brew.

A loud knock on the apartment door made him flinch and nearly spill beer all over the keyboard.

"All right already, hold your water," he muttered, dragging his focus away from the killer scene he'd just concocted. Slugging back the last of the bottle, he opened the door—no call for peephole-checking in this tiny town. It could be one of maybe five people anyway. But when he registered who it was, he choked and spluttered. Rosalee had to whack him on the back before he could speak.

"What are you doing here?" he asked, once he could talk again. His ears buzzed and his fingertips itched in a way he knew well and understood even better. But he shoved his hands in his pockets and kept plenty of distance, or as much as his three-room roach-motel of a place would allow. Dressed in her banker lady get up—slim skirt, plain blue blouse, modest heels with her riotous hair secured in a semi-severe bun—she was chewing on her lip and looking everywhere but at him. She seemed ragged out, not like a woman planning the happiest day of her life—something she and Antony had agreed would be on December seventeenth. A "Christmas wedding," that she claimed as something she'd always dreamed of as a little girl.

Aiden shook his head, hoping to clear it of the random wedding minutia he wished he didn't know. But his mother had gone into full-throated paroxysms of delight at the concept of a "red and green wedding," and since she'd recuperated so quickly, she and Rosalee had been planning like mad, or so Aiden assumed.

Making a valiant attempt to close his mind and senses to her—or at least put more space between them, he moved past her. When she grabbed his arm, he didn't resist, much. They froze, facing in opposite directions, joined by the touch of her palm to his skin.

"Don't," he whispered. Moving in a kind of weird slow-motion, he put his lips to her ear. "*Why* are you here?" She shut her eyes. Aiden stuck his nose closer, touched his lips to her neck, and tried not to lose it.

"We need to talk," she said, tightening her grip on his arm.

"Okay." He took her shoulders and moved her around to face him. "Go ahead. Talk. I'm listening." Moving fast, letting his body lead, he smiled and unfastened the first buttons of her bank-logo blouse, going slow until he had it open all the way, before flipping her bra open. She flinched and stepped back, but he held onto her, determined not to let this moment pass.

His brain lit up with purpose. This would go his way tonight, no matter what. He'd gotten sick and tired of dancing around it.

"We um, oh...." She blew out a breath when he put his palm around the warm curvature of her breast, flicking his thumb across the peaked nipple.

Watching her eyes, he kept teasing her with one hand and reached up under her skirt with the other. "You didn't come here to talk," Aiden insisted, his voice raspy. He kissed her then, forcing her lips open, making her take his tongue. Wrapping her arms around him, she made that maddening little sound in her throat, a sort of whimpering moan he'd heard way too many times down the hall at Antony's, and that night at his parent's house when Antony had run home to beg her to move up the wedding.

Aiden wanted to hear it, a lot, and only for him—he wanted to *own* that damn noise.

As he swept into her mouth with his tongue, he hooked a finger into her panties and gave a yank, ripping them in two. "You came here so I would do this, didn't you, Rosalee?" He slid both hands up to cup her breasts before diving down to suck first one then the other nipple into his mouth. She tasted so very good, like a real woman, not covered in lotions and perfumes like Renee.

Her lusty energy coiled up in his brain, fueling his determination as he grinned into her flesh and she fisted his hair, making that glorious sound again. Blind and deaf to anything but her, Aiden picked her up and set her on the kitchen counter, shoving up her skirt and kissing her again, licking, teasing, caressing her lips with his.

"Tell me why you're here." He ran a finger down her face, catching a tear. "No crying allowed." Keeping up his pressure down below, sensing her flesh filling and hardening under his touch, he took a long, shaking breath. "Because I think I know." He teased one breast with his other hand. "I think you're here because I have something you want."

"Yes," she muttered into his neck, tugging at his belt buckle and unzipping his trousers. "No. I'm not here to talk."

"So which is it?" Slow and determined, he slipped a finger into her, while keeping pressure on the outside, teasing her nipple with his other hand. He exhaled into her mouth then kissed her, unable to stop, loving the taste, the feel, the smell of her all over him.

"Which is what," she asked, angling her hips and moving closer.

He tugged harder on her nipple, watching her face, soaking up her reaction, reveling in her unbelievable perfection. Everything about the woman turned him on, on so many levels, it terrified and exhilarated him all at once.

"It is no?" Still rubbing and teasing he pressed his finger deeper into her. "Or...." He moaned into her mouth as she came, relishing the grip of the orgasm, the pulse against his hand, and that sweet, sweet noise she made. "Is it yes?" Whispering the last words, he put the finger he'd just had inside her to his lips. Shuddering, she tipped her head back, exposing the long porcelain line of her neck. The moment shimmered between them, ripe with possibility.

She jumped down and yanked him close, slanting her mouth over his, ripping at the undershirt he still wore, and shoving his khakis down. "Yes," she ground out, before going down on her knees and deep throating him so fast, he had to grip the counter top behind her and focus on conjugating Spanish verbs.

"Okay, okay, but here's the thing." On the ragged edge, he tugged her back to her feet. Furious with them both for what they were about to do, but helpless to stop it, he forced his mind to still. "I think we've been here, done this, know what I mean?" He placed his palm against her cheek, loving the potential, but needing more. "You say you came here for something I have. So, I say..." Her hair, once freed from its holder, fell around her shoulders. He threaded his fingers in its wild abundance and closed his fist, making her head fall back and a hiss escape her lips. His need to be inside her so badly, to be connected to her, consumed him, making his arms and legs shake.

His lips found her collarbone and he licked his way down to her breast. Her breath caught in her throat.

"Fuck me, Aiden," she whispered, bringing instant goose bumps to every inch of his skin.

"What's that?" he asked, nibbling his way back up her neck to her lips.

"I...need you...to fuck me." Her eyes were bright, but without tears. Her hands were on him, moving up and down his dick, cupping his balls. The scent of her lust coiled up in his head and blinded him in a way he should not be susceptible to as a grown man. But this, and her, and those lips....Grinning, he grabbed her hips. "Hang on tight," he said as she wrapped her legs around his waist and he walked the few steps to the couch he'd liberated from the Love lower basement. Still holding her close, he lowered them onto the cushion. Their lips hovered but didn't touch.

"This," he said with a sigh, shoving her skirt up so she could spread her legs wider. "This is what you wanted from me?" His voice hitched, but he clamped down on emotion, focusing instead on the pure eroticism of the moment.

She cradled his face between her hands and angled her hips taking all of him at once, making them sigh in unison.

"Yes. This is what I wanted. Is that bad?" When he reached down to tweak her nipples, teasing her in a way he'd learned she liked, she moved faster. "Oh. I'm gonna...." A noise rose in her throat and filled his ears. Tugging at her flesh, he met her with thrusts of his own. The orgasm hovered, taunting him.

"I love you," she gasped, then tilted her head back and cried out, gripping him so hard, he lost all control and pressed his face into her breasts, his hips moving fast. His vision darkened then lightened, and he heard her say it again.

"I love you."

They sat, joined, breathing heavy, arms wrapped tightly around each other. She moved first, standing up and nearly falling over. Useless to anyone at the moment, he sat, watching as she tugged her skirt back down and tried to refasten her bra with shaking hands. Remorse and gut-churning guilt roiled through him. Finally, he stood and found his pants, got mostly back together then grabbed some tissues.

She took them from him, but she wouldn't meet his eyes. And at that moment, he didn't want to see them. They'd only reflect back at him what they'd done, what he'd just done with Antony's fiancée.

He groaned and closed his eyes.

Damn her for coming here anyway. Damn me for being so weak willed.

"So, we cleared the air, I think." She tossed the used tissues into the garbage can then yanked her hair up more or less into the same arrangement she'd been wearing before he'd gotten his hands on her.

"Uh, yeah." He leaned against the kitchen counter, willing her to come to him so they could really talk. But wishing at the same time that she'd just go and leave him in peace. As she straightened her blouse, tucked her feet back in her shoes and faced him, Aiden had to chew on the inside of his cheek not to grab her, toss her in his bed and never let her escape.

"I am marrying Antony," she stated, unnecessarily. "We—you and me—are done."

He raised an eyebrow, noting how her hands shook when she messed with her hair. Words he should say died in the back of his throat.

"Stop smirking."

"I'm not. But, I really wonder how done you want us to be, Rosalee."

He took a step closer, which forced her backward, but she raised her hand as if to ward him off. Eager yet horrified at the same time, he grabbed it and slowly tugged her into his arms.

The sound of a key in the door made them leap apart. She pointed to his naked torso. Skin tingling, he ducked into the bedroom and grabbed a fresh T-shirt, emerging to find Renee in the doorway, staring at Rosalee then at him.

"Well, hey there," she said in a high voice, tossing her keys on the table and sauntering up to him. "Sorry for interrupting."

"You didn't," Rosalee squeaked out. "We were just talking about...Mrs. Love, and wedding stuff, and...Jeffrey."

Aiden sighed when Renee slipped an arm around his waist. He bent into her hair, feeling protected—from what, he wasn't sure, but the sensation was both pleasant and god awful all at once. She held him close, exchanged a few more pleasantries with Rosalee then bumped him with her hip once Rosalee made her frazzled exit.

"What the hell are you up to, Aiden Love?"

He dropped to his knees, gripping her waist, his lips pressed to the line of perfumed skin between her shirt and jeans waistband.

"Marry me, Renee."

She frowned and glanced at the door where Rosalee had just left.

"Get up, Aiden, seriously. You're actin' crazy."

He couldn't see, or hear, but his chest ached with guilt and horror at what he'd done—the ultimate betrayal of a sibling. And how badly he wanted to do it again. If it took a legal shackling to someone, someone nice, and easy, and simple, like Renee, well then, by hell, that's what he would do.

He stood and pushed her down in a chair before kneeling again in front of her.

"I'm not crazy. I'm not joking. Marry me. Please." He prayed that she couldn't hear the desperation in his voice.

Chapter Eighteen

• • • •

HALLOWEEN

Rosalee rolled her shoulders and got up from her teller station, eager for her shift to be done. The wedding to-do list still contained items like "decide about the flowers," and "pick the DJ," and lay there beneath her desk blotter like a beacon of shame. The rush to the altar had made this sort of thing more challenging, but it seemed even more necessary to her now. The sensation of trying to stay one step ahead of her own guilt over the ill-advised tryst with Aiden, but also of Antony's growing dependence on his therapist, made her a nervous wreck most days, and sleepless at night.

It had been a full month since the night she'd almost walked right in on the mysterious "something" between her fiancé and the woman who'd dropped into their lives at such an odd time, despite Antony's vehement insistence to the contrary.

She had planned to surprise Antony that night with the good news that she'd finally been promised a spot in management training at the bank. She'd rushed from work after confirming Paul's mom could pick Jeffrey up from daycare, and headed straight for the strip of offices, shops, and restaurants that housed Margot Hamilton, M.S.W., PhD, DD.

She'd spotted Antony's truck, and AliceLynn's subcompact in the lot, and sat in the car a few minutes, wondering how best to surprise him, proud of herself for being so grown up and mature about all of this. Especially considering that he seemed to enjoy his three hours a week with Margot more than the rest of the hours with her. She, Rosalee, had the man's ring, she said in her head, with a thoroughly immature and uncharacteristic mental jolt.

At the scheduled session-time ending, AliceLynn came barreling out the office suite's glass door, face streaked with tears. Rosalee watched her for a second then got out of her SUV.

"Go away," the girl screeched. "God, I don't want to talk anymore. All y'all do is talk me to death." She swiped her hand across her eyes then climbed into her car. Her stormy expression made her look so much like her mother, Rosalee hesitated. AliceLynn kept glaring at the door she'd exited. Finally, Rosalee knocked on her window.

"What?"

"Is your Daddy still in there?"

"Yeah." The sudden knowing glint in the girl's eyes had made Rosalee uncomfortable. "He's gotten hooked on...therapy. Now, if you'll excuse me please, I'm late for work."

Against her inner advice, Rosalee had walked up to the door and touched the cool silver handle. She'd been here once with Antony and his daughter. But it had seemed counter-productive. She hadn't known how to act and had clammed up. Antony had obviously been unhappy about including her in it, too, so Margot declared the session "over" after about twenty minutes.

Rosalee pushed the door open, figuring they'd be out in the main reception area by now. But it was deserted. Head pounding, she marched over to the closed door and paused, running a mental pep talk in a familiar loop through her brain.

She and Antony were going to be married soon. She had every right to be here, right then, to take him away for a nice dinner to celebrate the first bit of good news she'd gotten in while.

"I can't," she'd been shocked to hear Antony say, his voice rough in a way she had not heard in years, not since the news came about Crystal's accident. "I can't be this...person they want me to be. Not anymore."

"You don't have to be," Margot replied in a soft, soothing and thoroughly annoying voice. "Antony, look at me."

"Yes, I do. I can't....I—Oh shit—"

His words were cut off by a strange sort of silence, followed by the distinct sound of a kiss. Rosalee's brain processed it then she walked away from the door, wobbly-legged, drove down to the river, and sat for a while, not really thinking, not really upset, not really surprised. Then she went to Aiden's apartment, still dressed in her work clothes, claiming she wanted to "talk." Which he had translated, correctly, into something else within minutes.

She knew Antony Love well by now. She sensed his intensity with regard to the therapist. Unlike the comfortable, broken-in chair kind of relationship they shared, it represented something much more, based on the sort of lightning-bolt reaction they'd had to each other when they'd first met. She'd witnessed it, both at that party and later, in the visitor's lounge of the hospital. But the possessive female in her would not let him go. Not even after she'd committed the horrific sin of having sex with Aiden, at her instigation.

And now, here she was, a mature woman on the verge of marrying a man good for her, and she for him, even if they were both miserable at the thought of it.

But it was *the right thing. Just ask anybody.*

Most especially her future in-laws. Antony would not do anything to disappoint them, not for a million tall, blonde, sexy therapists. Not now that his mama seemed to be getting better, against all odds.

Rosalee sighed and turned to face her next, and hopefully final, customer, her mind already drifting to the things she had to do at the end of her short shift, including decorate for the Love's Halloween party.

"Hey." Aiden stood before her, dressed in his "professor costume" as Dom liked to call it—khaki trousers, light-blue button-down shirt, polished brown shoes, and matching belt.

She made the mistake of meeting his gaze, took in that crooked, boyish grin, and could taste and feel him all over again. "Hi. Whatcha got?" Her voice broke as she gestured for the paper in his hand, assuming it was a paycheck from the community college. "Nice shiner, by the way. Hope the other guy looks worse."

After he handed it over in silence, she processed it, keeping her eyes on the screen and off him then gave him the receipt. The closeness of the community and of the Love family in particular needled her then. Antony had wasted no time informing her that Aiden and the sexy spa owner Renee were engaged.

"Nope. But then, you would know, since you sleep with him every night." Aiden touched the nasty purple skin around his eye. "You know, just another friendly fraternal basketball game. I said something your fiancé didn't care for. He fouled me. With his fist."

"Oh. So, why come in? Don't you usually use the ATM?" Something selfish and horrible in her wanted to hear it.

"Wanted to see you. How's therapy going?"

She sucked in a breath at his obvious dig. "Great."

She had insisted on participating in the session after hearing the illicit kiss on the other side of the therapy door, if only to study the bizarre and sudden connection between Antony and Margot Hamilton, the divorcée. She'd only seen glimmers of it, when Antony would shoot the woman a shy smile—which infuriated her, irrationally, but enough to make her non-communicative the rest of the session.

"Ah, well, then it's good, I suppose." He lingered, the gaze that haunted her guilt-ridden nights focused squarely on her. "I'm happy for you, Rosalee."

"Stop it." She glanced around, hoping to find something to do so she could get away from him.

"Stop what?"

"You know." Shoving his elbows off her counter, she frowned in what she hoped was a firm, mature way. "Go."

"I miss you and Jeffrey."

"You're the one making yourself scarce, not me." Finding fake busy work closing down her station, she kept ignoring him. But he didn't budge. Finally she sighed and turned back to face him. "Jeffrey asks about you all the time. You'll be at your mama's Halloween party, I assume?"

"I'll be there. I wouldn't dare miss a Love Party production—too risky. See you then, I guess. Got to teach one more class still this afternoon. I'll be the big Batman. Thought Jeffrey might like that." He winked at her and she flinched. Then he walked out, leaving her breathless and wondering what in the hell had possessed her to even consider flirting with the guy. She grabbed her phone and sent Antony a text.

I'm going out to help decorate. Can you grab Jeffrey?

It took about twenty seconds for him to reply.

Can't, unless he can stay there until six. I've got a last-minute problem at garage. Just take him with you. Mama can handle him.

Rosalee blew out a breath at his casual assumption and answered back, trying not to sound as pissy as she felt.

I can't let him see us setting up the decorations and stuff. It will be like spotting you wearing a Santa Claus suit. You do have your costume with you, right?

She had found them Peter Pan-and-Tinkerbell-matching getups at one of those temporary costume shops near the mall. Hers looked a whole lot slutty, but his had green tights he swore he would never wear for anyone but her.

The Love family never missed the opportunity to throw a holiday-themed party. Since Halloween fell on a Friday that year, they were going all out despite Lindsay's ongoing cancer treatments. The barn had been converted into a child-friendly haunted house, complete with apple bobbing, pin the tail on the vampire, the usual. And it was costume-mandatory for adults and children. At last count, there were a dozen children of various ages coming, mostly from church, along with their parents, plus the family, their friends and—she assumed—fiancées.

Rosalee had convinced Lindsay to use a caterer for most of it, thank the good Lord. But they still had a ton of decorating and setting up to do. Cursing under her breath, she headed toward the daycare, already concocting potential distractions for Jeffrey. Maybe she'd get lucky and Dom or Kieran would be there to play with him. The pool remained open as the muggy mid-Kentucky summer had eased into the sort of autumn that made her bank customers talk about the old days, and her son a cranky, sweaty mess most afternoons.

Son retrieved and stuffed into car seat, she made a quick detour to her house for costumes and Jeffrey's swimsuit.

"Mommy!" he yelped when she got back in. The damn AC rarely worked anymore. It was like the inside of a tobacco barn in high-staking season in the SUV's cab. "Hot!"

"I know, baby. Sorry." She put all the windows down and cranked up his favorite Disney music.

The lack of recognizable cars in the Love family driveway did not bode well for Jeffrey-distracting potential. She set him on the gravel, and he immediately ran toward the glistening blue temptation of the pool.

"Stop!" she shouted, struggling with her bags of decorations and costumes. "Jeffrey. I mean it. I won't let you come to the party if you don't listen to me right now."

He stopped and glared over his shoulder at her. The stuck-out lower lip and the glistening eyes made her chest tight with frustration.

"Come on inside where it's cool, baby. I'll let you have some of Miss Lindsay's lemonade."

He didn't move other than crossing his arms and resembling her late husband when she'd ask him to help her clean the house. When he spotted the huge orange-and-black tent set up between the patio and pool he ran toward it.

"Mommy! A circus is here."

"No, Jeffrey, it's the Halloween party tent, remember? Antony told you about it last night at bedtime."

He threw out his arms and spun in a circle. "Halloween! Halloween! Hallo—Mommy did you bring my Batman costume?" He stopped turning and staggered around like a drunken sailor.

"Of course. Batman is right here." She jiggled the wardrobe bag where she'd hung both of their costumes after steaming out the wrinkles, and pondering sewing something more substantial into the cleavage of her sleazy Tink dress, before deciding she didn't care at that point. Jeffrey took off for the patio ahead of her, stopping to plunge both grimy hands into a huge bowl of M&Ms that had been placed on the table for reasons that escaped her.

She sighed. In honor of Halloween, she decided to let him keep the few he managed to cram into his mouth, before shooing him toward the open door. But he grabbed another fistful and ducked under her arm, knowing if he made it into the house and onto Lindsay's lap, she'd laugh and convince Rosalee to let him keep the damn things. Even though a sugar rush on top of his overtired state spelled disaster for anyone in a five-mile radius.

Rosalee adjusted the straps of the three decoration bags higher on her shoulder and followed him. When she heard a wail of dismay that could only be her son she ran the last few feet to the door, bags bouncing against her side, and spotted him sitting on his butt, glaring at something or someone inside the door.

As her eyes adjusted from the bright outdoor afternoon light, she saw the cool and classy Melinda, Kieran's lady lawyer fiancée, with blood covering her torso.

"Oh, my heavens, what...." She stopped. No, not blood, but an entire tray of Mrs. Love's secret-recipe baked beans. Rosalee dropped the bags and shoved Jeffrey out of her way so she could grab the huge glass container before it hit the floor.

The woman glared in horror down at her ruined clothes. Jeffrey was hollering about how the lady had run into him and dumped food on his head. One glance back at him proved him right. He had the amber-colored beans, flecked with bacon, green peppers and onions in his hair, with some dripping down his face.

"Can't you control him?" Melinda finally managed to say as she glared down at her once pristine-white, and probably silk, blouse. "This is BCBG," she muttered, taking a few swipes at her outfit. "I hope you have insurance."

Rosalee lost the inner politeness battle and burst out laughing which made Jeffrey burst into tears. Melinda glowered at them both then flounced toward the steps up to the kitchen muttering about "hillbillies," and wishing she'd never agreed to come out here to the boonies for the weekend.

"Come on, sweetie. I'll stick you in the shower. It will cool you off." Rosalee left the bags and costumes on the lower family room couch and picked up her squalling spawn. He wrapped his arms and legs around her, coating her cheek and shoulder with the delicious-smelling dish.

"That lady is mean," he mumbled around his thumb.

"Jeffrey, big boys do not suck their fingers."

"Yes, ma'am."

Antony had begun instilling a bit more politeness in him. But Jeffrey's relationship with him remained strained. Antony wasn't "fun" like Aiden, her son liked to remind her.

She kissed his bean-covered hair and bypassed the kitchen. "I need to shower him off," she called out.

"Do whatever you need to, honey. You know where the towels are."

After singing Lion King songs, washing and shampooing, drying, and re-dressing him in his batman costume, Rosalee plunked her son in front of the ancient TV/VCR combo in Antony's old bedroom, with a tape of Sesame Street, leaving him glassy-eyed and half-asleep before she left the room.

But when she saw the array of women at the table, she stopped and waited, taking it in. Renee sat with a tall glass of iced tea, perfectly put together as always. She'd been the captain of the cheerleading squad, the most popular girl, the girl Rosalee wanted to be, most days. Now, she appeared as if she'd been using a time machine. Her unlined, taut skin maintained a perfect shade of bronze. She'd straightened her dark-blonde hair for the occasion.

"I cannot believe Mama gave that punk our Nana's engagement ring," Antony had grumbled to Rosalee when he'd broken the joyous news of Aiden's pending nuptials. "But he always was her favorite."

The ring in question, a huge emerald, surrounded by perfect diamonds, mesmerized her. She gulped, and touched her throat, willing memories of Aiden out of her head.

Melinda sat there, too, utterly out of sorts in a Lucasville High basketball booster shirt instead of her BBG-or-whatever, fancy blouse, her face pinched and unhappy. Angelique was behind them, filling goodie bags with prizes and gifts.

Aiden's little sister caught Rosalee's eye and winked then tilted her head toward Renee and made a gagging motion with her finger. She jerked her chin toward Melinda and did it again. Rosalee frowned at her but then smiled, thankful the girl had taken a semester off school for her mama's sake.

"It's not like I'm gonna graduate with anything useful anyway," she'd said to Rosalee one night, when she'd come over to have supper with them.

"Unless you can get a degree in 'shitty boyfriend choices' or 'expensive car insurance,'" Antony had muttered into his iced tea.

Rosalee had smacked his arm, but noted the way his gaze softened when he smiled at his only sister.

"I am so lucky." Lindsay patted first Renee's then Melinda's hands. "I'm gonna have such successful and smart daughters-in-law." She met

Rosalee's eye. "All of y'all." She gestured for Rosalee to step into the kitchen.

She did, but couldn't help comparing her sweaty and frumpy self to the other two, even with Melinda sporting an old T-shirt.

"I hear the big bank that bought the Lucasville Savings and Loan is gonna start layoffs soon," Renee said, sipping her tea.

Rosalee tried not to glare at the woman who currently slept with and would soon marry Aiden. "Yes, that's the rumor." She smiled down at Lindsay. The woman's hair had thinned so she wore bandanas every day to cover it up. Todays had little, black jack-o-lanterns on a bright-orange background. Rosalee didn't feel like talking about the promised promotion. She didn't want to share anything with Renee. Truthfully, Rosalee didn't want the woman there, or anywhere near the Love family. She shook her head. Ridiculous and selfish behavior had become her thing lately and she didn't care for it one bit.

"They'll try to keep our Rosie, though," Lindsay insisted, tightening her grip on Rosalee's hand. "They'd be foolish to let her go."

"Well, I sure hope so, Miss Lindsay."

"Well, me, too, of course, Missus Love," Renee said brightly, sucking up in a way that made Rosalee's teeth ache.

"Nonsense," Lindsay favored Renee with a tight smile. "And don't be calling me that. You'll be one yourself soon enough."

Renee tapped her manicured fingernail on the family table's worn oak surface and widened her sugary-sweet smile at her future mother-in-law then threw ice-cold eyeball daggers across the table at Rosalee.

"I declare I don't know how my sons got so very lucky," Lindsay went on, sipping her tea.

Rosalee knew damn good and well Aiden's entire family believed he had knocked Renee up and wanted to do the right thing by her. And they had no explanation for "that Melinda," as she'd become known outside of Kieran's hearing. Angelique made a snorting sound. Her mother frowned at her.

"So, where is everyone?" Rosalee poured some of the lemony, mint-laced tea and sat, holding the cool glass to her forehead.

"Anton, Kieran, and Dom are out in the barn, prepping the haunted house," Lindsay said, frankly appraising the future in-laws at her kitchen table.

"Aiden is still at home." Renee pressed a linen napkin to her lips, her expression smug.

Rosalee raised an eyebrow at Lindsay, who shrugged.

"I won't let him out of the house until he sends that book out to more agents. It's not gonna sell itself, I tell him. I've been doing my research." She examined her perfect manicure. "Silly boy keeps telling me he wants to 'revise' it, but I tell him that's just making excuses. Rejection is hard, but I know how to console him. One of these times it's gonna hit, I just know it, and we'll be off to New York City for a fancy book-release party."

Rosalee let the last words flow through her like water until the throw-away "I know how to console him" comment stuck in her chest, making it hard to breathe. She stood, noting Angelique behind the other two future Mrs. Loves making cross-eyed faces.

"Well, you are a very successful businesswoman, Renee." Lindsay patted the woman's hand, making what Rosalee figured had to be a valiant effort not to rip into her for bossing Aiden around. "That *boy*," she emphasized the word while smiling, "can surely use your more *mature* advice."

Angelique snorted and Rosalee coughed to smother the urge to laugh at the not-so-subtle dig. Renee blinked. Lindsay Love had always been a force to be reckoned with. Even diminished by cancer, she remained bound and determined to conquer.

"You do realize," Melinda said. "That the odds of him actually getting a publishing contract, even after finding an agent are slim to nonexistent. We have a new partner at the firm who specializes in entertainment law, mostly music. He claims that the difference between the number of books that could be published, compared to the ones that are, is vast." She sipped her tea and somehow managed to appear superior to everyone in the room in her ragged out T-shirt.

"Oh, I have every faith in *my* Aiden." Renee spoke to Lindsay but kept her gaze on Rosalee, her emphasis on the possessive loud and clear.

"Okay, Mama," Angelique interjected, breaking the obvious awkward moment between the two women. "These are done. Where do they go?" She held a basket full of goodie bags.

"Oh, yes, all right then, let's take them out to the barn. Rosalee, why don't you come with us? These lovely ladies can hold down the fort a bit longer."

Melinda heaved a huge sigh. Renee frowned and tapped her finger on the table.

"Sure thing. I need to run those decorations out there anyway." Rosalee stopped, remembering Jeffrey, hopefully by now asleep. "Um." She sat, wondering which of these women she'd trust to watch out for her cat, much less her son.

"I'll keep an eye on him." Renee stood to rinse out her glass. "I just can't wait to get a sweet little baby of my own, you know."

Lindsay coughed then smiled at the room in general before ducking out into the hall.

"Thanks." Rosalee checked the time, making a mental note not to linger out in the barn long.

By eight o'clock the party was in full swing. Aiden arrived in his Batman costume. Renee had donned a slinky, tight, custom-made Catwoman suit. Melinda had found Kieran, and they were sitting in one corner of the barn in something resembling Popeye and Olive Oyl, holding glasses of lemonade. The woman had her upper lip curled in a permanent sneer at the chaos of kids, costumes, and candy.

Rosalee tried to ignore them all, but Renee had jumped in to help entertain, leading groups of squealing children through the makeshift, and apparently terrifying, haunted house in the back half of the barn. Between her tour-guide shifts, she sat on Aiden's lap, whispering in his ear or kissing him. The casual hand he kept on her inner thigh, his smile, all made Rosalee want to scream and run out into the warm October night. Mainly because, when not pawing at his fiancée, pissing his mother off with his inappropriate public display, he was staring straight at her.

"Where's Antony?" His voice so near her ear made her jump.

She'd been assigned the musical jack-o-lantern game, a sort of cross between a cakewalk and musical chairs. "Don't know." She blew the hair out of her eyes then sighed when it dropped back into the same place. "Lordy, it is hot in here. I'm sweatin' like a whore in church." She held the front of her skimpy Tinkerbell costume away from her breasts, and observed the next group who'd be playing her game before she caught her own gaffe.

But Aiden had disappeared and by the time she paid attention again, Anton, Kieran, Aiden, and Dom were rounding up anyone interested to load them onto the back of the wagon for a haunted hayride.

"Where is Antony?" Lindsay flopped down into a rented chair. "He's missed all the fun. Y'all will be as cute as a bug's ear in your costumes." She patted Rosalee's bare knee.

"Please. I feel like a five-dollar hooker with wings in this nasty thing." Hearing the distinct sound of her son whining about something outside, she rose, but Lindsay tugged her back to the chair.

"Aiden will handle him."

Rosalee glanced at her, alarmed. But Lindsay just kept her calm smile.

"But I will declare that it's time for a drink. Let's leave all this for later and go on over to the tent. That Melinda's supposed to be in charge of making sure the caterers get set up. I suppose she managed it without suing anybody, bless her heart."

Lindsay linked arms with her as they walked back toward the house and tent from the huge, now-empty barn. The tractor motor revved and she prayed Jeffrey would not freak completely out at the various mildly scary episodes he had in store. He'd never been fond of being startled on purpose, and lately awoke nearly every night, screaming from nightmares in his "new bed" as he called it—the one at Antony's house where they now stayed.

She could barely stand to drive by her old house anymore, with its "for sale" sign bearing the name of a Realtor she'd once gone to high school with, and who promised her they would get "real value" for the small place in the current market.

The theme from *Jaws* rolled out of the sound system, and the tables groaned with the food she'd helped Lindsay pick out for the party inside the well-lit tent. Kid-friendly mac and cheese, fried chicken strips and fries sat alongside delicious-smelling barbeque, slaw, and what remained of the secret-recipe beans. Every table had its own centerpiece made of a carved pumpkin and small bowls of candy. A bar, stocked with beer, bourbon, gin, root beer, iced tea, and lemonade, dominated one corner.

"I'll be back. Need to visit the powder room," Lindsay said as she passed through the tent.

Rosalee sighed and grabbed a cold Love Brewing lager bottle, holding it first to her forehead then downing half of it before meeting her fiancé's eyes across the empty tent. He had his hands on his hips and a small smile playing at his lips. She couldn't help but giggle at his full Peter Pan regalia, including green tights, tunic that barely covered his ass, and jaunty cap with yellow feather. The one thing he'd balked at were the silly slipper-like shoes, so he had on his Timberland boots instead. As always, he was a vision of masculine perfection, her man.

She patted the seat next to her. "Come on over here, Peter, and let me check what you're wearing under that dress."

After snagging a beer, he made his way over to her and took her outstretched hand. Smiling in that way that never reached his eyes, he kissed her fingers and sat, letting her keep her hand on his thigh.

"My brothers are going to have a field day with this," he muttered, tugging the short tunic down, or at least trying to.

"Who knew though? Green legs are a total aphrodisiac for Slutty Tinkerbell," she said as her hand traveled higher. He draped an arm around the back of her seat and turned to face her.

Relaxation coursed through her at the touch of his now-familiar lips to hers. He shifted, moving closer, deepening the kiss in a surprising, and not unpleasant, way.

"C'mere," he said, his voice rough as he pulled her over so she straddled his lap. Running his hands up the exposed outsides of her legs, he held her close. "Who knew," he whispered, his lips hovering over hers, "That you dressing up like a streetwalker with wings would give me a hard on."

"Mm hmm." She sighed with relief that he'd shown up and seemed glad to see her. "I can tell." She ground down onto his growing tights-covered erection as they kissed. Even after just one beer she had a sort of dizzy, drunk feeling in her head. He gripped her harder, digging his fingers into her ass, and encouraging her to rub against him. One hand let go of her backside and cupped her breast, thumbing her nipple that pressed against the cheap costume fabric.

She broke away, confused, anxious and more than a little turned on. His eyes had darkened with lust. His breathing quickened. But something about the whole scene had a distinctly off-kilter aura. Antony didn't engage in much PDA. The man would barely kiss her in public. He liked to "save it" for when they were alone. And here they sat, dry-humping in a tent that would, in a few minutes be teeming with people, including his parents.

"Antony," she gasped when the hand teasing her nipple slid down and under the short skirt between her legs. "Stop." She gasped when his finger found its target.

"Kiss me," he demanded. "Then come for me Rosie. I want to feel it."

Burying her hands in his hair, sending the silly hat floating to the floor, she covered his full lips with hers, opening her thighs slightly, shocked, but more than ready for all of it. She shivered, as the brightly lit tent dimmed, and her ears buzzed.

"Oh, Peter." She grinned when he took his hand out from under her skirt. "Tinkerbell likes it when you get all naughty." But he stayed quiet, his dark eyes narrowed, making her uncomfortable. "What?" When she heard voices, adult ones, getting closer she tried to get off his lap so she could get herself presentable.

But he held onto her even tighter, rock hard under that dumb tunic, and she admitted she wanted it, wanted him, needed him so badly she thought she might choke on it. His fingers threaded in her hair, which she'd kept down and loose as he put his lips on her sweaty neck.

"I do love you. I do."

Alarmed, hearing the "but" on the other end of that declaration, she tilted his face up to meet hers. His eyes reflected a sort of desperate unhappiness that made tears press against hers. They sat, silent, as words that required voice coiled up, unspoken between them.

When Aiden ran into the tent, she jumped up off Antony's lap as if it were forbidden for her to be there.

He spent a half second scowling at her as she tugged her skirt down then at Antony. "It's Jeffrey, he jumped off the wagon and lit out across the field."

Antony got to his feet, but Aiden ignored him—luckily, since there would be no hiding that raging erection in a Peter Pan costume.

Aiden grabbed her hand. "I think I know where he is. Come on."

She glanced back once at her fiancé. But Antony hadn't moved. His gaze remained on his brother and it held a strange, uncharacteristic sort of expression—almost wistful, but definitely not pleased.

"Go on." He waved them off. "If anybody knows all the hiding places around here, it's Aiden."

She blinked, unsure, panic rising in her throat—less at the thought of Jeffrey missing somewhere on the Love property, than of the way Antony seemed utterly detached from her at that precise moment.

Chapter Nineteen

They moved quickly out of the tent against the tide of traffic. Partygoers were filing in, lining up for food. Kids ran around yelling in the midst of serious sugar highs. Aiden held onto Rosalee's hand, dragging her past people she nodded and waved to. She saw more than one person look right at their joined hands. But nothing cut through the layer of ice that had formed around her, at the hard, cold fact of her new reality.

Antony didn't love her. She understood that now. Or, maybe he did, but not in the way he wanted to, not the same way he did Margot.

What to do about that, Rosalee had zero clue.

Her engagement diamond cut into her finger, but she endured the pain, considering it a small penance for her many transgressions. Her life, as she once knew it, had ended again, just like it had when she'd been visited by two uniformed Marines, her belly huge, and her heart broken by their presence.

She followed Aiden away from the tent, past the pool with the burning tiki torches reflecting in the still water. They hit the gravel drive on the other side, running, still hand in hand. Rosalee looked over at Aiden and tried to process his strange appearance—black cape, attached head covering with funny ears, mask dangling around his neck. When she touched her flaming-hot face, wetness from tears she hadn't realized she'd been shedding coated her fingertips.

He let go of her hand and slid the large door of the pole barn aside. When he flipped the light switch, the space flooded with bright fluorescence. The old Love family pick-up Antony had driven when she'd been with Paul in high school, sat alongside a horse trailer, a riding lawn mower, several bicycles, a four-wheeler, and a tidy stack of sleds.

A sob escaped her aching throat. What had she done? Had she pushed a perfectly fine man away from her, somehow? Did he sense what she wanted from Aiden—no, did he *know* what she had *gotten* from his own brother?

Oh, sweet Jesus, forgive me. Please let me salvage this with Antony.

Aiden glanced back at her and nodded at a set of stairs leading up to a storage space with a window she remembered from her high school partying days. The fact that she'd convinced Paul to take her virginity up there the summer between their junior and senior years, made the irony of all this too close for comfort.

But then she heard it—the distinct sounds of her son, Paul's son, the baby he would never hold, crying somewhere up in that darkness. She dashed up the steps ahead of Aiden.

"Jeffrey Paul Norris, are you up here?"

"No," his small voice called out.

She took a breath and forced her reply to sound casual and not blood-curdling furious at him. "Oh, well, honey, folks are kinda worried about you, running off like that and all. Can I tell them you're all right?"

"Don't care."

Aiden put a hand on her arm, restraining her from moving forward. "Hey buddy, you didn't tell me you were done with the hayride."

"Jeffrey doesn't like hayrides."

"That's cool. But it's time to eat. Aren't you hungry?"

"Had too much candy," he said, in a small and unhappy voice. "Got a tummy ache."

Something appeared out of the dark, dashed past her and attached itself to Aiden, who'd crouched down low. Hanging on to him, he took a seat on a nearby bale of hay. As her eyes adjusted, Rosalee saw them clinging to each other both dressed as batman. A slightly hysterical giggle bubbled into her throat. She forced it down when Jeffery's crying got louder. She sat next to them and draped her arm around Aiden's shoulders, her other hand on Jeffrey's small, warm back.

"Jeffrey wants to go home."

"Sweetie, the party is only halfway over. There's food and music and...."

"I wants to go home *now*." He raised his tear-streaked face. "I wants my old house and my old bed."

It didn't surprise her to hear that. Things at Antony's were, at best, strained between her son and fiancé. Whenever AliceLynn showed up, she'd distract and play with him, and had gotten them both in semi-trouble, swimming in the pond one night after dark. But the trade-off for AliceLynn's presence meant a near constant hum of anger between her and her father.

"Tell you what." Aiden patted the boy's back as he spoke. "You stick with me for a while. We'll get some mac-and-cheese and chicken, and have a root beer. It's Dom's root beer, the kind he makes. I know you'll like it. And you can sit with me the whole time, okay, buddy?"

"Mommy doesn't let Jeffrey have root beer," he mumbled. Aiden raised an eyebrow.

"It's okay tonight, baby." She tightened her grip around Aiden's shoulders. He moved so quickly she couldn't draw back before their lips met, briefly, making them both inhale at the same time. But a stone sat cold in her chest at the realization that Aiden remained lost to her, just like Antony, no matter how many more wedding details she formalized.

"Hey! You all in here?" A deep voice rose from downstairs.

"Yeah. Found him." Aiden got up, his eyes still on hers in the near dark of the pole barn's attic. Words shriveled and died in her throat.

"All right. Bring him on down. Mama's freaking out." Antony kept his voice calm in a way that should have given her clear warning.

Aiden led the way, and she emerged, shaking from the last hour's worth of drama. Still clad in his ridiculous Peter Pan gear, Antony was waiting, arms crossed, his glare reserved for Aiden.

"Give him to Rosie."

"No!" Jeffrey screeched, hanging onto Aiden's neck. "Jeffrey wants Aiden!"

Antony touched Jeffrey's back, which calmed him as he got handed off to Rosalee.

"Antony, let's just go...."

"Rosie, please take Jeffrey and go back to the party. Aiden and I need to talk."

"Honey, it's...." But she had nothing. What could she possibly say that would make sense? That she wanted only one of them, and not the one who she'd agreed to marry in less than two month's time?

She sucked in a breath. The men were staring at each other, both dressed for a costume party, with murderous intent on their faces. It would be funny, were it not so distressing.

"This is ridiculous." She shifted the floppy child to her other arm. "Stand down. I mean it."

Antony frowned at the tone of her voice. But he only gave her the briefest of glances before pinning Aiden to the wall with his dark, Italian glare. Aiden did not flinch, to his credit.

"We'll be along in a few minutes," Antony said, yanking her close and kissing her on the mouth then dismissing her in such an offhanded way it caused a wave of raw fury to crash through her brain.

"Will you please stop acting like some kind of Neanderthal?"

"It's okay, Rosalee. He's right. We're overdue for a chat." Aiden kept his gaze on his brother.

She stomped out and headed up the small incline near the pool, when she heard the first clear sound of flesh hitting flesh. Dropping Jeffrey to the grass, she said, "Run with me." He nodded, his eyes serious as if he understood the urgency.

As they burst into the tent, she wondered who best to grab for help. She spotted Dominic dressed as a vampire, his long blond hair slicked back, and his huge eyes framed by what had to be eyeliner. He'd gone into full, frontal flirt mode with some new woman in town, a teacher or something, who seemed well-matched for him in a slinky, lady-Dracula getup. Rosalee thought, not for the first time, she'd be hard-pressed to identify most of the guests as regulars at the Lucasville Episcopal Church.

She spotted Lindsay and Anton sitting with a few other older couples, eating and laughing, although Lindsay's eyes were tired. Kieran and Melinda sat alone, stiff and unhappy, with full plates of food in front of them. Renee sat at a table of her friends, giggling and admiring the Halloran family engagement ring.

Dom met her eyes, and she jerked her chin to indicate she needed him. He got up and headed her way, snagging Jeffrey, and slinging him up on his shoulders.

"Somebody needs a root beer." He grinned at Rosalee.

"Yeah, um, listen, I think you should go check on Antony and Aiden."

"Why? They'll pound on each other and get whatever it is—or whoever it is—out of their systems. It'll make for a better basketball game this weekend, trust me."

"No, I mean it. I...." She stopped when Lindsay walked up, carrying a fresh drink.

"Hey, honey. Where did you find this one?" She patted Jeffrey's leg.

"Pole barn." She bit her lip, picturing the carnage she'd left behind.

"Good. That's exactly where I sent Antony. Lots of great hiding places there."

At that moment, Rosalee would have given every penny in her paltry bank account to say to Antony's mother that there would be no holiday wedding. That the whole thing was the worst sort of farce. Somebody else's idea of a happily-ever-after she simply did not deserve. And one that Antony didn't want anymore—if he ever truly had.

Just as she opened her mouth to let the ugly truth fly, Renee appeared at her elbow.

"Did you manage to bring Aiden back with you?" she asked with arched eyebrows.

Rosalee's face flamed hot. She hated this bitch, and everything she represented for Aiden right then, good and bad.

"No actually," she ground out through clenched teeth. "He's down at the pole barn getting the crap kicked out of him by his older brother, if you must know."

This fact didn't seem to faze anyone in their circle. Renee sipped her gin.

Lindsay sighed. "Dom, would you?" she asked, reaching up for Jeffrey, who went eagerly into her arms. Rosalee tried to take him, knowing Lindsay had been weakened from her treatments. She just grinned down at him. "The day I can't hold a fine young man like this is the day you can plant daisies on me."

"This is your fault," Renee whispered before stepping away. "Your fault," she mouthed again behind Lindsay's back.

Dom winked at her, smacked Renee's leather-clad ass hard enough to make her squeal then motioned for his brother to join him. "Kieran, *vamanos*."

The tall, red-headed man leapt up, as if relieved to have an excuse to escape his present company. "Trouble *mi hermano*?"

Melinda's royally pissed-off face got even more pinched.

"*Si, con dos hermanos*."

Kieran shrugged at his unhappy future wife. "Sorry, babe. Family stuff." She waved him away. He blew her a kiss. She ignored him.

Rosalee tried to breathe, but the anxiety, guilt, and now anger at Renee's presumption about why the men were fighting, filled her lungs and wouldn't allow it. She dropped into a chair, while Renee and Lindsay walked with Jeffrey toward the bar, presumably to get him his forbidden root beer. After a few minutes, she dropped her head down on her arms and fought the urge to burst into tears.

Chapter Twenty

"**N**ow this is a sight you don't see every day." Dom stood in the pole barn doorway, arms crossed and wearing a scowl.

Aiden caught a glimpse of him before Antony lunged again, forcing him to focus on the task at hand. They faced one another, breathing heavily, both costumes ripped. He thought his shoulder might be out of its socket, it hurt so badly. They'd both sport black eyes by morning. But he'd gotten his licks in, by God. Antony might have a broken nose for his trouble.

Kieran was shoulder to shoulder with Dom. "I wish I had my phone. This would make a killer YouTube video. Peter Pan kicks Batman's ass around the pole barn." He laughed.

Aiden made the mistake of shooting him a dirty look, and Antony hit him hard and low in the side, driving him ass over elbow on a bale of hay. The breath left his lungs in a loud whoosh as Antony hauled back to pound his face. Cartilage snapped and his jaw moved sickeningly sideways. At that point, he had no pain. Pain would come later.

He lurched up, determined to head butt the asshole. But just as he hauled back to make likely ill-advised forehead-to-forehead contact, Antony disappeared. Aiden lay there, trying to breathe, and wondering if he would be in any way presentable for his class on Monday. Sounds of random scuffling and cursing grew closer to where he lay sprawled on the floor, one leg still propped on the hay bale, and he scrambled to his feet.

"Get off me, you shit," Antony yelled while Dominic hung onto his arms and tugged him backward. Kieran grabbed Aiden when he ran toward Antony, ready to use the brief respite to his full advantage.

"Don't touch me, you pussy-whipped son of a bitch," he spat out, breaking from Kieran's grip. "I'm not done with him." He cocked his not-aching left arm back, ready to plant his fist in Antony's nose again while Dom had the bastard restrained.

"What did you call me?" Kieran yelled yanking him around so fast, Aiden almost lost his balance. The fist he had ready for Antony glanced a blow off Kieran's cheekbone.

"Motherfucker!" Kieran shoved him to the floor. "You douchebags need to keep your fight to yourselves. No piece of ass is worth all this." He looked down at Aiden in disgust before kicking him hard in the thigh. "At least I'm not trying to steal my own brother's woman. I ought to let him do whatever he wants to you, punk."

Fury blinded him as he reached out and grabbed Kieran's calf, digging his fingers into the muscle.

"And you," Dom said as Kieran swayed and his legs buckled, bringing his six-foot-six-inch frame crashing down on top of Aiden, "You need to keep your goddamned eyes on the prize." Dom could easily hold Antony. Despite his shorter stature, he'd always been the toughest and most tenacious of all of them. "The prize that is Rosalee Norris."

Aiden shifted to avoid Kieran's grip and jumped up. "Yeah." He stomped over where Dom still had Antony's arms locked behind his back. He went right up in Antony's grill. "You know what she thinks, right? Rosalee thinks you," he poked a finger into Antony's chest, "are boning your goddamn therapist, even while you make noises about marrying her."

"Well, that sure would work out for you, wouldn't it, you punk shithead." Antony spat a stream of blood at Aiden's feet. "Then you'd be free to do whatever it is your dirty-little-boy mind wants to with *my* fiancée."

Dom blew out a breath of frustration then his eyes widened at something over Aiden's shoulder. "Kieran, Jesus don't make this worse than it already—duck!"

Aiden ducked, and Kieran's fist landed squarely on Dom's nose, forcing him to let go of Antony's arms and bend over. Blood spurted from between his fingers.

"You are such a pussy-whipped loser," he muttered as he climbed over Antony to get at Kieran. "Does she suck the chrome off your trailer hitch, ginger? I sure hope so."

Antony spun around and faced Aiden, his dark eyes full of anger, but also a tinge of remorse. "She's leaving town," he muttered, arms at his sides, fists clenched.

"Who is?" Aiden asked, backing away, but eyeballing Kieran and Dominic, who were now scuffling around on the floor, trying to best each other.

"Margot. She's moving back to Michigan. It's...it was...I'm...fuck you," he mumbled, rubbing the blood off his mouth. "I don't owe you shit. You're the one who's trying to scam on Rosalee. And I'm here to tell you, you are not man enough for her. Stick to your cougar-mama hairdresser. You put a ring on that shit, our Nana Halloran's ring. I suggest you—*oof.*"

Aiden heard nothing but the satisfying sound of Antony's lungs emptying of air when he planted his head into the man's midsection. They went over top of Dom and Kieran, but Aiden had the upper hand and had landed a couple of good blows to Antony's gut when a spray of freezing-cold water hit him straight in the face. He yelped, cursed, and struggled to his feet.

The water hit Antony next as he headed for Aiden, and he spluttered, letting loose a string of curse words to dye the very air blue. Aiden stood, dripping and shivering, his face a huge ball of agony, his shoulder screaming in pain.

Kieran and Dom got the water hose next, and they leapt apart to stand, dripping wet, hands on their hips, heads down. This particular treatment meant one thing.

Lindsay Love called from the doorway, holding the high-pressure hose nozzle in one hand. "Y'all had better have some kind of excuse for this behavior at my party, and open up your wallets. I'm gonna go on a real sweet shopping spree with the money you owe my swear jar."

Aiden sighed and rolled his shoulders, wincing, and trying not to moan from the pain. Bastard had pinned him and yanked his arm high up behind his back in the first five minutes of their fight.

"Mama," he spoke up first, figuring that begging was his role still. "We're...."

"Shut. Up." Antony's low, raspy voice gave Aiden an evil sense of triumph. He'd landed a couple of good blows to his throat. The rudeness garnered Antony the water hose right to his messed-up face.

"Ow! Mama! Goddamn it...I mean...cut it out!"

"Antony, I'm taking Jeffrey and going home. To my house." Rosalee's strained voice came from somewhere behind Lindsay. "You let me know when you're prepared to act like a grown-up in front of him."

"Aiden!" Jeffrey hollered from the darkness.

He sucked in a breath. His chest hurt, but not from the fight. "Go on with your mommy, Jeff. I'll catch up with you later."

Antony tensed next to him, but he ignored it in favor of shoving the man sideways hard enough to make him drop to one knee. That netted Aiden another chilling spray to his aching face.

"Aiden," Renee said in a tight voice. He groaned. His mama surely knew how to make an impression. She must have dragged all three women over from the tent to observe her water hose intervention. "That had to be the most immature display of...." She stopped. He could see her Catwoman silhouette next to his mother, and recalled thinking how hot she looked, and how much he couldn't wait to get her home and mess around with them still in their dumb costumes. "I'm going home," she declared after a bit. He knew how hard it was for her not to rip into him.

The brothers moved slightly closer together, as if forming a wall of resistance to the general female disapproval radiating from the doorway.

"Kieran," Melinda added in her nasally voice. "You need to—"

"Go home, Melinda," Kieran said through clenched teeth. "I'll call you tomorrow."

"I will not leave here without—"

"Melinda, just shut up and get your ass home. I'll call you tomorrow. Ow!" Water whooshed by Aiden and hit Kieran in the mouth.

Antony raised his eyes to Aiden's. Regardless of their anger, they gave each other a silent high five in honor of their brother's suddenly rediscovered balls.

"Chrome off your trailer hitch," Dom muttered under his breath. Kieran shoved him and they were at it again, fists flying.

Aiden heard his father before he saw him. His patented "fucking dumbasses" comment under his breath and out of his wife's hearing range, hit Aiden's ears in a familiar, almost comforting way, before the man dragged Dom off of Kieran.

"Go on." He pushed him toward Antony. "Go jump in the pool, all of y'all sorry excuses for men. Cool the hell off. You're ruining your mama's party."

"Watch your language, Anton," Lindsay said.

"Sorry, Linds, but I won't tolerate this bullshit—"

She sighed and let the water hose dangle from her fingers. "Cool off then family meeting in twenty minutes in the tent."

Anton gave each of them a hard shove toward the door. Lindsay disappeared, taking the water hose with her. Aiden stumbled out, noting the distinct lack of cars in the driveway, before running over the small hill, yanking off his ruined shirt and diving into the cool water.

By the time he emerged on the opposite side, Antony had joined him. Kieran and Dom were sitting, legs in the water, a good four feet of air between them. Aiden propped his elbows on the side of the still-warm concrete and touched his nose. Damn guy had broken it again most likely, and his left shoulder and upper arm were going numb pretty fast.

Antony emerged next to him, shook the water out of his hair, and climbed out without speaking or looking back.

Aiden sighed and let his body float behind him. He heard shouts and splashes, indicating Antony had shoved the other two into the water, so he got out, not eager to face either of them.

Grabbing a towel from the bin his mother kept stocked, he dried his hair then shucked out of his dark jeans and underwear before wrapping it around his waist.

"I'm going down there." He spoke to Kieran and Dom, who seemed intent on ignoring him while drowning each other. He'd never seen Kieran so worked up. Not that Dom had stated anything they hadn't all been thinking since meeting that Melinda bitch. "I can send Daddy back up for you two." That got their attention. They scrambled to the side and climbed out.

He wanted to bypass the tent and duck indoors for a pair of dry shorts, but Antony spotted him and waved him inside. He sat facing their parents, a healthy two fingers of bourbon in a glass in front of him. His father and mother sat close together. Anton had his arm around Lindsay's shoulders. Guilt flooded Aiden's aching head at the sight of her reddened eyes. Sitting two chairs away from his oldest, formerly favorite sibling, he accepted the drink his father poured him.

Kieran showed up next, his sailor suit dripping water, then Dom, wearing nothing but a pair of wet boxer shorts and an evil glare.

"Sit," their father commanded, preempting any requests for dry—or more—clothing.

They filled in the two spaces between Antony and Aiden, and took their drinks. Angelique appeared, still wearing her Glinda the Good Witch dress, her face tear-streaked. Aiden's chest constricted. Something else must be going on. Her siblings acting like idiots would never affect her that much.

"What's wrong?" He winced when the alcohol hit his sore tongue. It burned his throat going down, but lit a nice fire in his chest.

His sister stood behind and between her parents, a hand on either of their shoulders. "You stupid jerks ruined the party." She glared at each of them. Anton patted her hand while Lindsay focused on her untouched glass.

"The cancer—" Aiden said, needing to add words to the space.

"It's not getting any better," his father finished for him, knocking back his drink, and pouring another healthy portion. "We got the news two days ago, and your mama has been trying so hard not to ruin the party by telling you. But what do you collective group of knuckleheads go and do anyway...hmm?"

Lindsay kept her eyes on her sons while Anton gazed at her. The raw desperation and terror in his father's eyes scared the shit out of him. He gulped back his drink and shoved the glass forward. Anton refilled it.

"But I thought the surgery had been a success." Kieran's abraded fingers gripped his glass.

"They thought so, too, but at an eight week PET scan, they found more bad cells."

His mother placed both of her hands on the table. Transfixed by them, by the memory of them dressing him, brushing his hair, swatting his bottom, Aiden gulped. The backs of them were dark brown and dried from the sun, the fingernails short, but tidy. He grabbed for one and she gripped him then held out her other one toward her eldest son. Eyes dark and brooding, Antony placed his huge palm in her smaller one.

"It's gone to my ovaries. They want to do a radical hysterectomy, as early as next week. They think it's confined there, but...." She bit her lip and held tight to Aiden and Antony's hands. "You two are not helping me one bit. I don't know what it is for sure, although I have an inkling, and may I just say shame on you." She glared at Aiden, who shrunk back in his chair, while Antony swelled with righteous indignation at the other end of the row.

"It's not just me," Aiden insisted. "He is...he wants...well...." He stopped. How to explain what he suspected about Antony and Margot? That they had a bad case of the goo-goo eyes for each other? That he had some kind of crush on Margot, but still loved Rosalee? He shook his head.

"And you, Antony Ian Love, I'm just beside myself over this. You all are grown men now." Their mother's voice got stronger with every chastising word. "You don't solve problems with your dang fists."

"I don't give two shits what you dummies are fighting over, or why. All I know is you'd better sort yourselves out fast. Your mama needs you to be strong, together, a unit. The Love family will not implode this way because some broad can't make up her mind—*ow*!" Anton rubbed his shoulder where Lindsay had punched him.

She plunked the infamous swear jar down on the table then stood and met each of her sons in the eye before coming back to Aiden. He fidgeted in his seat. "I just have one question for you, Aiden, my sweet."

"Yes ma'am?" He slammed back his second drink dreading the question.

"Is that Renee going to be presenting me with a grandbaby in the next few months?"

Aiden frowned. The men all snickered. He ran a hand through his wet hair. "Um. No ma'am. At least, not to my knowledge. I mean, the wedding's not until June, the, uh, last I heard." His face flushed hot when Dom nudged his arm.

"Oh, well then. What a relief." She kept staring at him, saying more in those few, flat words than other women took paragraphs to state. She'd made her stance on Renee clear when he'd first returned home. A sick sort of dread rose in his throat.

"And you." She faced Antony, who sat chuckling into his glass. "You're the oldest, and meant to be an example. I operated under the apparent mistaken assumption you understood that."

"Yes, ma'am, I do. I've understood that my entire life." He scowled down the row at Aiden, who experienced a sudden flicker of sympathy for him.

"Really. Well then, perhaps you'd best start acting like the example. Rosalee Norris is a fine woman. And if I find out you are doing anything to disrespect her in any way whatsoever—" She let the other half hover, using one of her best guilt trips—the unspoken threat. They all knew it, and feared it.

"No, ma'am. But I will say you bringing her around to the pole barn to see us—"

"This is my house, Antony, and I will do what I see fit. She needed—they all needed—to get an idea what they were getting themselves into firsthand with you all sorry so-and-so's." Her eyes softened when they rested on Kieran. "Oh, my sweetheart, the peacemaker." She reached across the table to brush a lock of red hair off his forehead. He smiled at her, his face a mask of hopefulness for getting off the hook. She cupped his chin. Resentment rose in Aiden's gut at her coddling.

Lindsay smiled serenely, keeping her palm alongside Kieran's face. "I sincerely hope that Melinda has some kinda special skills for you in the boudoir. Oh, and you should let her know now that she'd better not ever keep me from your babies, either. I have a feeling she'd be the mama to try it. She's a right cunt, that one."

Aiden blinked, not quite sure he'd heard her correctly. Dom burst out laughing so hard, he tipped his chair and landed on his back.

"Mama!" Angelique squealed. But her lips were twitching in an attempt not to laugh. Anton scowled down into his drink, but Aiden saw him shaking.

"As for you, young man." She focused on Dominic then, once he'd managed to get up off the ground and sat once more between Aiden and a fuming Kieran. "Well, I just don't know what to say. I'm not sorry that hippy girl left town, but I sure do wish I could meet your son someday." Dom cleared his throat but wouldn't meet her eyes. "There's somebody right for you, Dominic Sean Love. I just know it. I wish it had been Diana Brantley. I'm not sure what your issue is with her."

"Well, you chased my new girl off from here tonight, Mama," he muttered into his drink, letting the comment about his on-again, off-again, oldest girlfriend go unaddressed. "She's even a teacher."

"Yeah, a yoga teacher." Kieran nudged him.

Dom shot him a murderous look then tilted his half-empty glass at the rest of the group. "Yeah. Lucky me. I like 'em bendy."

Everyone laughed. Peace, it seemed, would prevail, as it usually did after fists flew between them. Even Lindsay cracked a smile.

"I don't believe that you know what you want yet. But you will some day." She touched his face with her fingertips. "I'm tired, Anton." She slumped against her husband. "Please go with me into the house. You all be sure and fill this thing." Dropping her own dollar into it, she said, "Pardon my language. Make it overflow, Misters Love. I mean it." She shot them one more glare. And like that, their family meeting concluded.

Their father left the bourbon bottle in the middle of the table. "Finish it off if it'll help you all calm down." He glowered at them before taking Lindsay's arm. "Come on, Angelique," he said, gesturing for his beloved daughter. She gave him a hug, and her mother a perfunctory peck on the cheek, but stepped away from them.

"I'm gonna stay with the knuckleheads awhile longer."

Aiden observed his brothers, sitting all in a row. Each of them wore his own version of dismay at the sight of their strong mother being helped into the house. He got up, walked over to the bar, and snagged more Woodford.

"This is gonna take more than one bottle, I think." He glanced at Antony, who held up his glass by way of agreement. Angelique flipped on the music then grabbed her own glass and sat facing them.

"All right, assholes, let's get drunk," she said, dropping a dollar into the large, clear glass jar between them.

Chapter Twenty-One

Aﬀter a solid five days of ignoring him, Renee finally responded to a text.

You can come over tonight.

Aiden looked at the message then up at the classroom full of mostly grown-ups waiting for his next bit of advice about their first chapters. It had taken him a full twenty-four hours to recover from the brawl and the bourbon. They'd even issued a rare cancellation of the weekly basketball game, given that his shoulder still ached like a rotten tooth, and they were all black and blue that Sunday.

His mind still refused to accept any of his current reality. So he operated mostly on autopilot, moving from his tiny apartment to his classroom, home to his laptop, to bed then up again. Antony expected him back at the garage—the first day after the mess they'd instigated at the Halloween party. Aiden's stomach roiled the concept of facing Antony now. The hard fact of the matter that he didn't give an honest shit if he never saw Renee again didn't help his mood much.

Not a good frame of mind, considering you'll be marrying the woman in a few months.

Her next message made him feel even worse.

I don't forgive you, but I miss you more than I want to punish you. See you after the garage shift.

He dropped the phone on the desk, pondering how well she knew his schedule—many times better than he did—and focused on his job. As he headed toward Lucasville and the Love Garage, he sent her an answer.

Sure. See you then.

He parked around back and got out, noting the usual busyness of the shop on a Thursday afternoon. Antony had a reputation for brutal honesty with regard to car repairs, charged fairly, and fixed things right the first time. As a result, he had people come all the way out from the other side of Lexington to do business with him. Aiden admired it a lot, but when he saw his brother in one of the open bay doors, wiping his hands on a rag, he experienced a thrill of anger.

"Hey." He walked past him, heading for his usual first task, unpacking the day's worth of parts deliveries. Antony grabbed his arm and held him in place.

"You all right?" He nodded to Aiden's other arm that rested in a sling.

"Yeah, it just keeps pressure off the shoulder so it can heal." He took it off. "I can still work, don't worry."

"Good." Antony let him go. "Sorry," he spoke to the air slightly to Aiden's left.

"What's that?" Aiden asked, gritting his teeth.

"I said I'm sorry. You going up to the hospital tonight?"

Aiden blinked, trying to recall if he'd indicated he would, and coming up with nothing.

"Last night was a bad one." Antony tucked the rag into his front jeans pocket.

"Is Rosalee there?"

"Only when I'm not."

"Ah, well, okay. I can go if it's my turn. I thought I had the weekend though."

"Well, Daddy called and wants us to all go tonight." Antony focused down at his work boots. "I guess he didn't get a hold of you yet."

"Oh." Terror slithered down Aiden's spine. "She's...that bad?"

"I don't know." Antony slouched in the bay doorway, his face grim. "Go on and get some work done. We can ride up there together when we close up."

Aiden shot a quick text to Renee. *Can't come tonight. Need to go to hospital.*

I'll come with, she responded quickly. *I hope everything is OK.*

Don't know if it is. I'm riding with Antony after work. I'll let you know if you should come or not.

Waiting for her answer, expecting bossy indignation, he got nothing. He spent the rest of the day organizing the parts room after three large shipments were unpacked then helping one of the mechanics change the oil on a Volvo. After they shut the garage, he and Antony rode the thirty minutes to University Hospital in total silence.

Their father, Angelique, Dom, and Kieran were already there when they arrived. Aiden held back, his feet frozen at the sight of everyone gathered around their mother in a hospital bed. His heart thudded in his chest and his mouth dried up. Antony tugged him in.

"Come on," he insisted, reminding Aiden of all the times he'd dragged him along when they were younger, shielding him from Dom, taking him bike or horseback riding. "Be brave," he said, making Aiden do a double take at the sight of his encouraging face.

When their father looked at them, his expression made Aiden exhale.

"She's turned a corner. You just missed the doc. He said she's—" He stopped and Aiden came face-to-face with his very Italian, alpha male, in-control father, choking up with raw emotion.

Angelique flew to his side and buried her face in his chest. Anton held onto her, which seemed to calm him more than it did her. He sucked in a breath and swiped at his eyes. "They weren't sure early this morning. But they did a scan and say they got it all and her temperature is normal again."

"They were about to put her on a respirator I thought. That was some kind of miracle." Antony voiced what Aiden had been thinking.

"Yeah." Anton gave his daughter a squeeze then released her. "She's not going out of this world without a fight. You know that."

Aiden stood by the bed and watched her sleep. The beeps and pings of machines monitoring his mother's heartbeat and pulse barely registered. Relief made him weak in the knees, but he grinned at her when her eyes fluttered open and found his.

"Aiden? Baby?" she croaked between dry lips. "Mama needs a drink of water."

After a couple of hours, Lindsay shooed everyone away, insisting they sleep in their own beds. She'd bossed the nurses into giving her some real food, and had everyone declaring her a miracle, including her doctors.

Antony and Aiden walked to the elevator and rode down to the parking garage with their siblings. Aiden gave Angelique a hug before she got into their dad's car.

"I'll come back for him if he wants me to. I'm gonna stick around until at least the new year now, I think." She kept chewing on her lip and tugging at her long black hair.

"Yeah, but then you go back. You have to finish your degree."

"You should talk," she said, climbing into the car. "Besides I hear I can make great money dancing on a cruise ship, or at one of the big parks."

"I did finish, twice. I just didn't this last one—yet. But hey, I got a positive response from a small agency. They want the full manuscript. And I've decided if they pass, I'm gonna self-publish the damn thing. See if that'll work." He frowned and crouched down next to the open car door. "And somehow, I think dancing in a Cinderella costume is kind of a waste of your talent, so get that idea right out of your fool head."

She kept her eyes straight ahead, gripping the steering wheel. "I hope you're sorting things out with Rosalee."

"You mean Renee."

Her knowing gaze was so like their mother's it made him pause. "No, I don't. Move. I need to go home and sleep." He stood and waited until her car's taillights disappeared around the corner then climbed into Antony's truck and leaned his head back.

"Rosie still won't talk to me. Won't let me in the house, near her, or Jeffrey," Antony said as they waited in line to pay the parking-garage attendant.

"Renee is just now talking to me. I'm supposed to go over there." Aiden pulled his phone out of his pocket and switched it off. "But I think I'll just go home."

Antony raised an eyebrow at him. Aiden matched it. And the discussion choked and died from a lack of oxygen.

Chapter Twenty-Two

November

Rosalee watched from her kitchen window as Jeffrey climbed around on his Antony-installed backyard jungle gym. The warm weather so close to Thanksgiving gave her a welcome opportunity for her son to get outside and blow off steam. She sighed and ran a hand through her hair. A sharp rap at the door startled her out of the morning's fresh worry.

She opened it, leaving the screen door latched and looked at Antony without saying anything. The confusion in her heart and mind over him, Aiden, and that bizarre, ugly scene at the Halloween party still had her tied up in knots. She owed Antony a loosening, some forgiveness. She also owed him the truth.

"How's your mama?" she asked.

Coming just short of scuffing his feet on the worn porch, he clutched a huge bouquet of roses in one hand. "Better. The chemo is tearing her up, but she won't let Daddy check her back into the hospital. Wants to keep doing the outpatient. But it's rough on 'em. Angelique is helping, but I know Mama misses you."

Rosalee gritted her teeth and tried not to respond. She missed Lindsay, too. The woman had always been like a second mother to her. She was smart, funny, and practical in ways her own mother had not been. But although Rosalee had visited her in the hospital after her second surgery, she could not bring herself to go out to the Love family house.

"I miss you, Rosie." He kept dark eyes on hers. "I'm so sorry for how I behaved."

"I know you are." But she couldn't let him in. Her body already reacted to his presence but she kept a grip on it, unwilling to give in to her base need for his arms around her. She would not be with Antony again, would not have sex with him until she told him the truth about

Aiden—about what she had done with him. It had to be done, no matter how hard it would be or what might happen after.

"Mama wants me to bring Jeffrey out to my place. She's spending the day with Daisy and Lucy." He named Lindsay's two favorite show horses. "She owes him a horse ride, and she's feeling strong today, so she wants her animals. I guess. I don't know."

Rosalee smiled, softening despite her attempts not to do just that. He seemed lost, like a sad little boy in a large, nearly forty-year-old man's body. Her heart flexed, but she forced her gaze away from him.

"All right, he's around back." She opened the door. Antony moved forward, but she held up her hand. "I'll take those. And thank you." He handed her the flowers. Their perfume overpowered her.

"Rosie, I'm...we're still...shit. I don't even know how to have this conversation with you."

"I'll grab Jeffrey a change of clothes in case he gets muddy." Stepping back, she closed the door, cutting off her view of Antony's miserable face, and quieting the clanging guilt in her brain. Something had certainly gone on with him and Margot Hamilton. But her own tumbled, conflicted feelings about Aiden hardly gave her room to accuse.

Her innate competitive nature refused to accept Antony might have feelings for another woman, or that he might have actually acted on those feelings. At the same time, her conscience kept her awake at night, reliving the moment she'd first kissed Aiden, let him touch her, touched him, let him enter her body and, apparently, her soul.

Jeffrey squealed with delight when Antony got around back and told him they were going horseback riding.

"Will Aiden be there?" His voice carried through the open window at the back of the house.

Rosalee sucked in a breath and gripped the flowers so close the few remaining thorns poked through her shirt.

"No, but if you play your cards right, we'll get ice cream on the way home. How's that sound?"

"Yay! Ice cream!"

She put the flowers down and went to grab his spare clothes, noting she had a text on her phone as she passed by the hall table where she'd left it.

Aiden had messaged her: *We need to talk.*

She bit her lip and tucked the phone into her pocket. Antony had Jeffrey fastened into his car seat by the time she met him at the truck. Taking the backpack from her, he tossed it into the front seat then grabbed her so fast she squealed.

He held her close, his lips near her ear. "I love you, Rosie. Please forgive me. Please say we're still gettin' married. I can't stand this. I acted like such an ass."

She fought it a half second then went up tiptoes and wrapped her arms around his neck. This is what she needed in her life, this man, not his immature little brother. They were good together—she and Antony. She knew it—or at least she wanted to know it. His hands slid down her back to cup her ass as their lips met.

"Horsies! Horsies! Jeffrey wants horsies!"

Her sense of Antony going through motions, doing what people expected of him, still remained. She broke away and touched his rough cheek, knowing she'd crossed a line, and had no choice about going back.

"Bring him home in one piece, please."

Antony gripped her hand, kissed it, and looked so relieved, hysterical laughter threatened to burst from her lips. She closed her eyes a brief second, picturing Aiden. Guilt rose, choking off anything resembling happiness.

"I want to have a baby with you, Rosie," he said, surprising her. More children had never been a topic of conversation between them. He held onto her, despite Jeffrey's growing displeasure at the apparent delay of game. He put a hand on her stomach, and she got a chill, along with a strange surge of desire so strong she had to take a step back from him.

"You are so beautiful when you blush." He tucked a lock of hair behind her ear. "I love you."

"Antony, I...."

Before she could finish, he climbed into his truck. "Horsies, Jeffrey?" he asked, glancing into the rear view mirror.

"Horsies! Horsies!"

Rosalee propped her arms in the open window. "I'm not who you think I am," she insisted, her heart pounding so loudly it deafened her. "I'm not...I need to tell you—"

He grabbed her for another kiss, cutting her off.

"You are exactly what I want in my life, my bed, my world." His wild, desperate expression scared her a little. "I'll have him home in one piece, if a little dusty and full of ice cream. Oh, and we need to talk about Thanksgiving. I don't think Mama is up to feeding us all this year."

She stepped away and watched the truck drive out onto the street. By the time she stumbled back inside her own house, tears ran down her face in anticipation of the conversation she needed to have with Antony and Aiden's mother.

Chapter Twenty-Three

Thanksgiving

"I'm not lettin' her do anything," Rosalee insisted, hauling one of two huge turkeys out of the oven, and setting them on the counter already crowded with dishes.

Renee wrapped tin foil over one of the three pans of dressing. Angelique poured the gravy into a plastic pitcher for ease of transport. Jeffrey and Aiden were yelling at the television in the next room, playing some video game or another.

"But she wants to," Antony insisted. He held a box full of table linens she'd handed him. "I'm telling you not helping out is makin' her nuts."

Rosalee wiped the sweat off her forehead and made a mental calculation of the turkey poundage versus the number of people she had to feed for the thousandth time.

"Antony, please just pack the car. Your mama is coming off two days of chemo. Let her rest. Tell your daddy to get her to the garage at three o'clock like we told him."

She blew a lock of hair out of her eyes when Renee appeared in the doorway.

"Did you bring them?"

Renee smiled. They'd made a sort of peace during the last week's worth of planning for the Love family Thanksgiving dinner. Rosalee had initiated it, thinking it the mature, Christian thing, while choking on jealousy at the sight of the woman's emerald ring. But no matter her own misgivings about marrying Antony, she knew Renee didn't deserve to be in the middle of all the mess between her and Aiden.

"Sure did." The woman pointed to the small suitcase she'd parked by the fridge. "Who's first up?"

"Me, I guess." Dom appeared in the doorway, holding a beer, and running his hands through his long, blond hair. "You sure this is

185

really...." He stopped at Rosalee's glare. "Never mind. Let's get it over with."

Renee patted the chair on top of a big plastic tarp in the far corner of the kitchen and opened the case. "This won't hurt a bit, sweetie. Just leave it to me." Rosalee focused her attention back on the remainder of the meal prep and pack-up, knowing Renee had her part well under control.

The sound of a hair trimmer filled the air while she and Antony ferried food to the car. When Aiden headed toward Renee, Jeffrey barnacled onto him so tight he couldn't sit.

"Jeffery Paul Norris," Rosalee said, her nerves frayed, sweat dripping down her back. "You either let Aiden loose, or I'll have Miss Renee take your hair off, too."

Jeffrey studied Miss Renee to gauge her relative harmlessness. The woman smiled and crouched down, holding the trimmers. When she switched them on he flinched. Antony grabbed Rosalee's arm to keep her from leaping between them. He turned, shocked at how different he looked with a shaved head. He rubbed the stubble.

"It's just hair, Rosie. It'll grow back. Remember?" He parroted her words back at her. She frowned then took a step back.

"Come on, Jeff. We'll let Miss Renee take care of us both," Aiden said.

Jeffrey let go of Aiden's neck and flipped around without a second's hesitation. Renee looked to Rosalee for confirmation. She nodded and let Antony put his arm around her waist for a few minutes. The whole thing had been her idea. She'd been bound and determined to make this show of solidarity. Lindsay Halloran Love had never been vain by any stretch of the imagination, but the total loss of her thick mane of red hair had hit her hard this last round of chemotherapy.

Exhaustion pierced Rosalee between the eyes, and she swayed on her feet. Antony held onto her.

"Tired of resisting me yet?" His whisper made her shiver. She kissed him, knowing Aiden watched, but also knowing the statement required making.

"Maybe not," she said, smiling and touching his newly shorn head. "Might have to get a wig on you though, so I know who that is...you know...doing that to me."

He winked and smacked her butt in front of everyone, which took a lot for him.

"We're almost all packed up. Why don't you take the first bit over to the garage?" She sensed Aiden's eyes on her. The noise of the trimmer filled her ears again as she focused on packing up the two apple and two pumpkin pies in the last box, ready to serve at the tables she'd arranged for the rental company to set up in Love Garage.

He nodded, saluted, and headed out the door, followed by the equally bald Dominic. Kieran stood running his hands across his head.

"Melinda know about this yet?" she asked, handing him the box of pies.

He shrugged and flushed. Patting his cheek, she said, "We need to get going. I gotta change clothes." She took off her apron and saw Jeffrey, sitting terrified clutching Aiden's hand while Renee ran the trimmers over his hair.

On her way out the door, she snagged the bandanas she'd stitched up for everyone. After ordering special fabric covered with horses and shamrocks, she'd stayed up late the last three nights finishing them. Since she couldn't really sleep anyway, it seemed a good use of her time.

The brothers had laid out the food as she'd told them. She wanted it to be a dish-passing meal, not a buffet, with Anton carving both turkeys, as he did every year.

They had the beer flowing and the coffee made. She held Jeffrey's hand, taking in the flowers, the candles, the music piping through the garage sound system, all to her specifications.

After Aiden and Dom had spent hours scouring the floors and polishing every possible surface. Tears stung her eyes at the sight of the newly half-bald men, messing around the bar, laughing and acting like they'd not been at each other's throats three weeks prior.

"Mommy!" Jeffrey tugged on her hand. She crouched down to be on his level. His eyes were so huge and blue, even more so with his stubbly head, it made her throat ache with memory.

I love you, Paul Norris. I never loved anybody but you. And I hate you for leaving me now with this decision to make.

Jeffrey grabbed her face. "No crying, Mommy. It's Thanksgiving!" He grinned at her, and in his face she saw the man he would be someday.

Wiping her eyes, she gave him a bandana. "Here, hold this. I'll be right back to fasten it on your head."

She handed the rest of them out. Aiden smiled at her in a way that meant nothing, but ripped her heart in two. Then he frowned at something over her shoulder. Rosalee turned and saw Angelique standing with Renee, touching her pixie haircut self-consciously.

Renee had her arm around the younger woman. "Our girl here is donating her hair. I took care to keep her pretty, not that it took much."

Rosalee handed them both bandanas. She got hers on then Jeffrey's, and took a deep breath. Renee stood beside Aiden without touching him, her face set in unhappy lines.

Antony moved next to Rosalee. "This is incredible. You are incredible. I am a lucky man," he said, giving her a kiss on the cheek. He tucked her under his arm when they heard Anton's voice in the office area.

"No, honey, it's all taken care of, will you please just...."

Anton and Lindsay Love stopped in the door, eyes wide and jaws slack at the sight of at the beautiful table, and at the people gathered around, all wearing bandanas like the one Rosalee had given her just yesterday.

"Holy...haircut," Anton blurted out, before Lindsay burst into tears.

Chapter Twenty-Four

T he Saturday after Thanksgiving, Rosalee slept well past 10:00 a.m., waking only when Jeffrey ran in and jumped on her, demanding she get up and eat breakfast. She stretched and made him snuggle in next to her as delicious odors of coffee and bacon wafted into the bedroom.

"Antony says we'll horsie ride today again!" he yelled, before scrambling down and heading for the kitchen. She ran her hands down her sated body, recalling how sweet and loving Antony had been last night, when she'd finally acquiesced to his begging that they act like engaged grown-ups again.

"What? You think I'm that kind of girl? Having sex before my wedding night?" She'd teased, already giving in to him in her mind.

"I know you are. And it's one of my favorite things about you." He'd set his wine glass on the coffee table before pressing her down onto the couch and kissing her until she saw stars. She relished the reconnection to him. It was a new connection even, something that pleased her, because she understood it for the way things had to be. Her life now as wife to Antony, daughter-in-law to the volatile Lindsay and Anton, and sister-in-law to the young man who would not exit her fantasies.

She and Antony would marry then Renee and Aiden then Kieran and that Melinda, even though she'd thrown the hugest hissy fit when she'd made it in time for the Thanksgiving dessert at the garage, and had gotten a load of his bald head.

This had to be the way of the world now. Period. No ifs, ands, buts or take-backs. And no more messing around with Aiden.

Antony had gone a long way toward shoving Aiden out of her mind last night, to be sure. Although she'd insisted they sleep at her house, not his. She smiled and a flush crept up her face as she touched her bare skin under the blanket. Wincing at the pleasant soreness between her legs, she got up and grabbed her jeans and one of Antony's shirts, taking a deep breath of his scent as she buttoned it over her naked breasts.

Antony kissed her and handed her a cup of coffee when she wandered into the kitchen.

"Did AliceLynn check in last night?" She yawned. The girl had been sullen and quiet at the Thanksgiving dinner, but Rosalee had been too preoccupied to ask her why. Her role as future stepmother still made her nervous, but she figured she'd "been there, done that" as a rebellious teenaged girl, so she'd handle it, somehow.

"Yeah. She stayed over at Janey's." Antony set the food on the table and hollered for Jeffrey.

Rosalee grabbed him when he ran in and kissed his prickly scalp. "I may never get used to this."

"Stop it, Mommy," he said, wiggling out of her arms and getting in his chair. "The sooner we eat and clean up, the sooner we can horsie ride, right, Antony?"

"Yes, sir."

When they were done, Rosalee shooed them out, eager for some peace and quiet. "I'll tidy it up. Y'all go and ride, and say hi to Miss Lindsay for me, and mind your manners, young man."

"Okay," he said, heading out of the kitchen.

Antony stopped him and turned him back around to face her.

"I mean, yes, ma'am." He looked up at Antony for approval and received it.

Finally, they were out the door and in the truck. Rosalee sat nursing a cup of coffee and contemplating the next few weeks of wedding planning. Her mind spun with a thousand details, but her body felt strangely heavy—sated in more ways than one, and urging her back to bed for a little more sleep. It made sense. She'd been up nearly every night the week before Thanksgiving getting ready for that dinner. But it had been more than worth it.

She took a shower instead, hoping it would revive her. After she cleaned the kitchen and did a few loads of laundry she ended up staring out the window, dazed and groggy. When her phone buzzed with a text from Antony, she nearly jumped out of her skin.

Taking him to the house for early dinner. Mama says it's fine. She wants to do it.

Facing another hour or two alone, Rosalee settled in with a book and a cup of tea, and lost track of time until her phone rang. She grabbed it, but couldn't answer before Antony hung up. She hit redial.

"Good Lord, what time is it?"

"Almost eight," Antony replied. "Sorry. We ate then watched *Babe,* then played a video game. He's getting cranky, so I'm bringing him home. Got any more wine?"

"I think so." She cracked a huge yawn.

"Gee, sweetheart, sorry to keep you up."

"I'm not sorry. Or I won't be later, I'm guessing. You were pretty amazing last night."

"I have my skills, yes."

"So, I'm wondering something," she said, taking down a wine bottle and rooting around for the corkscrew. "What's going to happen with your therapy sessions?"

The question surprised her even as it exited her lips, and once the words were out of her mouth, she wished them back. Total silence filled her ear. She placed the wine bottle on the table.

"Why do you ask?" He voice sounded wary, as if testing the waters.

"You know why, Antony. I'm not playing games with this. I'm not comfortable with her, you know, around.... I told you that last night." She started shaking and had to clench her jaw to keep her teeth from chattering. What had possessed her to bring this up, she had no idea. She had something even more crucial to impart to him, but instead she'd decided to confront him? Way to deflect, she thought as she gazed at the wine bottle, wondering how much longer she could fake drinking along with him.

"Well, I'm not comfortable with Aiden around either. But I can't very well keep you from ever seeing him again. And I told you already—Margot is moving back to Michigan."

"That's not the same thing, and—"

"I'm not having this conversation on the phone with you."

She sighed. "Fine. I've opened the wine. I'll see you in a few."

After tossing the floppy, whining Jeffrey into bed, she stopped in the bathroom to study her image in the mirror and wondered did she really want to open this particular can of worms now.

She splashed water on her face and neck, feeling as antsy as a cat in a roomful of rocking chairs. Ridiculous. Frowning at her reflection, she headed toward the living room where Antony sat with his feet up and the TV tuned to an early-season basketball game.

She slipped in next to him and took the wine glass out of his hand. He grunted in surprise then smiled as she climbed onto his lap. Kissing him, she tasted wine and the cigar he must have had with his father. She wanted to cry, she wanted to scream, but mostly she wanted to tell the man the truth.

Paul had been a secret cigar smoker, or so he'd thought. He and Antony were alike in so many ways. Responsible, strong, mature, the one relied upon by others, lacking in spontaneity, and never ever out of control—well, except for that horrible Halloween party.

Antony slid his hands up under her shirt and flipped open her bra, going further with the kiss, deepening it, until she tingled with anticipation. He cupped a breast and kissed down her neck.

"I'm sorry," she whispered, holding his head as he bent down to capture her nipple between his lips.

"Hmm?" he muttered, giving the other one equal attention. "Now, about that baby I want...." That topic shocked her again, but he distracted her with his lips, and tongue, and hands that roamed down her back. But the sensation of putting on a show, of acting a certain way to make others happy clouded her brain.

"No talking," she insisted, moving back on his knees to unzip his jeans. She glanced up at him then dropped down to the floor and teased him with her lips, loving the way he groaned and angled his hips, thrusting into her mouth.

"Oh...God, Rosie." He fisted her hair as she took as much of him into her mouth as she could. She wanted him to come and be done, so she could...what? Sleep? Drink? Talk?

She kept up her suction and teased his balls, going through motions and counting the seconds. He pumped his hips and gripped her hair and groaned again just before he filled her mouth. Releasing him, she wiped her hand across her lips.

He sat, breathing heavily, fully dressed but for his wet, glistening dick. With a grin, she sat down primly and picked up his wine glass. His satisfied smile made her warm inside as he reached for her arm, muttering something about "pay back." When someone banged on the door hard, they both jumped. He rose and zipped up before opening it.

"Hey...uh...what the hell?"

Rosalee got up and spotted his friend Mark, the local cop, with AliceLynn and....

"Margot," Antony said, with a slight tremor in his voice. The expression on his face told her all she needed to know at that split second.

"Antony, may I come in?" Mark asked, politely, as if he could be refused entry like a vampire.

"Sure." Antony opened the door. Rosalee sat, her knees shaking and her head pounding. A strange, dizzy, queasy feeling bowled her over.

"Margot brought AliceLynn to me." Mark crossed his arms.

"Why," Antony began, but Margot interrupted him.

"She called me to come get her. She'd been at a party and had too much to drink and smoke, and thought she saw somebody drop

something into one girl's drink, so she hollered at him and he...."
Margot stopped and met Antony's eyes, her expression so intent it hurt
Rosalee all over.

Antony frowned at the surly teenaged girl. Rosalee sat on her hands
to keep from running over and shaking her. They had come a long way,
Antony and his daughter, but this sort of setback could put a real kink
in the progress.

"Are you all right?" Antony lifted his daughter's chin up. Rosalee
gasped when she saw the blood on her lip. "Goddamn it, Mark."
Antony shook with rage.

"They just tried to stop me from running away and telling the cops,
is all." The girl jerked her chin out of Antony's grip and glared down at
her tightly clenched hands. "I tripped and fell and bashed my face on
the concrete."

"We broke up the party. She told us where. A bunch of college boys,
home on break. "AliceLynn says no one...interfered with her."

"Why did she come to you?" Antony asked Margot, his dark eyes
pleading for something Rosalee did not want to know, but thought she
did.

Margot ignored him, hugged the girl then held her at arm's length.
"AliceLynn, I told you we should have come here first. Your daddy will
take care of you and won't be mad. It's not my place, or my role, to come
between you, to shield either of you from each other."

AliceLynn's eyes darkened. She yanked out of the woman's grip.

"Not your role." She wiped a shaking hand across her bloody lip.
"Not your place? What is it then? What is your role anyway, Margot?
I'm a little confused."

Margot took a step back, her eyes wide with dismay. Antony moved
slightly closer to her.

"Don't back talk," he warned AliceLynn.

Mark shot Rosalee a confused look, but the scene slowly unfolding
in front of her eyes had her mesmerized.

"You know what? Screw you, Daddy," AliceLynn said, her eyes flashing with anger. "Screw you, too, Margot. Because I think I know your *place*, and it's right where I found you." Her gaze softened ever so slightly when she focused on Rosalee. "I'm so sorry, Rosie." She glared back at Margot and Antony, who now were standing shoulder to shoulder. "Your *place* is apparently in my daddy's bed, isn't it, Margot? And your *role* is to fuck a man who is engaged to someone else."

Rosalee gasped. Antony lunged for her, but Margot grabbed his arm, and Mark stepped between them.

"I hate all y'all stupid, hypocritical adults. Yeah, even you, Rosie. I know how you really feel about my daddy *and* about Uncle Aiden." She sneered at her father. "Y'all are just a bunch of...immature...idiots."

She stomped out onto the front porch, whirling around at the top of the steps to face them. "Don't you dare to tell me to act like a grown-up when you can't act like a grown man. You won't even own up to how you feel about her." She pointed to Margot who seemed to be near tears in a rare cracking of her ever-cool exterior. "Or her." She lifted her chin toward Rosalee, whose ears had started whooshing in a scary way.

She rose, but the room faded. *Funny*, she thought as she dropped like a stone—*this is what fainting feels like.*

Chapter Twenty-Five

Aiden tried to grab Renee, to hide from the nightmares with her. But her side of the bed remained cold and unused. He shivered, and shifted to his back, staring at the peeling paint on the stained bedroom ceiling, reliving the last twenty-four hours.

He'd convinced Renee to come home with him Thanksgiving night, but she refused to have sex with him. They'd watched a movie, cuddled, and fell asleep on the couch.

When he woke up, she'd left, but not before covering him with a quilt and making coffee in his miniscule kitchen. She had left a note, reminding him to pick her up for their shopping trip into Lexington. He despised shopping almost as much as he despised doing laundry, but he'd agreed to it since it was one of her favorite activities. He owed her at least a shopping trip. Besides, he'd be lying if he declared himself above enduring the early holiday throngs for the sake of peace, not to mention getting laid.

He drove down to the salon to pick her up, but the girls there told him she'd gone home already, eyeballing him like he'd just murdered a nest of baby rabbits. As he meandered the few blocks to her fussily decorated, but tidy house, he pondered his make-up moves, discarding them one by one and settling on abject begging.

"Renee? Honey?" Dread settled in his chest at the silence that met his ears once he opened her front door.

"In here."

He followed the sound of her voice and found her in the bedroom, draped across the bed wearing a black-lace bra, garter belt, silk hose and high heels. Grinning, he walked over to her and dropped to his knees, yanked her hips forward, and dove into her with his lips and tongue, reveling in her, loving her smell, and taste, and the noises she made as she raked her fingernails over his bare scalp. Once she'd come a couple of times and ripped the back of his shirt with her heels, he grabbed a condom from the bedside drawer, rolled it on while she lay, breathing heavily, her eyes bright with unshed tears.

Without a word, she got on her hands and knees and tilted her ass up with the sort of sexy look over her shoulder that got him every time. Feeling only slightly manipulated, he grabbed her hips, losing all semblance of control, pounding into her, yanking her hair, smacking her ass, and coming so hard he nearly passed out. He dropped down over her back and held her close, kissing her shoulder.

"It's over," she said, moving forward so he slipped out of her body. He remained on his knees, heart pounding and wondering if he'd heard her right.

"Sorry. I was a little fast on the draw." He fell over onto his side, dragging her onto his chest. Even as she put her head on his shoulder he sensed the tension coiled between them like a poisonous snake.

"No, not that."

Already fighting off a looming nap, he blinked when she propped up on her elbow and cupped his cheek. "We are over." She dropped the Halloran family engagement ring in its antique box onto his chest.

"What are you talking about?"

Without a word, she reached down and tugged the condom off, wrapped it in a tissue and set it on the bedside table. When she climbed on top of him, the moist heat of her sex pressed against his, he dug his fingers into her thighs and swallowed hard. She took the ring and placed it next to the wad of Kleenex.

"You're real sweet, Aiden, and I do love how you make me feel—young, and pretty, and desirable." A single tear dropped from her lashes. Aiden got up on his elbows and opened his mouth, already begging her to stay in his mind. "No, don't talk because if you do, I won't be able to finish." She grabbed another condom and applied it in silence. Her blue eyes told him clearly that this was the end of a potentially pleasant beginning. But of what, he imagined would be a fraught few years, ending in a divorce. Then something else gripped him, and his body reacted in a purely primal way.

He flipped her over, pinned her arms up over her head, taking her with a long stroke that made them both shudder.

"You *are* pretty...you're sexy and incredible." He sighed and bent down to kiss her, letting his lips hover over hers. "I do love you, Renee."

She nodded and wrapped her legs around his waist, drawing him deeper. "I know that, Aiden. But you love her more." She arched, rising to meet him again and again, until they both cried out together. He kissed her at the last minute and the salt he tasted on his lips he realized didn't only come from her tears.

And now his bachelorhood seemed firmly entrenched once more, with just a few more weeks until he had to stand and watch Antony marry Rosalee—the woman he wanted more than he wanted to draw his next breath. He sat, head drooping between his shoulders, able to see, smell, taste, feel, and hear her in his memory. He shivered and got up to take another cold shower.

Chapter Twenty-Six

D *ecember Seventeenth*
Rosalee straightened her dress and took in the room full of family and friends, all there for this special day. Her heart fluttered and her temples pounded. Butterflies slammed around in her stomach, making her wish for a stiff drink—three or four stiff drinks.

She spotted AliceLynn at the front, near the altar, beautiful and grown up in her sleek, silver-gray dress, her hair piled up in a fancy do. The candles made her eyes glimmer. When she caught Rosalee's gaze, the girl gave her a thumbs-up.

Rosalee gulped and gripped her flowers, the urge to bolt from the church and run far away never stronger than at that moment. She shook her head.

"What's wrong, honey?" Lindsay touched her freezing-cold arm. "Jitters?"

Rosalee nodded, unable to speak. Her tongue was stuck to the roof of her mouth and her cheeks seemed packed with cotton. They'd done a quick rehearsal, but it had been such a blur, she barely remembered it. At that second, she figured she'd screw everything up by passing out again, or something equally embarrassing.

Lindsay held onto her and Rosalee let the tears flow, acknowledging her gut-deep happiness with how things had turned out. But her chest ached, and her throat closed up in panic. Angelique hovered, blotting her makeup and offering her sips of water as they lingered in the church's vestibule.

The crowd grew quiet. She peeked back through the window and saw that the men had gathered near the preacher. They were arrayed together, heads still stubbly, reminding her of Paul, who never had his hair an inch longer than high and tight from the second he'd joined the Marines.

She sucked in a breath, touched her stomach, and thought through a quick prayer for strength. The sight of Jeffrey in his mini-tuxedo and his own shaven head made her smile then burst into irrational tears.

"Oh, sweetheart." Lindsay held her tighter. "There's plenty of time for crying over them later. Trust me, I know. I married the original Love brother, remember?" She kissed Rosalee's cheek and handed her a bouquet of deep-red roses bound with an emerald-green silk ribbon. The music shifted to something Rosalee vaguely remembered being chosen for the bridesmaids and mothers. She gripped Lindsay's arm.

"I'm real sorry about all this. Truly."

"Don't be silly. There's nothin' for you to be sorry about." Lindsay took her husband's arm to proceed down the aisle, leaving Rosalee hyperventilating, tears running down her cheeks.

"Hey, there's my wife." A voice from behind her made her jump. She sighed and pressed her face into Aiden's tuxedo-clad chest. "I heard you were back here blubbering and besmirching the family name." He tilted her chin up and wiped her tears with his thumbs. "Chill, Missus Love. We have a wedding to attend." He tucked her hand into his elbow then whispered in her ear. "I can't wait to get you home. Let's get this over with, shall we?"

She nodded at him, took a breath then walked into the church, ablaze with light and music. They parted at the altar, taking their places on either side, facing the back as the music changed. The organ music soared and Rosalee smiled when Margot emerged, looking for all the world like she'd just stepped off the cover of *Bride's* magazine. Tears glimmered in her eyes, but she kept them pinned to one man, standing at the front, waiting for her.

Once Margot made it to the altar, Rosalee took the long dress trail and arranged it behind her then watched as Antony took her hand, gazed into her eyes, and mouthed, *I love you.* Rosalee caught Aiden's eye over Antony's shoulder. He winked, and mouthed, *I can't wait to get you home.* She grinned and blew him a kiss.

What would be a weird moment suddenly seemed right. Relief that she had recognized it and acted quickly and decisively surged through her.

As Antony repeated vows he had exchanged a week before, Aiden kept his gaze on Rosalee.

Rosalee Love.

His wife.

He had come so close to missing this moment. Fate had such a way of tugging folks along in its wake, heedless of anyone's desire to stop it. But luckily, this time, they'd all come to their senses, dropped an anchor, and halted the whole thing before it wrecked everyone's lives.

Antony took Margot's hand, slid a ring onto her finger, and she his. Then they kissed so long the crowd cheered. He worried about Rosalee some, knowing how very strange this must be, but thanking God in his heart and mind, again and again, that he'd been able to halt fate's

inexorable progression.

That Saturday after Thanksgiving, he'd been sulking, drinking beer, and feeling sorry for himself when his phone rang. He'd ignored her first two calls then answered it.

"What's wrong?" he'd asked.

"I need to see you. Now."

"I'm home."

She'd arrived in minutes, and he caught her as she fell into the living room, crying and saying something about "Margot, and Antony, and AliceLynn."

He'd poured them both a bourbon, but she'd set hers down and taken his hands. "I love you, Aiden," she'd declared in a shaking voice, making his heart pound at the sight of her wild curls and tear-streaked face.

"Thank the Lord." He folded her into his arms. "Because I was about to move back to Iowa to avoid watching you marry him." He cupped the back her neck and kissed her, picking her up and carrying to his unmade bed. She'd ripped at his clothes. Hers had disappeared. And he'd been over her, kissing her, inside her, loving her, and knowing, finally, he had found his home.

Later, she'd lain on his chest, and he'd been running his hands through her hair, wondering what in the hell would happen now when his life changed forever at her next words.

"I'm pregnant," she'd muttered into his neck. "It's yours."

"How...I mean...but...uh...Antony is...." His throat had closed up, but a sense of perfection had surged through him at the same time.

"Antony always wore a condom. At least he did after our first time, and that would be too long ago." She'd taken his hand and placed it on her stomach. Aiden had contemplated his hand then when he thought he could speak, looked back up at her. She'd nodded, biting her lip in the way that drove him mad with lust.

"Well, I guess I need to make an honest woman out of you then?" He hadn't been able to stop grinning.

"Yes, but not until after we talk to your parents. All of us. You, me, Antony, and Margot. Together. It's the only right way to handle this mess."

"Wow, that will be interesting."

"Something tells me your mama won't be surprised," she said, before climbing on top of him and dropping down to curtain them with her thick fall of her hair, shrinking the world to just the two of them—exactly the way he liked it.

Lindsay Love didn't even blink when confronted by the four of them, arrayed around the living room in varying couples. Antony held tight to Margot's hand as if afraid she'd disappear otherwise.

"It's all right," Rosalee stated to him, and to everyone in the room. She made a point to meet Margot's eyes, which were wide and terrified. "It's all right. I'm happy for you both."

Aiden tugged her back to his side, loving her more than ever at that moment.

"I always knew having a bunch of boys would be complicated," Anton grunted, before pouring them all a drink. "Never thought I'd be on the receiving end of this particular conversation though." He raised his glass. "Here's to two weddings."

Lindsay held hers up, too, but eyeballed Rosalee when she didn't partake, just clinked then set the glass down. Aiden took her glass from her, leveling his gaze to his mother's, as if daring her to say anything. Antony took Margot's from her, too, shrugged, and held it up to repeat the toast.

"Two weddings. Two birthdays," the oldest Love brother said with conviction.

"Oh, for Christ's sake."

"Take the Lord's name in vain over our grandbabies one more time, Anton Love, and I will throw you out in the barn with the horses."

"Dollar in the swear jar, Daddy," Aiden said, making everyone laugh with relief.

Chapter Twenty-Seven

July

"Goddamn it, Dominic," Aiden grunted when the man ran over him in his quest for the dunk. The hotter-than-hell Sunday afternoon didn't do its job—distracting Aiden from his near-constant anxiety. He'd left Rosalee at his parents' house after church and dinner and got dragged into the weekly basketball game only because his wife insisted on it.

"Get him out of my face, please," she had begged everyone. "I swan but he is gonna worrywart me straight into labor."

He'd touched her giant, terrifying stomach, and kissed her. "Sorry. Rookie error," he said, barely able to disguise the panic dancing around in his chest at the thought of becoming a father. Not that he didn't already feel like one to Jeffrey. Although they had established a new relationship, still buddies, but without tolerance for being treated like a babysitter. He'd been splashing around with AliceLynn in the pool, newly liberated from his floaties at Aiden's insistence.

Margot reclined on a lounge nearby, her equally huge belly a convenient shelf for her book. She'd waved at them as they passed, accepting Antony's blown kiss.

With extreme reluctance, he let Antony drag him to the truck, and then to the park, where they unloaded the cooler full of water for now, beer for later, and drew straws for teams.

"How are you so calm?" he asked, glancing for the millionth time at his phone, expecting The Text from her.

"These things will happen in their own time, and all will be well—punk," Antony said, before lobbing the ball into his gut. "Now get out there and draw some fouls."

Thirty minutes into the game, he did forget it all—the stress over moving into her house, the self-publishing venture that had, amazingly, landed him an agent, the trips back and forth to New York without her.

"Yo, Mister Mom, stop draggin' ass," Antony yelled helpfully, as he passed over Dom's head. Aiden grinned and used his size to his advantage, darting under Dom and Kieran's outstretched arms for a layup, tying the game.

Rosalee had gone through management training and been promoted to a branch of the newly merged Lucasville Bank and the national chain. They'd even talked of moving her up to the regional office in Louisville after her maternity leave. Aiden had let his mother read his manuscript which she'd declared "sappy," and helped set him straight regarding the fact that she had chased Anton and lured him into temptation, not the other way around.

Once he'd gotten over the extreme embarrassment when his father had chuckled and admitted that Lindsay Halloran had taken it in her head that the stable hand should be her "first," and that their many intimate encounters in the haymow of her father's fancy horse barn had been at her insistence, Aiden had revised and self-published his book, *Family Love*. He released it under the name, "A.L. Amatore," taking back his family's original Italian.

It had captured the eye of a New York agent, pure luck, he fully acknowledged. The man had just started negotiating print rights with a large publishing house. Aiden still taught one class at the community college, but would be done with that once his daughter decided to make her appearance. Truth be told, his relief knowing they'd be having a girl had been boundless, despite Antony's warnings about their teenaged difficulty.

In short, he wanted to be home with baby Amanda Lindsay, named for her two grandmamas, full time. And he wanted to keep Jeffrey home, too, the year before he went off to kindergarten. Rosalee warned him he might regret that, but had cancelled Jeffrey's place in the daycare beginning in August. He'd concoct his next book around being home, taking care of his children, he insisted, ignoring his mother's and wife's scoffing disbelief.

When Dom ran into and over him, he shoved the man off, pushing him into the fencing hard enough to hear it rattle. Aiden glared at him, but Dom just grinned and tossed him the ball.

"I can't beat the almost-daddy into the dirt today. Wouldn't be right, now would it?"

Kieran grabbed the ball and headed in the other direction in silence. The three remaining brothers eyeballed each other. Kieran's wedding had not gone off without a hitch. It had not gone off at all. They'd had a talk the previous week about it, when Kieran had skipped the game, claiming he had a torn hamstring. But none of them knew what to say or do to help. So they just played ball, glad to have the peacemaking member of the family back in their midst.

Aiden paused, catching his breath and wiping sweat from his face, pondering what a major shift had occurred in a single cycle of the calendar. He was so happy to have a home with his family, and anticipating something that excited, and terrified him to the point of paralysis at the same time.

"Oh, it sucks, dude. Don't kid yourself. Those lucky assholes who got to sit in the waiting room puffing cigars had it too easy," Antony had told him last week over post-basketball game bourbons. "So much screaming, pain, blood, and shit—no, actual shit. It's the worst thing ever. You may never recover from it." He'd draped a friendly arm around Aiden's shoulders. "The concept of a son from my loins makes me a little queasy."

Antony and Margot were having a boy—already named Joshua Anton for his two granddaddies. Josh and Mandy Love were both due within three days of one another, exactly one week from today.

But Aiden couldn't wait to hold his baby daughter, his and Rosalee's child. He shook his head at his own sappiness, shivering when a breeze blew up, sending the sun behind a scrum of dark clouds. Thunder sounded, and he watched the sky change as it will on a summer day in Kentucky, going from dark blue to gray in minutes. Lightning flashed, followed by another loud clap of thunder.

The rain hit fast and hard, drenching everyone before they could run for their vehicles. Aiden tilted his face back and let it cool him, opened his mouth to it, tasting the perfection of water from the sky, peace in his soul for the first time in his life.

Until he heard it—the loud honking of his father's truck as it raced into the parking lot, shattering his illusion of peace forever.

"Aiden!" He heard his sister's voice call through the deluge, and ever-increasing thunder claps. He ran full-out for the truck, heart racing with dread of what lay ahead.

He skidded to a stop at the back passenger door of his father's truck. Angelique sat at the wheel of the empty cab.

"Where's...." He gasped around the anxiety closing in on his throat.

"Daddy took them, both of them. Damn, it sure was some wild and crazy shit. Get in. Antony! Get your sorry ass over here!"

Antony dropped the basketball. His jaw dropped along with it.

"Let's go!" Aiden yelled over the storm. "Love babies wait for no man, or thunderstorm!"

"Go on!" Dominic replied. "We're right behind you with the cooler."

Aiden took a breath, and gripped the headrest as Antony leapt into the car, his eyes wild.

"I'll drive," he told Angelique.

She rolled her eyes. "The hell you will. Daddy's words. Settle back, knuckleheads. I've got this."

The End

Sneak Peek at
Coach Love

• • • •

CARA CAUGHT A FLASH of red hair atop a tall, familiar body
the second she looked away from her computer. Face flushed hot, she
glanced down at the screen to reabsorb the alarming news that not
only would she be now taking on patients at three different locations,
the clinic owners had reneged on her raise. Warring emotions made
her stomach churn. But when she met Kieran Love's deep green eyes,
twinkling as usual and focused solely on her, it sent a jolt of serenity
through her psyche.

"Hey gorgeous," he said, as he slipped out of his sweatshirt. "Ready
for the torture session?"

She blew out a breath and got to her feet, wishing she'd worn
her newer scrubs today, even as she shook her head at such an absurd
thought. He'd already climbed onto the tall treatment table in
anticipation of their hour or so together. She must have sighed out loud
because he frowned and put a large palm over hers.

"What's up, sweets? Why the heavy sighs? Wedding planning got
you down?"

Focusing down on their hands that now rested on his
once-shattered knee, she flinched, and pulled away fast—too fast.

"Sorry. Awkward." He tucked his arm behind his head and trained
his gaze toward the ceiling. Her face flamed hot all over again.

"It's all right." She got to work putting him through the therapy
paces, admonishing him for continuing to play basketball and run on
the leg that had been broken on national television during his rookie
season in the NBA. They had history—plenty of it—but it remained
firmly in their mutual past. Especially now that they were both engaged
to other people.

"Ow, easy there, sweetheart," he muttered, dragging her from the zone-out she entered every time she treated Kieran Love, mainly to distract herself from the fact that she got to touch him, three times a week. His face, so close to hers as she manipulated his leg, bringing his knee toward his chest made her a little dizzy. "I'm not made of rubber. My hammies are tight."

"Because you played again yesterday," she said, bushing to the roots of her hair at his wide, wicked grin. "Dumbass." She smacked his shoulder and got out of his away so he could head over to the treadmill.

"What can I say? The Love family traditions will not be hampered by me and my bum leg."

"Yeah, well you ought to think before you worry about your stupid traditions. You're never gonna fully heal if you don't."

After programming the treadmill for a light jog, she observed his footfalls and hips while he ran, knowing she'd see the same thing she saw every time—that he favored his left knee so much he'd thrown off his cadence and risked injuring his other leg, the stubborn so-and-so. But she had to admit, seeing him again had lifted her saggy spirits.

They bantered while he ran. When she had the nerve stimulation machine running along the ugly scar he got quiet. Unusual, since the man could and would talk the birds right out of the trees.

She watched his face for a few seconds, biting the inside of her cheek to keep from asking about his wedding plans. It was a real downside of moving home after she'd gotten her sports med certification in Michigan—knowing more than she cared to about her first boyfriend and his future wife.

"Cara." Her colleague's voice interrupted her rising, irrational jealousy. "Kent's on the phone. Says it's urgent. I can take this one." The woman pointed to Kieran's leg.

"Oh, um, okay." Cara headed for the desk in their shared office.

"Hi, hon." Her fiancé's voice made her wince. The man had no volume control sometimes. "Whatcha doing?"

"Working. You know that. What's so urgent?" She clenched her jaw against the urge to apologize for snapping at him.

"Well, the boys want to meet up and I know we still have to do the caterer thing and settle on the menu and all." He trailed off, unwilling to impart the obvious news—that he would be leaving her to make the final decisions on some important aspect of their looming, giant, over-the-top wedding. She counted to ten. "Honey?" her successful husband-to-be pleaded, waiting for her to relieve him of the burden of saying *you're on your own, kid.*

"That's fine. I'll pick the menu but you're not allowed to complain about any aspect of it."

"Deal. You're such a sweetheart."

"Glad you think so, considering I'm about to marry you and all."

She caught sight of her former boyfriend flirting mercilessly with the younger, cuter-than-her girl running the machine over his knee. Pausing to issue another mental reminder that she'd caught a live one in Kent Lowery Jr., she forced thoughts of her stupid, high school obsession with the funny, lanky, redheaded man lying on the treatment table across from her out of her head. The irony that both she and Kieran were about to marry attorneys did not escape her. Never mind that his soon-to-be-spouse was a high-powered corporate somebody and her future husband a classic ambulance chaser with billboards blaring out *Call Kent 1800lawsuit* all over Interstate 64 between here and Louisville.

"Dinner still on tonight?"

She blinked and refocused on the voice in her ear.

"Sure," she said, leaning against the edge of the cluttered desk. "I found out I'm not getting that raise, though. So we should..."

"I told you that doesn't matter." An ugly edge crept into his voice. One she'd only heard a few times and did not care for in the slightest. "My wife won't have to work."

"This isn't the fifties. Stop acting like it doesn't matter. It matters to me."

"Oh hon, you know I'm messing with ya. Besides, once I get you knocked up, you'll have to stay home."

Cara's face burned. Kent's old-fashioned ways sometimes shocked her. While she appreciated his romanticism, she had to admit that their courtship had been of the whirlwind variety—well, the "courtship" after she'd had drunk sex with him in a bar bathroom in Lexington that is. But he'd been full-frontal, lots of roses, wine and fancy dates after that. The whole thing had the aura of fantasy, most days. By way of anchoring in the here-and-now, she focused on her giant engagement ring.

"You're so cute when you go all feminist. I can feel you fuming through the phone." He chuckled. "Relax, Gloria Steinem. I'm kidding."

Problem being of course, he only half-meant it. The Lowerys were old school Republicans with generations of money propping them up. Kent had grown up on the wealthy side of Louisville but had founded his practice here in the new suburbs of Lexington after graduating from law school. Claiming that her red hair would be *good luck* for the Lowery family, his brittle, patrician mother had swept Cara and her own mother into her ritzy social circle so fast neither of them could protest.

Two separate bridal teas in Louisville loomed on her horizon, one at the Lowery family estate on Riverside Drive and the other at the downtown Louisville Athletic Club. Both of which would be crowded with people she didn't know but who'd clutched her short, less than perfect-figured, redheaded self to their collective bosom as if she'd been born with her own silver spoon. Which she most definitely had not.

"I love you, babe. See ya tonight. Wear a nice dress... one with sleeves."

Cara clenched her jaw against the urge to remind him that she understood the dress code for the country club when she realized the phone had already gone dead. Kieran stuck his head around the corner, surprising her.

"Gotta run. Mama Love's dinner waits for no late sibling." His crooked smile sent a spike of long-forgotten longing through her gut.

"How is she doing?"

His grin widened. "Great, especially now that there are two grandbabies to spoil."

She waved as he ambled toward the front door of their strip mall PT clinic wondering not for the first time why she'd dumped him all those years ago.

• • • •

YOU KNOW YOU WANT TO get your hands on Kieran's story....

And be sure to get the rest of the series in this order:

COACH LOVE (Kieran's story)

LOVE BREWING (Dominic's story)

FAMILY LOVE (Angelique's and Lindsay's stories)

About the Author:

Liz Crowe is a Kentucky native and graduate of the University of Louisville living in South Carolina. She's spent her time as a three-continent expat trailing spouse, mom of three, real estate agent, brewery owner and bar manager, and is currently a digital marketing and fundraising consultant, in addition to being an award-winning author.

The Liz Crowe backlist has something for any reader seeking complex storylines with humor and complete casts of characters that will delight and linger in the imagination long after the book is finished.

Her favorite things to do when she's not scrolling social media for cute animal videos is walk her dogs, cuddle her cats, and watch her favorite sports teams while scrolling social media for cute animal videos.

• • • •

FOLLOW ALONG WITH LIZ online:

@lizcroweauthor on Facebook, Instagram, Twitter, Tiktok

Lizcrowe.com for all other news